BOOK THE THIRTEENTH

THE END

A SERIES OF UNFORTUNATE EVENTS

BOOK THE FIRST
THE BAD BEGINNING

BOOK THE SECOND
THE REPTILE ROOM

BOOK THE THIRD
THE WIDE WINDOW

BOOK THE FOURTH
THE MISERABLE MILL

BOOK THE FIFTH
THE AUSTERE ACADEMY

BOOK THE SIXTH
THE ERSATZ ELEVATOR

BOOK THE SEVENTH
THE VILE VILLAGE

BOOK THE EIGHTH
THE HOSTILE HOSPITAL

BOOK THE NINTH
THE CARNIVOROUS CARNIVAL

BOOK THE TENTH
THE SLIPPERY SLOPE

BOOK THE ELEVENTH
THE GRIM GROTTO

BOOK THE TWELFTH
THE PENULTIMATE PERIL

BOOK THE THIRTEENTH
THE END

A Series of Unfortunate Events

Book the Thirteenth

THE END

by

Lemony Snicket

Illustrated by
Brett Helquist

EGMONT

EGMONT

We bring stories to life

First published in the USA 2006 by HarperCollins Children's Books
First published in Great Britain 2006 by Egmont Books Limited
The Yellow Building, 1 Nicholas Road, London W11 4AN

This edition published 2012 by Egmont Books Limited

Published by arrangement with HarperCollins Children's Books
A division of HarperCollins Publishers, Inc.
1350 Avenue of the Americas
New York, New York, USA

ISBN 978 1 4052 6618 5

A CIP catalogue record for this book is available from the British Library

Printed and bound in Great Britain by the CPI Group

43533/9

For Beatrice –

I cherished, you perished.

The world's been nightmarished.

www.lemonysnicket.com

THE END

CARMELITA
Count Olaf

CHAPTER
One

If you have ever peeled an onion, then you know that the first thin, papery layer reveals another thin, papery layer, and that layer reveals another, and another, and before you know it you have hundreds of layers all over the kitchen table and thousands of tears in your eyes, sorry that you ever started peeling in the first place and wishing that you had left the onion alone to wither away on the shelf of the pantry while you went on with your life, even if that meant never again enjoying the complicated and overwhelming taste of this strange and bitter vegetable.

In this way, the story of the Baudelaire orphans is like an onion, and if you insist on reading each and every thin, papery layer in A Series of Unfortunate Events, your only reward will be 170 chapters of misery in your library and countless tears in your eyes. Even if you have read the first twelve volumes of the Baudelaires' story, it is not too late to stop peeling away the layers, and to put this book back on the shelf to wither away while you read something less complicated and overwhelming. The end of this unhappy chronicle is like its bad beginning, as each misfortune only reveals another, and another, and another, and only those with the stomach for this strange and bitter tale should venture any farther into the Baudelaire onion. I'm sorry to tell you this, but that is how the story goes.

The Baudelaire orphans would have been happy to see an onion, had one come bobbing along as they traveled across the vast and empty sea in a boat the size of a large bed but not nearly as comfortable. Had such a vegetable appeared, Violet, the eldest Baudelaire, would have tied up her hair in a ribbon to keep it out of her eyes, and in moments would have invented a device to retrieve the onion from the water. Klaus, the middle sibling and the only boy, would have remembered useful facts from one of the thousands of books he had read, and been able to identify which type of onion it was, and whether or not it was edible. And Sunny, who was just scarcely out of babyhood, would have sliced the onion into bite-sized pieces with her unusually sharp teeth, and put her newly developed cooking skills to good use in order to turn a simple onion into something quite tasty indeed. The elder Baudelaires could imagine their sister announcing "Soubise!" which was her way of saying "Dinner is served."

But the three children had not seen an onion. Indeed, they had not seen much of anything during their ocean voyage, which had begun when the Baudelaires had pushed the large, wooden boat off the roof of the Hotel Denouement in order to escape from the fire engulfing the hotel, as well as the authorities who wanted to arrest the children for arson and murder. The wind and tides had quickly pushed the boat away from the burning hotel, and by sunset the hotel and all the other buildings in the city were a distant, faraway blur. Now, the following morning, the only things the Baudelaires had seen were the quiet, still surface of the sea and the gray gloom of the sky. The weather reminded them of the day at Briny Beach when the Baudelaires had learned of the loss of their parents and their home in a terrible fire, and the children spent much of their time in silence, thinking about that dreadful day and all of the dreadful days that had followed. It almost would have been peaceful to sit in a drifting boat and think about their lives, had it not been for the Baudelaires' unpleasant companion.

Their companion's name was Count Olaf, and it had been the Baudelaire orphans' misfortune to be in this dreadful man's company since they had become orphans and he had become their guardian. Olaf had hatched scheme after scheme in an attempt to get his filthy hands on the enormous fortune the Baudelaire parents had left behind, and although each scheme had failed, it appeared as if some of the villain's wickedness had rubbed off on the children, and now Olaf and the Baudelaires were all in the same boat. Both the children and the count were responsible for a number of treacherous crimes, although at least the Baudelaire orphans had the decency to feel terrible about this, whereas all Count Olaf had been doing for the past few days was bragging about it.

"I've triumphed!" Count Olaf reiterated, a word which here means "announced for the umpteenth time." He stood proudly at the front of the boat, leaning against a carving of an octopus attacking a man in a diving suit that served as the boat's figurehead. "You orphans thought you could escape me, but at last you're in my clutches!"

"Yes, Olaf," Violet agreed wearily. The eldest

Baudelaire did not bother to point out that as they were all alone in the middle of the ocean, it was just as accurate to say that Olaf was in the Baudelaires' clutches as it was to say they were in his. Sighing, she gazed up at the tall mast of the boat, where a tattered sail drooped limply in the still air. For some time, Violet had been trying to invent a way for the boat to move even when there wasn't any wind, but the only mechanical materials on board were a pair of enormous spatulas from the Hotel Denouement's rooftop sunbathing salon. The children had been using these spatulas as oars, but rowing a boat is very hard work, particularly if one's traveling companions are too busy bragging to help out, and Violet was trying to think of a way they might move the boat faster.

"I've burned down the Hotel Denouement," Olaf cried, gesturing dramatically, "and destroyed V.F.D. once and for all!"

"So you keep telling us," Klaus muttered, without looking up from his commonplace book.

For quite some time, Klaus had been writing down the details of the Baudelaires' situation in this dark blue notebook, including the fact that it was the Baudelaires, not Olaf, who had burned down the Hotel Denouement. V.F.D. was a secret organization that the Baudelaires had heard about during their travels, and as far as the middle Baudelaire knew it had not been destroyed—not quite—although quite a few V.F.D. agents had been in the hotel when it caught fire. At the moment, Klaus was examining his notes on V.F.D. and the schism, which was an enormous fight involving all of its members and had something to do with a sugar bowl. The middle Baudelaire did not know what the sugar bowl contained, nor did he know the precise whereabouts of one of the organization's bravest agents, a woman named Kit Snicket. The children had met Kit only once before she headed out to sea herself, planning to meet up with the Quagmire triplets, three friends the Baudelaires had not seen in quite some time who were traveling in a self-sustaining hot air mobile home. Klaus was hoping the notes in his commonplace book would help him figure out exactly where they might be, if he studied them long enough.

"And the Baudelaire fortune is finally mine!" Olaf cackled. "Finally, I am a very wealthy man, which means everybody must do what I say!"

"Beans," Sunny said. The youngest Baudelaire was no longer a baby, but she still talked in a somewhat unusual way, and by "beans" she meant something like, "Count Olaf is spouting pure nonsense," as the Baudelaire fortune was not to be found in the large, wooden boat, and so could not be said to belong to anyone. But when Sunny said "beans," she also meant "beans." One of the few things the children had found on board the boat was a large clay jar with a rubber seal, which had been wedged underneath one of the boat's wooden benches. The jar was quite dusty and looked very old, but the seal was intact, a word which here means "not broken, so the food stored inside was still edible." Sunny was grateful for the jar, as there was no other food to be found on board, but she couldn't help wishing that it had contained something other than plain white beans. It is possible to cook a number of delicious dishes with white beans—the Baudelaire parents used to make a cold salad of white beans, cherry tomatoes, and fresh basil, all mixed together with lime juice, olive oil, and cayenne pepper, which was a delicious thing to eat on hot days—but without any other ingredients, Sunny had only been able to serve her boat mates handfuls of a bland, white mush, enough to keep them alive, but certainly nothing in which a young chef like herself could take pride. As Count Olaf continued to brag, the youngest Baudelaire was peering into the jar, wondering how she could make something more interesting out of white beans and nothing else.

"I think the first thing I'll buy for myself is

a shiny new car!" Count Olaf said. "Something with a powerful engine, so I can drive faster than the legal limit, and an extra-thick bumper, so I can ram into people without getting all scratched up! I'll name the car Count Olaf, after myself, and whenever people hear the squeal of brakes they'll say, 'Here comes Count Olaf!' Orphans, head for the nearest luxury car dealership!"

The Baudelaires looked at one another. As I'm sure you know, it is unlikely for a car dealership to be found in the middle of the ocean, although I have heard of a rickshaw salesman who does business in a grotto hidden deep in the Caspian Sea. It is very tiresome to travel with someone who is constantly making demands, particularly if the demands are for utterly impossible things, and the children found that they could no longer hold their tongues, a phrase which here means "keep from confronting Olaf about his foolishness."

"We can't head for a car dealership," Violet said. "We can't head anywhere. The wind has died out, and Klaus and I are exhausted from rowing."

"Laziness is no excuse," Olaf growled. "I'm exhausted from all my schemes, but you don't see me complaining."

"Furthermore," Klaus said, "we have no idea where we are, and so we have no idea which direction to go in."

"I know where we are," Olaf sneered. "We're in the middle of the ocean."

"Beans," Sunny said.

"I've had enough of your tasteless mush!" Olaf snarled. "It's worse than that salad your parents used to make! All in all, you orphans are the worst henchmen I've ever acquired!"

"We're not your henchmen!" Violet cried. "We simply happen to be traveling together!"

"I think you're forgetting who the captain is around here," Count Olaf said, and knocked one dirty knuckle against the boat's figurehead. With his other hand, he twirled his harpoon gun, a terrible weapon that had one last sharp harpoon available for his treacherous use. "If you don't do what I say, I'll break open this helmet and you'll be doomed."

The Baudelaires looked at the figurehead in dismay. Inside the helmet were a few spores of the Medusoid Mycelium, a terrible fungus that could poison anyone who breathed it in. Sunny would have perished from the mushroom's deadly power not so long ago, had the Baudelaires not managed to find a helping of wasabi, a Japanese condiment that diluted the poison.

"You wouldn't dare release the Medusoid Mycelium," Klaus said, hoping he sounded more certain than he felt. "You'd be poisoned as quickly as we would."

"Equivalent flotilla," Sunny said sternly to the villain.

"Our sister's right," Violet said. "We're in the same boat, Olaf. The wind has died down, we have no idea which way to go, and we're running low on nourishment. In fact, without a destination, a way of navigating, and some fresh water, we're likely to perish in a matter of days. You might try to help us, instead of ordering us around."

Count Olaf glared at the eldest Baudelaire, and then stalked to the far end of the boat. "You three figure out a way to get us out of here," he said, "and I'll work on changing the nameplate of the boat. I don't want my yacht called *Carmelita* anymore."

The Baudelaires peered over the edge of the boat, and noticed for the first time a nameplate attached to the rear of the boat with thick tape. On the nameplate, written in a messy scrawl, was the word "Carmelita," presumably referring to Carmelita Spats, a nasty young girl whom the Baudelaires had first encountered at a dreadful school they were forced to attend, and who later had been more or less adopted by Count Olaf and his girlfriend Esmé Squalor, whom the villain had abandoned at the hotel. Putting down the harpoon gun, Count Olaf began to pick at the tape with his dirt-encrusted fingernails, peeling away at the nameplate to reveal another name underneath. Although the Baudelaire orphans did not care about the name of the boat they now called home, they were grateful that the villain had found something to do with his time so they could spend a few minutes talking among themselves.

"What can we do?" Violet whispered to her siblings. "Do you think you can catch some fish for us to eat, Sunny?"

The youngest Baudelaire shook her head. "No bait," she said, "and no net. Deep-sea dive?"

"I don't think so," Klaus said. "You shouldn't be swimming down there without the proper equipment. There are all sorts of sinister things you could encounter."

The Baudelaires shivered, thinking of something they had encountered while on board a submarine called the *Queequeg*. All the children had seen was a curvy shape on a radar screen that resembled a question mark, but the captain of the submarine had told them that it was something even worse than Olaf himself. "Klaus is right," Violet said. "You shouldn't swim down there. Klaus, is there anything in your notes that might lead us to the others?"

Klaus shut his commonplace book and shook his head. "I'm afraid not," he said. "Kit told us she was going to contact Captain Widdershins and meet him at a certain clump of seaweed, but even if we knew exactly which clump she meant, we wouldn't know how to get there without proper navigation equipment."

"I could probably make a compass," Violet said. "All I need is a small piece of magnetized metal and a simple pivot. But maybe we shouldn't join the other volunteers. After all, we've caused them a great deal of trouble."

"That's true," Klaus admitted. "They might not be happy to see us, particularly if we had Count Olaf along."

Sunny looked at the villain, who was still scraping away at the nameplate. "Unless," she said.

Violet and Klaus shared a nervous glance. "Unless what?" Violet asked.

Sunny was silent for a moment, and looked down at the concierge uniform she was still wearing from her time at the hotel. "Push Olaf overboard," she whispered.

The elder Baudelaires gasped, not just because of what Sunny had said but because they could easily picture the treacherous act Sunny had described. With Count Olaf overboard, the Baudelaires could sail someplace without the villain's interference, or his threats to release the Medusoid Mycelium. There would be one fewer person with whom to share the remaining beans, and if they ever reached Kit Snicket and the Quagmires they wouldn't have Olaf along. In uneasy silence they turned their gazes to the back of the boat, where Olaf was leaning over to peel off the nameplate. All three Baudelaires could imagine how simple it would be to push him, just hard enough for the villain to lose his balance and topple into the water.

"Olaf wouldn't hesitate to throw *us* overboard," Violet said, so quietly her siblings could scarcely hear her. "If he didn't need us to sail the boat, he'd toss us into the sea."

"V.F.D. might not hesitate, either," Klaus said.

"Parents?" Sunny asked.

The Baudelaires shared another uneasy glance. The children had recently learned another mysterious fact about their parents and their shadowy past—a rumor concerning their parents and a box of poison darts. Violet, Klaus, and Sunny, like all children, had always wanted to believe the best about their parents, but as time went on they were less and less sure. What the siblings needed was a compass, but not the sort of compass Violet had mentioned. The eldest Baudelaire was talking about a navigational compass, which is a device that allows a person to tell you the proper direction to travel in the ocean. But the Baudelaires needed a moral compass, which is something inside a person, in the brain or perhaps in the heart, that tells you the proper thing to do in a given situation. A navigational compass, as any good inventor knows, is made from a small piece of magnetized metal and a simple pivot, but the ingredients in a moral compass are not as clear. Some believe that everyone is born with a moral compass already inside them, like an appendix, or a fear of worms. Others believe that a moral compass develops over time, as a person learns about the decisions of others by observing the world and reading books. In any case, a moral compass appears to be a delicate device, and as people grow older and venture out into the world, it often becomes more and more difficult to figure out which direction one's moral compass is pointing, so it is harder and harder to figure out the proper thing to do. When the Baudelaires first encountered Count Olaf, their moral compasses never would have told them to get rid of this terrible man, whether by pushing him out of his mysterious tower room or running him over with his long, black automobile. But now, standing on the *Carmelita*, the Baudelaire orphans were not sure what they should do with this villain who was leaning so far over the boat that one small push would have sent him to his watery grave.

But as it happened, Violet, Klaus, and Sunny did not have to make this decision, because at that instant, as with so many instants in the Baudelaire lives, the decision was made for them, as Count Olaf straightened up and gave the children a triumphant grin. "I'm a genius!" he announced. "I've solved all of our problems! Look!"

The villain gestured behind him with one thick thumb, and the Baudelaires peered over the edge of the boat and saw that the CARMELITA nameplate had been removed, revealing a nameplate reading COUNT OLAF, although this nameplate, too, was attached with tape, and it appeared that yet another nameplate was underneath this one. "Renaming the boat doesn't solve any of our problems," Violet said wearily.

"Violet is right," Klaus said. "We still need a destination, a way of navigating, and some kind of nourishment."

"Unless," Sunny said, but Count Olaf interrupted the youngest Baudelaire with a sly chuckle.

"You three are really quite slow-witted," the villain said. "Look at the horizon, you fools, and see what is approaching! We don't need a destination or a way of navigating, because we'll go wherever it takes us! And we're about to get more fresh water than we could drink in a lifetime!"

The Baudelaires looked out at the sea, and saw what Olaf was talking about. Spilling across the sky, like ink staining a precious document, was an immense bank of black clouds. In the middle of the ocean, a fierce storm can arrive out of nowhere, and this storm promised to be very fierce indeed—much fiercer than Hurricane Herman, which had menaced the Baudelaires some time ago during a voyage across Lake Lachrymose that ended in tragedy. Already the children could see the thin, sharp lines of rain falling some distance away, and here and there the clouds flickered with furious lightning.

"Isn't it wonderful?" Count Olaf asked, his scraggly hair already fluttering in the approaching wind. Over the villain's nefarious chuckle the children could hear the sound of approaching thunder. "A storm like this is the answer to all your whining."

"It might destroy the boat," Violet said, looking nervously up at the tattered sails. "A boat of this size is not designed to withstand a heavy storm."

"We have no idea where it will take us," Klaus said. "We could end up even further from civilization."

"All overboard," Sunny said.

Count Olaf looked out at the horizon again, and smiled at the storm as if it were an old friend coming to visit. "Yes, those things might happen," he said with a wicked smile. "But what are you going to do about it, orphans?"

The Baudelaires followed the villain's gaze to the storm. It was difficult to believe that just moments ago the horizon had been empty, and now this great black mass of rain and wind was staining the sky as it drew closer and closer. Violet, Klaus, and Sunny could do nothing about it. An inventing mind, the notes of a researcher, and surprisingly adept cooking skills were no match for what was coming. The storm clouds unfurled wider and wider, like the layers of an onion unpeeling, or a sinister secret becoming more and more mysterious. Whatever their moral compass told them about the proper thing to do, the Baudelaire orphans knew there was only one choice in this situation, and that was to do nothing as the storm engulfed the children and the villain as they stood together in the same boat.

CHAPTER Two

It is useless for me to describe to you how terrible Violet, Klaus, and even Sunny felt in the hours that followed. Most people who have survived a storm at sea are so shaken by the experience that they never want to speak of it again, and so if a writer wishes to describe a storm at sea, his only method of research is to stand on a large, wooden boat with a notebook and pen, ready to take notes should a storm suddenly strike. But I have already stood on a large, wooden boat with a notebook and pen, ready to take notes should a storm suddenly strike, and by the time the storm cleared I was so shaken by the experience that I never wanted to speak of it again. So it is useless for me to describe the force of the wind that tore through the sails as if they were paper, and sent the boat spinning like an ice-skater showing off. It is impossible for me to convey the volume of rain that fell, drenching the Baudelaires in freezing water so their concierge uniforms clung to them like an extra layer of soaked and icy skin. It is futile for me to portray the streaks of lightning that clattered down from the swirling clouds, striking the mast of the boat and sending it toppling into the churning sea. It is inadequate for me to report on the deafening thunder that rang in the Baudelaires' ears, and it is superfluous for me to recount how the boat began to tilt back and forth, sending all of its contents tumbling into the ocean: first the jar of beans, hitting the surface of the water with a loud *glop!*, and then the spatulas, the lightning reflecting off their mirrored surfaces as they disappeared into the swirling tides, and lastly the sheets Violet had taken from the hotel laundry room and fashioned into a drag chute so the boat would survive its drop from the rooftop sunbathing salon, billowing in the stormy air like jellyfish before sinking into the sea. It is worthless for me to specify the increasing size of the waves rising out of water, first like shark fins, and then like tents, and then finally like glaciers, their icy peaks climbing higher and higher until they finally came crashing down on the soaked and crippled boat with an unearthly roar like the laughter of some terrible beast. It is bootless for me to render an account of the Baudelaire orphans clinging to one another in fear and desperation, certain that at any moment they would be dragged away and tossed to their watery graves, while Count Olaf clung to the harpoon gun and the wooden figurehead, as if a terrible weapon and a deadly fungus were the only things he loved in the world, and it is of no earthly use to provide a report on the front of the figurehead detaching from the boat with a deafening crackle, sending the Baudelaires spinning in one direction and Olaf spinning in the other, or the sudden jolt as the rest of the boat abruptly stopped spinning, and a horrible scraping sound came from beneath the shuddering wood floor of the craft, as if a gigantic hand were grabbing the remains of the *Count Olaf* from below, and holding the trembling siblings in its strong and steady grip. Certainly the Baudelaires did not find it necessary to wonder what had happened now, after all those terrible, whirling hours in the heart of the storm, but simply crawled together to a far corner of the boat, and huddled against one another, too stunned to cry, as they listened to the sea rage around them, and heard the frantic cries of Count Olaf, wondering if he were being torn limb from limb by the furious storm, or if he, too, had found some strange safety, and not knowing which fate they wished upon the man who had flung so much misfortune on the three of them. There is no need for me to describe this storm, as it would only be another layer of this unfortunate onion of a story, and in any case by the time the sun rose the next morning, the swirling black clouds were already scurrying away from the bedraggled Baudelaires, and the air was silent and still, as if the whole evening had only been a ghastly nightmare.

The children stood up unsteadily in their piece of the boat, their limbs aching from clinging to one another all night, and tried to figure out where in the world they were, and how in the world they had survived. But as they gazed around at their surroundings, they could not answer these questions, as they had never seen anything in the world like the sight that awaited them.

At first, it appeared that the Baudelaire orphans were still in the middle of the ocean, as all the children could see was a flat and wet landscape stretching out in all directions, fading into the gray morning mist. But as they peered over the side of their ruined boat, the children saw that the water was not much deeper than a puddle, and this enormous puddle was littered with detritus, a word which here means "all sorts of strange items." There were large pieces of wood sticking out of the water like jagged teeth, and long lengths of rope tangled into damp and complicated knots. There were great heaps of seaweed, and thousands of fish wriggling and gaping at the sun as seabirds swooped down from the misty sky and helped themselves to a seafood breakfast. There were what looked like pieces of other boats—anchors and portholes, railings and masts, scattered every which way like broken toys—and other objects that might have been from the boats' cargo, including shattered lanterns, smashed barrels, soaked documents, and the ripped remains of all sorts of clothing, from top hats to roller skates. There was an old-fashioned typewriter leaning against a large, ornate bird cage, with a family of guppies wriggling through its keys. There was a large, brass cannon, with a large crab clawing its way out of the barrel, and there was a hopelessly torn net caught in the blades of a propeller. It was as if the storm had swept away the entire sea, leaving all of its contents scattered on the ocean floor.

"What is this place?" Violet said, in a hushed whisper. "What happened?"

Klaus took his glasses out of his pocket, where he had put them for safekeeping, and was relieved to see they were unharmed. "I think we're on a coastal shelf," he said. "There are places in the sea where the water is suddenly very shallow, usually near land. The storm must have thrown our boat onto the shelf, along with all this other wreckage."

"Land?" Sunny asked, holding her tiny hand over her eyes so she might see farther. "Don't see."

Klaus stepped carefully over the side of the boat. The dark water only came up to his knees, and he began to walk around the boat in careful strides. "Coastal shelves are usually much smaller than this," he said, "but there must be an island somewhere close by. Let's look for it."

Violet followed her brother out of the boat, carrying her sister, who was still quite short. "Which direction do you think we should go?" she asked. "We don't want to get lost."

Sunny gave her siblings a small smile. "Already lost," she pointed out.

"Sunny's right," Klaus said. "Even if we had a compass, we don't know where we are or where we are going. We might as well head in any direction at all."

"Then I vote we head west," Violet said, pointing in the opposite direction of the rising sun. "If we're going to be walking for a while, we don't want the sun in our eyes."

"Unless we find our concierge sunglasses," Klaus said. "The storm blew them away, but they might have landed on the same shelf."

"We could find anything here," Violet said, and the Baudelaires had walked only a few steps before they saw this was so, for floating in the water was one piece of detritus they wished had blown away from them forever. Floating in a particularly filthy part of the water, stretched out flat on his back with his harpoon gun leaning across one shoulder, was Count Olaf. The villain's eyes were closed underneath his one eyebrow, and he did not move. In all their miserable times with the count, the Baudelaires had never seen Olaf look so calm.

"I guess we didn't need to throw him overboard," Violet said. "The storm did it for us."

Klaus leaned down to peer closer to Olaf, but the villain still did not stir. "It must have been terrible," he said, "to try and ride out the storm with no kind of shelter whatsoever."

"Kikbucit?" Sunny asked, but at that moment Count Olaf's eyes opened and the youngest Baudelaire's question was answered. Frowning, the villain moved his eyes in one direction and then the other.

"Where am I?" he muttered, spitting a piece of seaweed out of his mouth. "Where's my figurehead?"

"Coastal shelf," Sunny replied.

At the sound of Sunny's voice, Count Olaf blinked and sat up, glaring at the children and shaking water out of his ears. "Get me some coffee, orphans!" he ordered. "I had a very unpleasant evening, and I'd like a nice, hearty breakfast before deciding what to do with you."

"There's no coffee here," Violet said, although there was in fact an espresso machine about twenty feet away. "We're walking west, in the hopes of finding an island."

"You'll walk where I tell you to walk," Olaf growled. "Are you forgetting that I'm the captain of this boat?"

"The boat is stuck in the sand," Klaus said. "It's quite damaged."

"Well, you're still my henchpeople," the villain said, "and my orders are that we walk west, in the hopes of finding an island. I've heard about islands in the distant parts of the sea. The primitive inhabitants have never seen civilized people, so they will probably revere me as a god."

The Baudelaires looked at one another and sighed. "Revere" is a word which here means "praise highly, and have a great deal of respect for," and there was no person the children revered less than the dreadful man who was standing before them, picking his teeth with a bit of seashell and referring to people who lived in a certain region of the world as "primitive." Yet it seemed that no matter where the Baudelaires traveled, there were people either so greedy that they respected and praised Olaf for his evil ways, or so foolish that they didn't notice how dreadful he really was. It was enough to make the children want to abandon Olaf there on the coastal shelf, but it is difficult to abandon someone in a place where everything is already abandoned, and so the three orphans and the one villain trudged together westward across the cluttered coastal shelf in silence, wondering what was in store for them. Count Olaf led the way, balancing the harpoon gun on one shoulder, and interrupting the silence every so often to demand coffee, fresh juice, and other equally unobtainable breakfast items. Violet walked behind him, using a broken banister she found as a walking stick and poking at interesting mechanical scraps she found in the muck, and Klaus walked alongside his sister, jotting the occasional note in his commonplace book. Sunny climbed on top of Violet's shoulders to serve as a sort of lookout, and it was the youngest Baudelaire who broke the silence with a triumphant cry.

"Land ho!" she cried, pointing into the mist, and the three Baudelaires could see the faint shape of an island rising out of the shelf. The island looked narrow and long, like a freight train, and if they squinted they could see clusters of trees and what looked like enormous sheets of white cloth billowing in the wind.

"I've discovered an island!" Count Olaf cackled. "I'm going to name it Olaf-Land!"

"You didn't discover the island," Violet pointed out. "It appears that people already live on it."

"And I am their king!" Count Olaf proclaimed. "Hurry up, orphans! My royal subjects are going to cook me a big breakfast, and if I'm in a good mood I might let you lick the plates!"

The Baudelaires had no intention of licking the plates of Olaf or anyone else, but nevertheless they continued walking toward the island, maneuvering around the wreckage that still littered the surface of the shelf. They had just walked around a grand piano, which was sticking straight out of the water as if it had fallen from the sky, when something caught the Baudelaire eyes—a tiny white figure, scurrying toward them.

"What?" Sunny asked. "Who?"

"It might be another survivor of the storm,"

Klaus said. "Our boat couldn't have been the only one in this area of the ocean."

"Do you think the storm reached Kit Snicket?" Violet asked.

"Or the triplets?" Sunny said.

Count Olaf scowled, and put one muddy finger on the trigger of the harpoon gun. "If that's Kit Snicket or some bratty orphan," he said, "I'll harpoon her right where she stands. No ridiculous volunteer is going to take my island away from me!"

"You don't want to waste your last harpoon," Violet said, thinking quickly. "Who knows where you'll find another one?"

"That's true," Olaf admitted. "You're becoming an excellent henchwoman."

"Poppycock," growled Sunny, baring her teeth at the count.

"My sister's right," Klaus said. "It's ridiculous to argue about volunteers and henchpeople when we're standing on a coastal shelf in the middle of the ocean."

"Don't be so sure, orphan," Olaf replied. "No matter where we are, there's always room for someone like me." He leaned down close to give Klaus a sneaky smile, as if he were telling a joke. "Haven't you learned that by now?"

It was an unpleasant question, but the Baudelaires did not have time to answer it, as the figure drew closer and closer until the children could see it was a young girl, perhaps six or seven years old. She was barefoot, and dressed in a simple, white robe that was so clean she could not have been in the storm. Hanging from the girl's belt was a large white seashell, and she was wearing a pair of sunglasses that looked very much like the ones the Baudelaires had worn as concierges. She was grinning from ear to ear, but when she reached the Baudelaires, panting from her long run, she suddenly looked shy, and although the Baudelaires were quite curious as to who she was, they also found themselves keeping silent. Even Olaf did not speak, and merely admired his reflection in the water.

When you find yourself tongue-tied in front of someone you do not know, you might want to remember something the Baudelaires' mother told them long ago, and something she told me even longer ago. I can see her now, sitting on a small couch she used to keep in the corner of her bedroom, adjusting the straps of her sandals with one hand and munching on an apple with the other, telling me not to worry about the party that was beginning downstairs. "People love to talk about themselves, Mr. Snicket," she said to me, between bites of apple. "If you find yourself wondering what to say to any of the guests, ask them which secret code they prefer, or find out whom they've been spying on lately." Violet, too, could almost hear her mother's voice as she gazed down at this young girl, and decided to ask her something about herself.

"What's your name?" Violet asked.

The girl fiddled with her seashell, and then

looked up at the eldest Baudelaire. "Friday," she said.

"Do you live on the island, Friday?" Violet asked.

"Yes," the girl said. "I got up early this morning to go storm scavenging."

"Storm scavawha?" Sunny asked, from Violet's shoulders.

"Every time there's a storm, everyone in the colony gathers everything that's collected on the coastal shelf," Friday said. "One never knows when one of these items will come in handy. Are you castaways?"

"I guess we are," Violet said. "We were traveling by boat when we got caught in the storm. I'm Violet Baudelaire, and this is my brother, Klaus, and my sister, Sunny." She turned reluctantly to Olaf, who was glaring at Friday suspiciously. "And this is—"

"I am your king!" Olaf announced in a grand voice. "Bow before me, Friday!"

"No, thank you," Friday said politely. "Our colony is not a monarchy. You must be exhausted from the storm, Baudelaires. It looked so enormous from shore that we didn't think there'd be any castaways this time. Why don't you come with me, and you can have something to eat?"

"We'd be most grateful," Klaus said. "Do castaways arrive on this island very often?"

"From time to time," Friday said, with a small shrug. "It seems that everything eventually washes up on our shores."

"The shores of Olaf-Land, you mean," Count Olaf growled. "I discovered the island, so I get to name it."

Friday peered at Olaf curiously from behind her sunglasses. "You must be confused, sir, after your journey through the storm," she said. "People have lived on the island for many, many years."

"Primitive people," sneered the villain. "I don't even see any houses on the island."

"We live in tents," Friday said, pointing at

the billowing white cloths on the island. "We grew tired of building houses that would only get blown away during the stormy season, and the rest of the time the weather is so hot that we appreciate the ventilation that a tent provides."

"I still say you're primitive," Olaf insisted, "and I don't listen to primitive people."

"I won't force you," Friday said. "Come along with me and you can decide for yourself."

"I'm not going to come along with you," Count Olaf said, "and neither are my henchpeople! I'm Count Olaf, and I'm in charge around here, not some little idiot in a robe!"

"There's no reason to be insulting," Friday said. "The island is the only place you can go, Count Olaf, so it really doesn't matter who's in charge."

Count Olaf gave Friday a terrible scowl, and he pointed his harpoon gun straight at the young girl. "If you don't bow before me, Friday, I'll fire this harpoon gun at you!"

The Baudelaires gasped, but Friday merely frowned at the villain. "In a few minutes," she said, "all the inhabitants of the island will be out storm scavenging. They'll see any act of violence you commit, and you won't be allowed on the island. Please point that weapon away from me."

Count Olaf opened his mouth as if to say something, but after a moment he shut it again, and lowered the harpoon gun sheepishly, a word which here means "looking quite embarrassed to be following the orders of a young girl."

"Baudelaires, please come with me," Friday said, and began to lead the way toward the distant island.

"What about me?" Count Olaf asked. His voice was a little squeaky, and it reminded the Baudelaires of other voices they had heard, from people who were frightened of Olaf himself. They had heard this voice from guardians of theirs, and from Mr. Poe when the villain would confront him. It was a tone of voice they had heard from various volunteers when discussing

Olaf's activities, and even from his henchmen when they complained about their wicked boss. It was a tone of voice the Baudelaires had heard from themselves, during the countless times the dreadful man had threatened them, and promised to get his hands on their fortune, but the children never thought they would hear it from Count Olaf himself. "What about me?" he asked again, but the siblings had already followed Friday a short way from where he was standing, and when the Baudelaire orphans turned to him, Olaf looked like just another piece of detritus that the storm had blown onto the coastal shelf.

"Go away," Friday said firmly, and the castaways wondered if finally they had found a place where there was no room for Count Olaf.

C H A P T E R

Three

As I'm sure you know, there are many words in our mysterious and confusing language that can mean two completely different things. The word "bear," for instance, can refer to a rather husky mammal found in the woods, as in the sentence "The bear moved quietly toward the camp counselor, who was too busy putting on lipstick to notice," but it can also refer to how much someone can handle, as in the sentence "The loss of my camp counselor is more than I can bear." The word "yarn" can refer both to a colorful strand of wool, as in the sentence "His sweater was made of yarn," and to a long and rambling story, as in the sentence "His yarn about how he lost his sweater almost put me to sleep." The word "hard" can refer both to something that is difficult and something that is firm to the touch, and unless you come across a sentence like "The bears bear hard hard yarn yarns" you are unlikely to be confused. But as the Baudelaire orphans followed Friday across the coastal shelf toward the island where she lived, they experienced both definitions of the word "cordial," which can refer both to a person who is friendly and to a drink that is sweet, and the more they had of one the more they were confused about the other.

"Perhaps you would care for some coconut cordial," Friday said, in a cordial tone of voice, and she reached down to the seashell that hung around her neck. With one slim finger she plucked out a stopper, and the children could see that the shell had been fashioned into a sort of canteen. "You must be thirsty from your journey through the storm."

"We are thirsty," Violet admitted, "but isn't fresh water better for thirst?"

"There's no fresh water on the island," Friday said. "There's some saltwater falls that we use for washing, and a saltwater pool that's perfect for swimming. But all we drink is coconut cordial. We drain the milk from coconuts and allow it to ferment."

"Ferment?" Sunny asked.

"Friday means that the coconut milk sits around for some time, and undergoes a chemical process making it sweeter and stronger," Klaus explained, having learned about fermentation in a book about a vineyard his parents had kept in the Baudelaire library.

"The sweetness will wash away the taste of the storm," Friday said, and passed the seashell to the three children. One by one they each took a sip of the cordial. As Friday had said, the cordial was quite sweet, but there was another taste beyond the sweetness, something odd and strong that made them a bit dizzy. Violet and Klaus both winced as the cordial slipped thickly down their throats, and Sunny coughed as soon as the first drop reached her tongue.

"It's a little strong for us, Friday," Violet said, handing the seashell back to Friday.

"You'll get used to it," Friday said with a smile, "when you drink it at every meal. That's one of the customs here."

"I see," Klaus said, making a note in his commonplace book. "What other customs do you have here?"

"Not too many," Friday said, looking first at Klaus's notebook and then around her, where the Baudelaires could see the distant figures of other islanders, all dressed in white, walking around the costal shelf and poking at the wreckage they found. "Every time there's a storm, we go storm scavenging and present what we've found to a man named Ishmael. Ishmael has been on this island longer than any of us, and he injured his feet some time ago and keeps them covered in island clay, which has healing powers. Ishmael can't even stand, but he serves as the island's facilitator."

"Demarc?" Sunny asked Klaus.

"A facilitator is someone who helps other people make decisions," the middle Baudelaire explained.

Friday nodded in agreement. "Ishmael decides what detritus might be of use to us, and what the sheep should drag away."

"There are sheep on the island?" Violet asked.

"A herd of wild sheep washed up on our shores many, many years ago," Friday said, "and they roam free, except when they're needed to drag our scavenged items to the arboretum, on the far side of the island over that brae over there."

"Brae?" Sunny asked.

"A brae is a steep hill," Klaus said, "and an arboretum is a place where trees grow."

"All that grows in the island's arboretum is one enormous apple tree," Friday said, "or at least, that's what I've heard."

"You've never been to the far side of the island?" Violet asked.

"No one goes to the far side of the island," Friday said. "Ishmael says it's too dangerous with all the items the sheep have brought there. Nobody even picks the bitter apples from the tree, except on Decision Day."

"Holiday?" Sunny asked.

"I guess it's something of a holiday," Friday said. "Once a year, the tides turn in this part of the ocean, and the coastal shelf is completely covered in water. It's the one time a year that it's deep enough to sail away from the island. All year long we build an enormous outrigger, which is a type of canoe, and the day the tides turn we have a feast and a talent show. Then anyone who wishes to leave our colony indicates their decision by taking a bite of bitter apple and spitting it onto the ground before boarding the outrigger and bidding us farewell."

"Yuck," the youngest Baudelaire said, imagining a crowd of people spitting up apple.

"There's nothing yucky about it," Friday said with a frown. "It's the colony's most important custom."

"I'm sure it's wonderful," Violet said, reminding her sister with a stern glance that it is not polite to insult the customs of others.

"It is," Friday said. "Of course, people rarely leave this island. No one has left since before I was born, so each year we simply light the outrigger on fire, and push it out to sea. Watching a burning outrigger slowly vanish on the horizon is a beautiful sight."

"It sounds beautiful," Klaus said, although the middle Baudelaire thought it sounded more creepy than beautiful, "but it seems a waste to build a canoe every year only to burn it up."

"It gives us something to do," Friday said with a shrug. "Besides building the outrigger, there's not much to occupy us on the island. We catch fish, and cook meals, and do the laundry, but that still leaves much of the day unoccupied."

"Cook?" Sunny asked eagerly.

"My sister is something of a chef," Klaus said. "I'm sure she'd be happy to help with the cooking."

Friday smiled, and put her hands in the deep pockets of her robe. "I'll keep that in mind," she said. "Are you sure you don't want another sip of cordial?"

All three Baudelaires shook their heads. "No, thank you," Violet said, "but it's kind of you to offer."

"Ishmael says that everyone should be treated with kindness," Friday said, "unless they are unkind themselves. That's why I left that horrible man Count Olaf behind. Were you traveling with him?"

The Baudelaires looked at one another,

unsure of how to answer this question. On one hand, Friday seemed very cordial, but like the cordial she offered, there was something else besides sweetness in her description of the island. The colony's customs sounded very strict, and although the siblings were relieved to be out of Count Olaf's company, there seemed something cruel about abandoning Olaf on the coastal shelf, even though he certainly would have done the same to the orphans if he'd had the opportunity. Violet, Klaus, and Sunny were not sure how Friday would react if they admitted being in the villain's company, and they did not reply for a moment, until the middle Baudelaire remembered an expression he had read in a novel about people who were very, very polite.

"It depends on how you look at it," Klaus said, using a phrase which sounds like an answer but scarcely means anything at all. Friday gave him a curious look, but the children had reached the end of the coastal shelf and were standing at the edge of the island. It was a sloping beach with sand so white that Friday's white robe looked almost invisible, and at the top of the slope was an outrigger, fashioned from wild grasses and the limbs of trees, which looked nearly finished, as if Decision Day was arriving soon. Past the outrigger was an enormous white tent, as long as a school bus. The Baudelaires followed Friday inside the tent, and found to their surprise that it was filled with sheep, who all lay dozing on the ground. The sheep appeared to be tied together with thick, frayed rope, and towering over the sheep was an old man smiling at the Baudelaires through a beard as thick and wild as the sheep's woolly coats. He sat in an enormous chair that looked as if it were fashioned out of white clay, and two more piles of clay rose up where his feet should have been. He was wearing a robe like Friday's and had a similar seashell hanging from his belt, and his voice was as cordial as Friday's as he smiled down at the three siblings.

ever come for me. I do remember he said he was in a new-ish temple about twenty minutes' drive from town, and he was often there by himself. But he was talking about his students, so I'm guessing it's a temple that doubles as a school."

Siri considered where the Lao monk might go. It would be somewhere low key. Probably deep in the countryside.

"I don't suppose there's a town near here called Nam Som?" he asked.

"There is," said Looi. "It's about two hours west of Udon."

Daeng smiled. "You think the Sangharaj was telling you where he was going?" she said.

"'You couldn't find a thank you in a glass of ginseng juice,' was what he said on the bus," said Siri. "There's the word *'pra'*—a monk—in *'koprakoon'*—thank you. And *nam som* is ginseng juice. And, to tell the truth we haven't got anything else to go on."

The local bus to Nam Som was the type to make a Lao doubt the stories about Thai development. It was like being dragged over rocks on a tin tray. There were taxis—some of them forty years old—that ferried passengers to the ferry at Tardeua, but even those had suspension. This country bus was as stiff as a box cart. No longer able to tolerate the pummeling to her tail, Madam Daeng had resorted to standing. She held onto the seat in front and bent her knees like a charioteer. Siri had one arm around her waist, but he lost her a couple of times when the bus left the ground and landed nose first on the gravel road. Even Ugly growled in frustration at the quality of service.

It took three punishing hours in all. They'd never been so delighted to get off a bus. Nam Som had only recently been upgraded to a district. At first glance it appeared that the upgrading had been largely on paper. It was a sleepy, slow-moving place with nothing to distinguish it from the other small towns they'd passed. Once the knots had been shaken out of their joints, Siri and Daeng went directly to the motorcycle *samlor* stand at the bus stop. None of the three drivers seemed that interested in hustling for passengers or taxing their brains. When Daeng had finished explaining that they were looking for a comparatively new temple some twenty kilometers from Nam Som, perhaps with just the one abbot in residence who taught school, they all shook their heads. Something about the shaking suggested they knew of the place but had no intention of going there.

"My husband only has three days left to live," said Daeng. "It's his last wish to visit his son at the temple and beg forgiveness for casting him out of the house when he was just a child. He's been searching for him for a year. Please help an old man fulfill his dying wish."

Siri coughed and held his heart.

The drivers exchanged glances.

"I'll take you as close as I dare," said the most ragged of the three.

There were two short wooden benches behind the motorcycle with just enough space for Siri and Daeng with Ugly at their feet. The engine sounded like an ancient machine gun. They had to shout to be heard.

"Why is it always me who's about to die?" said Siri.

"Look at you," said Daeng. "Who'd ever believe a woman in my condition only had three days to live?"

"What do you suppose he meant by, 'as close as I dare'?"

"No idea."

They arrived, not exactly in the village, but at a signpost that said SAWAN. It was a metal sign peppered with small-bore bullet holes. The driver told them the road from there on was impassable by vehicle, but the village was only half a kilometer around the bend. They would come to the temple before that. So the three adventurers set off on foot. The dirt road didn't appear to deteriorate at all after they rounded the first bend. In fact, with few ruts and tire tracks, it seemed to improve. They walked along what might one day be a dotted line at the center and enjoyed the cries of the birds and beasts. It was evening, and as they walked the other sounds were drowned beneath the late chorus of cicadas.

"You do realize," said Siri, leaning into his wife's ear, "that we'll probably get to the temple and discover the abbot's never heard of our Sangharaj and he was just visiting Laos for a little female companionship."

"For a man who grew up in a temple, you aren't very respectful, are you, Dr. Siri?" she replied.

"Grew up there?" said Siri. "I was dumped by some mysterious relative who didn't want me."

"But you were a novice. You learned the precepts."

"The way a Catholic learns catechisms. It was rote. It was a school. I was a rebel. I concentrated on the skills that would get me out of the place as soon as possible rather than the ones that would leave me a prisoner there for life. I was a scientist long before I knew what science was. I'd heard that scientists debunked religion, so I wanted to sign up."

Daeng smiled. "If I remember rightly, this is the point where you start talking about lotus flowers and onions," she said.

"Too right I do," said Siri. "In the lycée I charged through anything that could be proven and resented the time I'd wasted in the temple school dancing on lotus flowers. Then I'm in France, and they want me to juggle onions because they were paying the bill. They called it Catholicism, but I recognized it soon enough as their version of lotus dancing. Over in England they were juggling potatoes. The Arabs were jumping camels through hoops. In Israel they were climbing walls with their lips. Everyone had to have a cabaret act. So I'd juggle with my left hand and learn how to sew up bodies with my right. I did my tricks, Daeng, but they never got me in the circus."

Daeng squeezed his hand. "Remind me where my tail and your inner-shaman come in the program of circus events," she said, although she'd listened to his philosophy many times before.

"Now there's a conundrum," he said. "The religions, you see, they let you leave. They don't even put up a fight. So when you realize they're useless you can just move on. But the spirits? They really are annoying. They're the clowns perhaps. The harder you laugh at them and tell them they aren't real, the more times they trip you up and leave you flat on your face. My science can make a fool of any religion, but I can make no sense at all of the power the spirits have over me."

The half-kilometer to the temple turned out to be a lot farther. They'd been walking for forty minutes, and they could see the distant sun quartered and diced as it sank behind the leafless forest ahead. The birds and animals had uttered their last chorus for the day, and, as one, the cicadas fell silent.

"I don't see the road becoming impassable, do you?" said Daeng.

"Just endless," said Siri. "Those Thais. Any excuse to save a liter of benzene."

With night approaching, Siri wondered how much longer they'd have to walk but said nothing. Neither did he mention the reaction of the white talisman that hung from his neck. It had been selected for its sensitivity to the paranormal and blessed to ward off evil spirits. It was nonsensical but had, on occasions, saved his life: the scientist's paradox. And here it was, hot against his chest, alert, vibrating a warning. Ugly, who had spent much of the walk far out in front, now dropped back to be with his master. His ears and his tail were down, and he growled quietly.

"What's wrong with him?" Daeng asked.

"He's a dog," said Siri.

"You don't say? And there I was thinking he's a can of pickles."

"It's a phrase that explains itself," said her husband. "It's like saying, 'That Dr. Siri, he's a man.' You see? And every woman for kilometers around understands the meaning."

Siri was talking for talking's sake. He could feel a nervous tingle in his wife's fingers. He could sense that she too was on alert. Yet neither of them said anything about it.

Ugly stopped dead in his tracks. He refused to walk another step. Siri's amulet was fluttering beneath his shirt like a warm bat. The sun had sunk and left a mauve hangover along the horizon. The road ahead bled into it and disappeared. At their backs the moon had not yet put in an appearance. Daeng stopped and reached into her shoulder bag. She produced a flashlight, flicked the switch and a long wormhole of white light reached off into the distance. And at its farthest point it briefly made out two pink eyes caught in its beam. At that second the light gave out and left them there in a moonless blot.

"Shit," said Daeng, and she rattled the flashlight and turned the switch on and off with no result.

Ugly began to howl the way city dogs howled, collecting other voices one by one, until the neighborhood was awash in one pitiful chorus. But here, Ugly howled alone.

"All we need is a slither of lightning and a burst of thunder, and we'd have a Hammer film," said Siri, his impenetrable funny lines all but exhausted.

"I just put new batteries in this thing in Nong Khai," said Daeng, slapping the flashlight against her thigh. Ugly's howl turned to a bark, and he ran in front of them. Two silent pink lights were coming toward them along the road ahead. Ugly danced left and right, his bark more desperate.

"I don't suppose you remembered to pack the shotgun?" said Daeng.

"Then I wouldn't have had room for the whisky," said Siri, who did however have a scalpel in his hand. Daeng held a penknife. Neither were much use if they were about to get shot.

◘ ◘ ◘

"They're all raving mad," said Civilai. "A deserted village. A reluctant would-be Buddha who may or may not have been lying about his father. And now the Virgin Mary joins the cast. What's going on here?"

The guesthouse was a block away from the bank of the Xan River, but that's where Civilai and Madam Nong decided to sit. Running water helped them concentrate and relax at the same time. The owner loaned Civilai an ice-cream vendor's bicycle horn to beep whenever they needed another drink or a snack. His wife was glad to run back and forth with a tray.

"I don't see why we can't go home together tomorrow," said Nong. "You write your report that you found no evidence of a reincarnation, and we forget all this nonsense."

"You know why I can't," said Civilai.

"Because you're meddlesome," she said. "You picked it up from Siri."

"I did not. I've always been meddlesome. He's the cantankerous one."

"Tell me, what's so fascinating about this place you'd want to stay another night? Don't tell me you're still miffed that they didn't have a reception for you."

"That's part of it," said Civilai. "There's a system, you see. The ministry contacts the provincial office to say a bigwig is coming to visit. The provincial office passes this on to the regional council. The regional council informs the village and provides a budget. The village prepares for the visit, not because they're excited at the thought of seeing me, but because it's what they are supposed to do."

"I thought you didn't approve of unnecessary pomp and ceremony?"

"I don't. Complete waste of money and manpower. But the protocol exists, and tomorrow I'll go to the regional office to see why it broke down. And, to be honest, in the light of our Mary's story, I think I'd like to have another chat with Comrade Maitreya."

"Surely you didn't believe the word of a seventy-year-old virgin, Lai. Her hospital report was handwritten on a lined page torn from a school exercise book. It was in English, but the birth predated any American hospital aid projects. And if they had been here they would have made a song and dance about an immaculate conception in the third world. They would have sent reports to every medical journal, *The Times*."

"And who would have believed it?"

They reverted to staring at the river. A bicycle ice-cream vendor rode past beeping his horn, and two minutes later the wife of the guesthouse owner arrived breathless with two new beers. Civilai and Nong were only halfway through the first round, but they accepted the fresh bottles and ordered more food.

"And the thing is we still have no idea who contacted the Supreme Sangha Council in Thailand to make this claim," said Civilai. It wasn't the Buddha himself because he isn't the least bit interested. The headman was so lukewarm about it he didn't even bother showing up. But they wouldn't have counted anyway. The Supreme Sangha Council is a bit like the Vatican. The Italians wouldn't rush off into the jungle to see whether Mother Theresa was worthy of a sainthood unless a credible source could vouch for the fact she hadn't spent all her time with her feet up drinking gin and tonic. They're not going to sanctify her because her auntie said she was a good girl. No, whoever contacted Bangkok wielded some influence, and I want to know who it was . . . and why."

"Meddlesome," said his wife.

"Aren't you even a little bit curious?"

"I have to be back for my Women's Union meeting on Tuesday."

"But if you didn't . . . ?"

"Then, no. Not in the least. There are far more important things in life to be curious about."

7
Felonious Monk

Siri and Daeng had slept well in the guesthouse of the temple in Sawan, although the bags under Ugly's eyes suggested he'd been up all night. They'd been met on the road by the Supreme Patriarch and his friend Abbot Rayron carrying mountain salt lamps. The Sangharaj was an entirely different character than the mellow lump of stone they'd traveled with from Nong Khai. Siri had passed the test and was granted access to the man inside the rank. Old Sangharaj was a lad. He was funny and had a keen intellect, and he announced he'd already heard Civilai's jokes—perhaps even the dirtier versions. When asked what it was he'd said to the coach boy on the Udon-bound bus, he confessed that he might have threatened to punch the boy on the nose if he harmed the dog. They'd talked long into the night, although the topic had been mostly Siri and Daeng.

"I knew it," said the Sangharaj. "I knew if I antagonized and tested you a little your curiosity would get the better of you. And here you are. Remarkable. All those stories are indeed true."

"What stories?" asked Daeng.

"Do I really need to retell them?" said the monk. "Daeng, the famous fleur-de-lis of the Free Lao underground movement. Dr. Siri, who saved so many on the battlefront then solved impossible mysteries as the national coroner. And who knows what celestial contacts you two have amassed."

"Wait," said Siri, "haven't you been in the stockade since '75? Where do you hear all these rumors?"

"The legends existed long before I was decommissioned," said the Sangharaj. "Temples have been the grapes on the vine for centuries. It's a worldwide saffron network. We attract all sorts—or used to. Intellectuals who've given up on the material world, old soldiers, frustrated shamans, murderers. Can you imagine the stories we hear around the campfire? It's destiny that you should be here with us now. I can think of no two people more qualified to address the chaos we have in Sawan."

"My husband isn't so big on destiny," said Daeng.

"Then let's call it something else. How about coincidence?"

"That's even worse," said Siri.

"Then let's not call it anything at all. You're here, and you'll help us. And for that we thank you."

"We're here because we agreed to deliver you to the Thais," said Daeng.

"Following your defection," added Siri.

The Sangharaj laughed. "Ah, yes. My defection. What say we discuss that later this morning over breakfast? The Thais are very generous when it comes to alms. Goodness, Abbot Rayron even had a pot of fresh strawberry jam yesterday. Can you believe it? A monk could actually put on weight here."

"All right," said Siri, "if you're sending us to bed early, how about a little story to lull us to sleep?"

"Which one would you like to hear, Brother Siri?"

"The one where the Supreme Patriarch flees Udon bus station on a motorcycle and heads for a temple in the middle of nowhere because there's chaos he presumably knew of long before he got there."

"It's complicated."

"Give us the simple version."

"Very well," said the monk. "At the root of the chaos there is a simple drama. A suspected murder. There sits the accused."

They all turned around to look at the abbot who had posed as a life-sized ornament in the shadows since their arrival. He was slim and sinewy and looked as if he could account for himself in a fist fight. He was very quiet and seemed embarrassed by the sudden attention, but allowed himself a slither of a smile.

"This," said the Sangharaj, "is Abbot Rayron. He has run this temple since it was erected ten years ago. He used to be well respected in the region, but over the last three months, he's murdered three people."

The Sangharaj paused here for effect.

"And, according to one of our village shamans," he continued, "the murderer will kill again before the new week begins. So I suggest you wedge a chair under your doorknob when you go to sleep . . . which will be right now."

"A lapsed Catholic, a thousand-year-old shaman and a homicidal Buddhist monk walk into a bar. And the barman says, 'We only serve spirits in here.' So the Catholic says, 'We have the biggest spirit of all. The Holy Spirit. So I should get a glass of your best scotch . . .'"

It was the beginning of a joke that wouldn't have worked in Lao, so Auntie Bpoo was telling it in French. Siri had no idea she could speak French, and perhaps she couldn't because this was a dream . . . possibly. In dreams, miracles happened. Miracles like when a man's just about to give up attempting to speak on a long distance line, and suddenly the signal's as clear as a bell.

"I've heard it," said Siri, even though he hadn't. He was back in the connecting door space and the gap between the doors was getting narrower.

"What?" said Auntie Bpoo.

"I said I've heard the joke before."

"Alleluia," said Bpoo in whatever language *alleluia* was supposed to be.

"Alleluia, what?" asked Siri.

"Don't you notice anything different?"

"There's a handle on the door behind me," said Siri. "So presumably I can go back to bed anytime I like."

"Old dog, you're so hard to please. Can't you hear we're talking?"

"I've had these two-way dreams before," said Siri. "I've had conversations. I once spent the night wining and dining Audrey Hepburn."

"Siri, you absolute idiot," said Bpoo, "that was you talking to yourself pretending to be someone else. That's not a dialogue. That's a monologue with you doing all the voices. This is real. This is your breakthrough."

A huge sense of relief washed over Siri like a spicy nasal spray. "So I can only speak to spirits in French?" he said.

"I don't know. I can't speak French."

"Then what's this?"

"We don't do languages here."

"Then, what . . . ?"

The signal began to break up. It deteriorated so rapidly Siri was left in the connecting doorway yelling at himself.

"Wait," he said. "I lied. I haven't heard it. What's the end of the joke?"

But he was alone.

He contemplated opening the door behind him and curling up beside his warm wife, but he gave the door ahead one last push.

And it opened.

He was in an unfamiliar room, and it was nighttime. He stepped through the door. The room was lit only by a street lamp outside the window. Flying insects gathered there in such numbers that the lamplight danced around the room. On the glass windowpane a battalion of lizards dined on the insects. As lizards have no self-control they too would be dead by morning. Stuffed to oblivion.

Siri stood in the room, knowing that he was on the other side for the first time. But there was nobody to talk to. Fearing the visit might be a fleeting one he endeavored to take in as many facts as he could. It was an office. A calendar on the wall told him he was in Thailand as he recognized the photograph of the king. The last date marked was February 7th. There was a desk with drawers, but as Siri wasn't actually there he couldn't open them. Nor could he pick up papers or thumb through the books on the shelves. All he could do was observe and remember. There had to be a reason for his being there. On the parquet flooring in front of the desk he noted a large stain the shape of Africa. He memorized the books, mostly academic: history, politics, engineering, science, literature. Most were in Thai, but there were some in English. Some had no lettering on the spine and seemed to contain files.

Near the far door there were chips of plaster that had fallen from the wall. He looked through the window beyond the insect carnage and saw a line of individual houses. Not luxurious but sturdy. Jeeps or pickup trucks parked outside them on a tarmac road. Front garden plants mostly in pots, suggesting the residents didn't expect to stay long, or the owner did not allow landscaping. Wires overhead. A cat sleeping. Bins for garbage.

One more circuit of the room. Leather chair behind the desk with the stuffing coming out. Guest chair opposite. Lamp with a chain pull. No carpet. He knelt at the litter basket beside the desk, infuriated that he couldn't unscrew the balls of paper there. Only one envelope offered a clue. It had been ripped in half but was clearly visible. An address was written on it: *Than Kritsana Mukum, Dusit Insurance Company, Suan Dusit, Ban . . .* There was an error. The Thai word for Bangkok was misspelled, crossed out and scribbled over as if in anger.

There was only one more oddity in the neat office. Siri was on his hands and knees looking under the sofa that was still wrapped in plastic. Beneath it was a hole puncher. It probably had been dropped there and forgotten. He lay on the floor and looked up at the non-moving ceiling fan, and a hand reached out from under the sofa. It stroked his skin before taking hold of his arm.

"Siri," said Madam Daeng, "I think we should get up now."

He awoke like a man who had jogged to Bangkok in his sleep. His joints and muscles ached. His first conscious uttering of the day was a groan. He would happily have rolled over and made another attempt at a peaceful sleep. His night's slumber had begun badly. The almost full moon through the window had been annoyingly hypnotic, and the amulet burned so hot against his chest he'd been forced to take it off and lay it on the floor beside his pillow. Had this led to the breakthrough in the dream audio and the nocturnal trespass?

They sat together at the rattan table, and he told Daeng all about it. They came to the same conclusion. Yes, it must have been the amulet that blocked his communication with the other side. Sure, it kept him alive, but if he really wanted answers to his myriad questions, he had to break his dependence on it from time to time. They just had to be sure they were in an area low on malevolent spirits, and this certainly wasn't the place to be experimenting.

Siri patted Ugly on the head and walked to the pretty temple garden. The Sangharaj was sitting in the lotus position on an enormous slab of slate beside a pond. His robe was off his shoulders and Siri could see the hieroglyphics of war and age and abuse etched across his back. He was probably in his late eighties, but, unlike the pensioners in fat cities, frugality and common sense had kept him fit and clear-headed.

"Hey, Granddad," said Siri.

"Go away. I'm meditating," said the monk.

"No you're not. You're reading a magazine. I wouldn't be surprised if there were a few glamour girls in those pages."

The Sangharaj put down his newspaper. "What would someone my age need a glamour girl for?" he asked.

Siri sat beside him on the black slab and looked out

over a pond of carp, some big enough to feed a family of ten for a week. "I imagine it mounts up," he said. "All those years of abstinence."

"The secret is to abstain from only those supposed pleasures that have been promoted beyond their true value. The advertisers and the pornographers have created needs in us that don't actually exist."

"Including lust?"

"Especially lust. Lust is not a necessary thing."

"I'll inform Madam Daeng of your ruling."

"She's a levelheaded woman, Siri. She knows."

"Even orangutans scream with pleasure when they mate."

"Perhaps they're screaming with joy because they're propagating the species," said the monk.

"I doubt I'd be too exited if I came back as a monkey," said Siri. "Isn't it funny how it works that way? Man has a good chance to come back as man, or, at a pinch, some superior animal species, but you lot make it hard for a turtle to climb the ladder. I mean, what exactly would an orangutan have to do to amass enough credit to come back as a pornographer?"

"I doubt any self-respecting orangutan would consider that to be an incentive."

Siri laughed and threw a pebble in the pond. The fat fish gathered around it.

"Ah, Siri," said the Sangharaj, "I feel you and I will have such fun discussing our relative values. Me explaining the simplicity of religion. You being wrong about everything."

"You've spoiled that confrontation, I'm afraid," said Siri. "Because it would come down to me sticking to my principles and you floating away from yours on a plastic boat."

"Are you a good Communist, Siri?"

"That's a non sequitur to take my mind off your defection."

"It's relevant, trust me. Do you believe everything they tell you? Are you convinced the system works? Are there times when you're embarrassed to represent the doctrine you've dedicated your life to?"

In his mind, Siri knew the answers, of course. He'd been a paid-up member of the Communist Party since Paris, and there were times when it was beautiful, when he and his colleagues were genuinely excited at the potential. They believed all of the unfairness of the world could be fed into the big pork mincer of Communism and come out fine and dandy. And it would fit burger-sized into buns to feed the poor. And everyone would be full and equal. But it didn't happen. And he wasn't about to spill his ideological guts to the Sangharaj on their first date. He threw in his own non sequitur.

"Haven't you ever sinned?" he asked.

"Unless you're seeking a confession, what would your point be in asking that question?"

"If I really need a point, perhaps it's that nothing is pure. That mankind is basically flawed. That we all pretend to believe in something but we realize it isn't exactly right, or even necessary. Everything's a compromise. There are blemishes and stains, but we ignore them because we desperately want to experience that trust. It's natural. Faith should be at the top of Maslow's hierarchy of needs. We're so desperate for it we gladly allow ourselves to be short-changed just so we can believe in something."

The two men watched the carp roll over each other.

"And love?" asked the Sangharaj.

"The ultimate compromise," said Siri. "It's so important to have a partner that we cut and shape our tastes and likes and dislikes and go to great lengths to tolerate differences. We do this so we have someone beside us. In this insane quest for institutional faith we need a sidekick: somebody to give us a daily burst of faith at the grassroots level. A little shot of home belief. In that way when our religions and our politics and our doctrines disappoint us it isn't so important because we have love. My planet is parched and crumbling, but my bedroom is in full bloom."

"That's the part I was waiting for," came a voice from behind them.

They turned around to see Madam Daeng leaning against a flowering plumeria. The blossoms formed a halo. The monk smiled.

"If only I'd had you two as neighbors in Luang Prabang," he said, "I might have survived. But all I had was sycophants to the right of me and agnostic cadres to the left. Nobody with me in the middle."

"We could have had cocktail parties," said Daeng. She joined them at the pond, keeping a respectful distance from the monk. Her stomach rumbled loudly as she watched the delicious fish, reminding her she hadn't eaten. But Siri appeared not to share her hunger.

"Suppose you tell us about your friend, the abbot," he said.

"You really came all this way to help him?" asked Daeng.

The monk studied the bushy tail of a passing cloud. "I came to offer support," he said. "I'm not sure how much help I can be. We're Lao, and we have no legal right to interfere here. But the abbot is in a terrible fix. It all started in the Western New Year period. There was a murder in this village. Abbot Rayron told me about it on his last visit to Luang Prabang. An ascetic monk had been staying here at the temple. You'll learn today just how . . . different this village is. It attracts a number of tourists and researchers and thrill seekers. The visitor was collecting information to better understand religions and had asked to stay for a week. Abbot Rayron is generally here alone, so he appreciates company. They found the young man's body on the track. It's a sort of shortcut between the village and the temple, but few people are brave enough to use it. The villagers claim it passes through a part of the forest that is densely populated with ghosts. The monk had been hit on the head with a rock that was found lying nearby.

"The police captain came from Nam Som to investigate. Gumron, he's a career policeman. Very thorough. He asked around the village, took statements. He took the rock away as evidence even though there are no questions you can ask a rock to learn who wielded it."

"Fingerprints," thought Siri to himself. He was a great fan of fingerprinting as a crime-solving method and had used it in the past to prove points. He wondered how advanced a rural Thai police officer might be in forensic skills.

"There was no conclusion," said the Sangharaj. "The traveling monk had been here for too short a time to have antagonized anyone. He had nothing to steal and was, according to the abbot, a thoroughly likeable fellow. There were no witnesses, no suspects and the case was suspended."

Ugly staggered across the lawn, looked unenthusiastically at the fish, and crashed sideways into the long grass beside the pond.

"And the second murder?" Daeng asked.

"Exactly a month later," said the monk. "I suppose it couldn't be described as a murder as the victim was already deceased. There's a tradition in the village that dates back to before the temple was built. This compound is comparatively new, you see? It was built in the sixties. Before its arrival the dead would be laid out in a gazebo behind the headman's house. It was a convenient place from which to carry the body to the pyre. The deceased was a young man who'd died mysteriously in his sleep. It happens a lot here in the northeast. They say it was the work of an evil witch who makes love to sleeping men, but I heard he'd been drinking some locally produced hooch of questionable quality. Anyway, the family came in the morning to take the body to the pyre only to find him on the platform with a ceremonial knife buried in his heart."

"What type of knife?" asked Siri.

"I believe it was a prop once used for exorcisms."

"And where might that have come from?"

The monk smiled. "You'll see," he said.

"So two criminal acts a month apart but no evidence they were connected," said Daeng.

"No. But on this occasion there was a witness. A young girl had been doing her ablutions late at night behind her hut. Through the gaps in the bamboo shower room she saw a monk."

"But it would have been dark," said Siri.

"Full moon," said the Sangharaj. "Just as the murder of the traveling monk had been on the night of the full moon a month earlier."

"Not the most sensible night to be doing evil deeds," said Daeng. "No cover of darkness."

"The same police captain came," said the old monk, "Gumron. He asked around again, but this time he wasn't satisfied with the answers. He interviewed Abbot Rayron and asked him why he was in the village late at night. The abbot said that he wasn't. As the abbot was the only monk known to be in the vicinity at the time, either he or the girl was lying. The inquiry again ground to a halt for lack of evidence, but the seeds of suspicion had been sown."

"And the third murder was also on a full moon?" said Daeng.

"A month ago," said the Sangharaj. "The village elders had been playing cards and drinking and getting raucous as they do. Most rowdy of them all was Loong Gan, age ninety-seven, oldest man in the village, illegitimate children in the hundreds. Abbot Rayron had cornered him earlier in the day and told him it wasn't too late to change his ways. Of course it was, but it's a standard pep talk to steer him from the hells. We're obliged to run it by those of little hope. They'd had one of their customary slagging matches, and Rayron had perhaps uttered one or two small insults that he hadn't learned from the temple.

"The next day they found Loong Gan facedown in a paddy, strangled with his own loincloth and slashed to pieces. And here everything comes together. Not one but three witnesses saw drunken Loong Gan being helped back to his hut on the arm of Abbot Rayron. And in front of the police captain one shy boy stepped up to admit that on the night of the death of the wandering monk, the first murder, he'd seen two monks, one following the other in the direction of the temple path. So it was all cut and dried. The captain arrested Abbot Rayron and took him to the police station in Nam Som. There is no tradition here of allowing a suspect one phone call. A local man would rely on his family to prove him innocent as nobody can afford a lawyer. But the abbot was familiar with the head of the police, who allowed him to make a call to a number in Nong Khai to explain his plight. The jungle telegraph carried that message all the way to me in Luang Prabang."

"Why isn't he still in jail?" asked Siri.

"Because, for as long as it lasts, I'm the Supreme Patriarch of Laos, and the police lieutenant is a very religious man. I vouched for the abbot, and he is here under my house arrest, at least until the judge gets here."

"Judges do house calls?" said Daeng.

"Not exactly," said the Sangharaj. "It's complicated. They aren't exactly judges, more like traveling public prosecutors with the right to make judgments on certain issues."

"Like Judge Bao Gong," said Siri who was a huge fan of the stories of the Chinese street judge. "He travels the land dispensing wisdom and justice in even measures. A pleasantly mannered man who can hang you."

"I don't think they can carry out the executions themselves," said the Sangharaj. "But they can refer you to courts in the cities where the prosecutor's assessment of a case is invariably not questioned. So I don't think I'm understating their power."

"So how long do we have to sort this all out?" asked Daeng.

"Prosecutor Suthon will be hearing the abbot's case tomorrow afternoon. They have a sort of courtroom in Nam Som."

"That's not much time, is it?" said Siri. "As I see it, there are two possibilities. The first is that he did it, which makes him a nutcase who deserves whatever the Thai justice system doles out to him. The second is that he's being framed. It really isn't that hard to shave your head and get ahold of saffron robes. They give them away at temple fetes. At night, even under a full moon, all you ever notice are the body shape, the shiny head and the robes. So the method's simple enough. All we need then is motive. Do you suppose there might be anyone in the village with a grudge against the abbot? Anyone who might see the temple as a threat to traditional beliefs? Any possible conflicts of faith?"

The Sangharaj turned to Siri, and another laugh rose from his gut. It was an infectious bronchial chortle, the type you'd expect from quarry workers or smokers who drank too much. He probably hadn't found a lot to laugh about of late, so Siri didn't begrudge him. But they had no idea what he was laughing about. It took some minutes for the rapture to die down.

"I think it's time you visit Sawan Village," said the Sangharaj.

For the first time since his rescue, Ugly the dog wasn't at Siri's heel when he set off along the shortcut trail to the village. The dog sat and stubbornly refused to take another step. So unexpected was it that Siri didn't even notice his absence until they were halfway along the track. He whistled. The dog didn't come.

"Weird," Daeng told the monk. "That dog goes everywhere with the doctor. If he wasn't afraid of being inside buildings I'm sure he would sleep with us."

"It won't be the last weirdness you see today," said the Sangharaj.

"I have to warn you we're rather hard to shock," said Siri.

He had no doubt there was heavy supernatural activity all around them. He could see the spirit shadows in the forest. They looked up nervously like deer when he passed. They were merely ghosts with no ill intentions, but his talisman told him of a deeper presence, one that couldn't be seen. The stone had ceased to be a chunk of rock and had taken on animate qualities. It squeezed his chest like a hand. It squirmed like a warm rattlesnake beneath his shirt. It was alive.

"Why was the temple built so far outside the village?" Daeng asked.

"Neutral ground," said Siri. "It was the only plot left unoccupied."

"By whom?" Daeng asked.

"The bad ghosts. The *phibob.*"

"I see," she said. "So we're heading off into another Siri moment. Marvelous."

Before she was reunited with Siri a few years earlier, Daeng had paid homage to her ancestors and shown respect to the spirits of the land. She'd had no personal dealings with any of them, but it was what her parents and grandparents had done. Just as a Muslim child has no doubt there is Allah, so little Daeng never questioned there were spirits. It hadn't been necessary to touch or be touched by them. But then came Siri with his entourage. Whether it was magic or hypnosis, it mattered not. She had a tail, and the tail had rid her of a debilitating infliction. Her husband saw ghosts. It was merely a confirmation that millions of spirit worshippers in the world were as sane as anyone else.

The trail opened onto the type of village they'd seen thousands of times in their travels. Bamboo and wood houses on stilts with grass roofs, large concrete water pots, pigs, antique-looking farm implements, dirt, fenced-in vegetables, neat gardens and a well-kept village center with a court for rattan ball. Daeng saw nothing immediately threatening about the place, but she turned to Siri, and his face was as white as coconut meat.

"Siri, are you all right?" she asked.

"I feel like an outlaw who's just ridden into town and seen his face on a hundred wanted posters," he told her.

She had no idea what he meant.

Sawan's headman was standing by the rattan ball net with a toothless smile. He was about fifty, muscular and had a face abused, perhaps, in Muay Thai tournaments. Time had healed over the beatings like an ancient ruin covered in moss.

"Welcome," he said, putting his hands together in a *nop* the Thais called a *wai.* Siri and Daeng responded in kind. The Sangharaj did not respond because, well, he was supreme. Daeng wondered how the headman had known to expect them.

"I'm Tham," said the headman.

"This is my wife, Daeng," said Siri. "And I am . . ."

"You are Yeh Ming," said Tham. "Of course. We've been expecting you."

It happened often. Yeh Ming was the name of Siri's resident shaman who had hopped from body to body for a thousand years. Siri had told few living beings about his possession, yet he often ran into those who felt the presence of the old Hmong before they saw the doctor. The Sangharaj raised what used to be eyebrows and smiled in admiration.

"He's mistaken me for someone else," said Siri.

"I don't think so," said the monk.

"Let me show you our dear Sawan," said Tham like a proud parent introducing a new baby.

It was only when they came close to the houses that they could see just how bizarre the village was. Every hut was adorned with some kind of supernatural paraphernalia. But there was no cultural uniformity. It was as if each resident had decided which spirit to worship and which to be afraid of. It was like an open-air museum of paranormal paranoia. There were Hmong gates and bridges for the lost souls to find their ways home, and glass ornaments and mirrors to ward off unwanted spirits. There were smelly portals of dried garlic and gardens of straw or taro root dolls like regiments of tiny terracotta warriors. There were white cotton strings looping down beside the entryways and stuffed animals with looks of horror on their faces. Some huts displayed old coconuts made up to look like shrunken heads, and even though they were five hundred kilometers from the sea there were garlands of seashells strung out on posts.

And, in front of every hut there was a hand-painted board with a menu of services and their costs:

FINDING LOST OBJECTS/PEOPLE—30 baht
FAMILY SÉANCE—50 baht
CURSES AND GOOD WISHES—20 baht

Villagers sat on rocking chairs or on their front steps waving at the visitors, announcing their skills and calling out special offers. Siri couldn't believe his eyes. This was a tourist town: the Disneyland of animism. But it wasn't a scam. He could feel the power. He was certain country folk would travel here to solve their problems. Yet he remembered how the taxi driver had been afraid to bring them. Only the desperate would come. There was something sad about the services they offered. It was as if the true potential of the village was being constrained. Something was holding these folk back.

All around, he could see or sense the limbo people. They leaned against trees, sat on the branches, sunbathed on the grass waiting for assistance that never came. And permeating all of this was a dark fog, a stratum of malevolence where the *phibob* lurked. He could feel their anticipation, the excitement of some impending disaster. He knew his arrival had created a murmur that would change everything in Sawan.

The Sangharaj called a halt to the tour. "Tham," he said, "I believe you have morning tea arranged for your guests."

"Indeed I do," said Tham.

Tea was in the gazebo where, normally, the bodies were laid out before the pyre. As it was impossible for everyone in the village to meet Yeh Ming, they whittled the reception down to nine. They lined up like actors being introduced to royalty. Tham introduced them by specialty followed by name. Tham himself was the senior exorcist, quick to point out that he was retired.

The diviner, Song, was a tall woman with teary eyes and hair streaked white like Frankenstein's bride. The intermediary, Cham, had a shaved head and was fey bordering on effeminate. His superior, a full-fledged medium, was Tian. She was an older woman not unlike Daeng in appearance, with the same unruly mop of short white hair and a wicked smile. Then there were the shaman brothers, Phi and Lek, who were responsible for making bargains with the spirits. They were both missing their left legs, although Tham didn't bother to explain why. The village priestess was Thewa, who had probably been cherubic in her youth but now looked like a potato. The herbalist, Ya, was perhaps the youngest of the group and resembled one of the handsome stars of a Thai television drama. This left only the fortune-teller, Doo. He was stocky and unpleasant both in looks and in nature. His hair was in clumps as if he'd cut it with blunt scissors, and he had a goiter the size of a ripe papaya on his neck. He refused to join the queue to shake the visitors' hands and grumbled continuously under his breath.

Siri and Daeng would have no problem remembering them, as they were named in Thai language after their roles and most of them looked the part. They were dressed in their respective costumes and were a colorful bunch. Tea was served along with a tasteless doughy cake that had no purpose other than to soak up the tea. All but Doo clamored around Siri with the adoration usually reserved for rock stars. The Sangharaj and Daeng were largely ignored.

"I have to begin by asking how you all came to be in this village," said Siri. "I can tell from your ethnicity and accents that you've traveled from far and wide. Why did you settle here?"

He'd planned to avoid mentioning the claustrophobic presence of the *phibob*, but in company such as this, where everyone communicated on non-verbal levels, it was a foolish plan.

"The thing we have in common," said Priestess Thewa, "is that we were all banished from our own villages."

"Because we were possessed by *phibob*," said Intermediary Cham.

"All of you?" said Siri, dumbfounded.

"The first two generations," said Headman Tham. "They haven't got to our grandchildren yet."

"And never will," grumbled Doo.

"We were like lepers," said Medium Tian. "It didn't even have to be proven. You know what it's like in the countryside, Yeh Ming. There's a suspicion that turns into a rumor that overnight becomes a fact."

"Then you weren't all possessed?" said Siri.

"Not completely," said Shaman Phi.

"Perhaps a little," said Shaman Lek. "From time to time. We were all in the spirit trade, you see? There were a lot of currents and waves passing through us. It's likely we'd pick up a *phibob* or two."

"But it's more like the flu than cancer," said Headman Tham. "You get over it."

"Some get it like cancer," grumbled Doo.

Siri had learned his lessons in *phibob*ery very quickly. They were not the spirits of the deceased. Neither were they, strictly speaking, the spirits of the forest. They were the ghosts that existed as a result of the destruction of nature. In a previous incarnation they may have been placid tree-dwellers. Then, one day, their home was gone, their roots lost. And they began to wander aimlessly and became more and more volatile. And as more forests were destroyed, so the *phibob* joined forces and became powerful. They did their evil by possessing a living being like a hand inside a sock puppet. The demoniacs rarely knew they were possessed unless they had their own channel to the spirit world.

Madam Daeng had never attended a meeting such as

this, and she was quite plainly thrilled by the ridiculousness of it all. She smiled at the Sangharaj, who replied with a slight tilt of his brow. She noticed how Medium Tian, the oldest woman in the group, would strain her neck from time to time to get a better look at Daeng's backside. The woman would give her a knowing smile before returning her attention to the meeting. The thought that her tail might be visible to this crowd made Daeng feel oddly self-conscious.

"Look, let's get to the point," said Doo.

"And what might the point be?" asked Priestess Thewa.

"The point," said Doo, "is not to discuss our origins. These outsiders are here because one of theirs is about to be executed for murder."

"Oh, do shut up," said Diviner Song.

Doo ignored her. "They're here to find a scapegoat," he said. "His high and mightiness there thinks we're expendable because we're clay doll worshippers. He thinks he can dangle one of our names in front of the judge, and they'll do a deal. Free the monk; shoot the village idiot."

"Then that would have to be you," said Headman Tham.

"Why else would they be here lording over us?" asked Doo. "Looking down at us like all those fancy abbots in Bangkok."

"Sorry," said Headman Tham to the Sangharaj. "He can see the future, so I suppose he doesn't have much to be positive about."

"But he does have a point," said Shaman Lek. "Given the Sangha's views on the occult, how can the Sangharaj be here with an open mind?"

"We really don't want to insult our guests," said Headman Tham.

"No, actually I don't mind at all," said the Sangharaj. "I'd like a chance to clear my name."

"It's not nec—"

"Really," said the Sangharaj. "I wonder if our learned fortune-teller realizes that there are as many members of the Thai Sangha Council who condemn our Lao version of Buddhism as those who make fun of your pagan rituals."

"I'm no pagan," said Doo.

"Nor am I," said the monk. "Animism had existed for centuries in my country long before Buddhism arrived. We are a fragmented nation of hundreds of different ethnic groups, each with its own beliefs. All of them were convinced of the existence of a spirit or a soul. Buddhism in other places denied the existence of a self—said that a soul is the source of suffering—but we didn't want to alienate those tribes, did we now? Didn't want to steamroll through centuries of culture. So we conceded that there is such a thing as a soul. That immediately pitted us against the mainstream. There were other contentious differences. Gods, for example. Our deities reside in their own heaven, whereas world Buddhism emphasizes impermanence. There was no room for compromise. We had defied our own order. So you see, in the Sangha's eyes I'm no less a heathen than you."

That was the moment when Siri and Daeng became aware that the Sangharaj had no intention of defecting to Bangkok.

"In conclusion," said the monk, "I am here because my friend is in trouble. I like and trust the abbot, so I have traveled far to be here in order to help prove him innocent. Does anybody here honestly believe a dedicated man such as Abbot Rayron would suddenly go rogue for no reason?"

This sparked a general discussion on both the good works of the abbot and a good-natured free-for-all examining the facts and putting forward new theories. There was nothing insightful nor particularly brilliant about the comments. Siri was always surprised by the day-to-day simplicity of the men and women who, with the right stimulus, tackled demons and rode on the back of stallions to the otherworld. But this was not a philosophical gathering. It was a collection of facts. They agreed that the girl who claimed to have seen a monk at night had no reason to lie. In fact, her future depended on her honesty. Her ambition was to join an order. In Thailand, a woman wishing to become a nun was like a man dreaming of becoming a street sweeper. There was nothing in the way of respect or financial gain to be had by joining a nunnery. Buddhism was an unashamedly misogynistic religion. Women were told that to become enlightened they would first have to be reborn a man. But she didn't seem to care. As lying was sinful she admitted that although she had seen a monk walk away from the village, she could not be certain it was Abbot Rayron.

The boy who had seen two monks walk to the shortcut on the night of the first murder was also unlikely to have lied. It was the abbot himself who had persuaded him to step forward with his eyewitness account. The lad studied at the temple and was one of the abbot's brightest. The village was too far from the nearest government school, so the children in Sawan studied in the temple. All the abbot's students adored him. The parents were pleased he didn't proselytize but instead encouraged the children to form their own view of the world by listening to all sides of a debate, religion included.

"So the abbot incriminated himself," said Daeng. "That hardly sounds like the action of a guilty man."

"Murderers can be devious," said Doo.

"Oh, shut up," said almost everyone.

"But that brings us to the night when your eldest villager was killed," said Siri.

"Nobody mourned that man," said Diviner Song.

"Evil piece of shit," said Shaman Phi.

"That doesn't excuse drowning him in his own paddy and gutting him," said Headman Tham.

"Who was he drinking with?" Siri asked.

Headman Tham, the shaman brothers and Doo put up their hands.

"I liked him," said Doo.

"It's a small village," said Shaman Lek. "If you like a drink you either indulge at home alone and get nagged at by the wife, or you come here to the gazebo."

"This is your pub?" said Daeng.

"We have a communal still out back," said Headman Tham, glancing at the Sangharaj hoping for forgiveness and not receiving it.

"So Loong Gan staggered out of here the way we came in," said Siri. He stood and went to the entrance, retrieving his sandals on the way out. The others followed.

"He went that way," said Shaman Phi, pointing across the clearing beyond the rattan ball court. "We all followed him out."

"And where was he when the monk came to help him?"

"Just at the tree line."

"Even with a full moon it's quite a distance to make a clear identification," said Siri. "And I assume you were all drunk."

Daeng stood scratching her head. "Was it closing time?" she asked.

"What?" said the headman.

"You all left at the same time," she said. "Did they close the bar?"

They laughed.

"It's not the type of bar that closes," said the headman. "You come and you go as you please."

"Then why did you all leave together?" she asked.

They all looked at each other but nobody had an answer.

Then, one of the shamans said, "The whistle."

"That's right," said Doo. "There was a whistle. I'd completely forgotten about that."

"What whistle?" asked Siri.

"It was like a police whistle," said the headman. "Loong Gan left and we heard this whistle, and the first thing we thought was that he'd been arrested. Now, thinking back, that doesn't make any sense because who's going to arrest him late at night for being drunk in his own village? And we have no local policeman. But, well, we were all in our cups. So we ran out."

"And that's when you saw him meet the monk?" said Siri.

"That's right."

"Interesting."

Before he retired for the night, Siri decided now was a good time to have a chat with the quiet abbot. He found him in the prayer hall reading by candlelight.

"Are you busy?" Siri asked, sitting opposite the monk without waiting for an invitation.

The abbot put down his book and removed his glasses. "Please," he said.

"Did you kill those people?" Siri asked.

"That's your first question?" said the abbot.

"Always good to get that one out of the way first," said Siri.

The abbot took some time to reply. "What do you think?" he asked.

Siri smiled. "Well, son, that really was the wrong answer. I hope for your sake the judge doesn't ask you that question. I don't know you. I don't know anything about you. So if you ask me what I think, looking at the evidence, I'd say you're as guilty as sin."

He looked around to give the abbot time to rethink his answer. They were sitting cross-legged in the prayer hall. The Buddha image looked down on them, jolly in its new coat of yellow paint. The wall murals depicted scenes of what Civilai called the Indian music hall version of Buddha's life: flying through the air and bursting into flames, taking on Angulimāla, the killer of thousands, walking through mountains.

"Then, no," said the abbot at last.

"Well, somebody's trying really hard to make us believe you did," said Siri. "So if you can think of anyone who might want you put away for life, now's the time to remember."

The long gaps between question and answer were vexing. Siri drummed his fingers on his knees.

"I'm a Buddhist monk in an animist village," said the abbot. "I have a big fine palace to live in because the Buddhist Council has a budget for buildings and ornaments. It's possible the spirit worshippers in the village resent this opulence because in their eyes I'm just another shaman. Brother Ya mixes potions that make a man irresistible to women. Sister Song selects a spot to dig a well. Abbot Rayron performs at funerals. I could branch out. There are monks who bless airplanes and provide lottery numbers and tell fortunes. But I do not. I don't step on anyone's toes. I adhere to my scriptures. I teach. I lead by example. I try to steer the villagers in the direction of better decisions on health and personal relationships and management of resources. But I don't preach. It's not our way. I tell stories. I hope to inspire. But I've never had a heated debate on the benefits of my religion. If you ask me if I'm respected here, I'd say I hope so. If I'm liked? I hope so. If I've angered a man enough to wish me dead? That, I hope not."

Siri shifted his numb buttocks and stretched his spine. One gentle crack echoed through the hall. He stared at the abbot. He was what Madam Daeng referred to as "eventually handsome": a face you don't immediately consider to be good-looking but which grows on you. He was about forty with a body that left no evidence of the sugars and alcohol and starches and fats and tobacco the twentieth century inflicted upon the weak.

"Then what about your personal life?" Siri asked.

"I'm a monk. I don't have a personal life."

"But you did. Before the monkhood."

"Oh, such a distant life. How is that likely to help us, Doctor?"

"In your defense? Probably not at all. But in understanding you there's gold to be panned in a man's origins."

"Then I think your pan might be empty. I was abandoned at the temple when I was eight."

"Really?" said Siri. "Me too. See? Our first scoop, and we come up with empathy. Eight must have been the fashionable age to dump young boys."

"But you broke away, Doctor. I remained with the Buddha because he was the only father I knew. I'd been raised by a woman I loved and who apparently loved me. And then suddenly she wasn't in my life. People I didn't know took over her duties. Then one day a man came to the house. He looked Chinese, but he spoke Thai. He was well dressed. He put me in the backseat of his car. There was a small paper bag beside me that contained my clothes. I'd never been in a car. It was like flying in a magic device. And he dropped me at the temple, told me to be good for my mother's sake, mussed my hair and flew off. Thanks to the mode of my arrival I was instantly popular with the novices."

"Do you know where the temple was?"

"Of course. It was my home as a child. Wat Po in Udon Thani."

"And did you ever return there later in life to ask about the man with the car?"

The abbot contemplated his fists for a long time. "Not until it was too late. The monks I served as a novice were all dead, and there was no record of deliveries. Today people drop off dogs at the temples when they can no longer cope with them or are too poor to feed them. Back then the same applied to male children. I was an unwanted stray, but I found acceptance and peace."

"Until now."

"This is my destiny."

"Oh, don't give me that karma rot."

But this was to be the night when destiny demonstrated her power. It was beneath the light of a single moon that three unrelated women lost their lives: one on the outskirts of Vientiane, one in Pak Xan and one in a village of sleeping shamans. It was midnight and Madam Daeng was woken by the word *"merde"* repeated several times. She opened her eyes to see her husband hurriedly putting on his trousers by the light of the full moon. As she was not unused to emergencies in their relationship, she immediately stood and began to throw on her clothes as well.

"Where are we going?" she asked.

"To the village," he said.

"What's wrong?"

"My brain. I can't believe how stupid I am."

"Anytime you need reminding, feel free to ask."

They were already on their way out of the door with their bags over their shoulders.

"Five years, Daeng," he said. "Five years I was at that temple. They told us those damned stories over and over again until they were big chunks of unwanted gunk lodged in our memories. The Buddha stories. The son of a king decides to renounce his wealth and head off into the world leaving footprints and body parts from Nepal to China."

Daeng's flashlight worked that night although the full moon was bright enough to see the eyelashes on a mosquito. They were out of the temple compound gate and on the haunted path. Again, Ugly balked at the start of the track. The couple ran at a sort of geriatric road-walk pace ignoring the howls and groans coming from the jungle on either side. Siri's lungs weren't what they used to be, and Daeng had only recently reclaimed her leg muscles.

"I wish I'd brought the Triumph," he said.

"And what was it the Buddha did that was so important we need to risk heart attacks?" wheezed Daeng.

"The four . . . things."

"What four things?"

"The things the Buddha saw that made him realize the world wasn't all frangipani leis and champagne cocktails. He climbed over the palace wall and went into town to see what his parents had been shielding him from. And that's when he saw them."

"What? Who?"

"An ascetic, a corpse, an old man . . ."

They were too late for the sick woman. She'd been given some sort of fast-acting poison. When they arrived at her hut, her lips and the inside of her nose had already turned greyish white, and there was some bubbling around her mouth. Siri had seen her earlier in the day when he'd offered to take a look at the village sick. He'd found the elderly folk to be in remarkably good shape. The old woman was the only serious case that the herbs of young brother Ya had been unable to help, and Siri had treated her for hepatitis. The Buddha had seen a sick man on his fact-finding mission, but as there were none available, in this case, a sick woman would have to suffice.

Following Siri's alert, the villagers headed off with their weapons to find the murderer. Some voiced their opinions that they'd find the culprit back at the temple where he'd come from. An old witch suffering from insomnia had been rocking on a chair on her porch when the monk walked past in the direction of the dead woman's house. She had no doubt whatsoever in her mind that the monk was Abbot Rayron.

◎ ◎ ◎

Humnoy, the man who currently ran the Lao national police force, was neither a policeman nor a military man. Nor was he an academic versed in the laws of the country because they were yet to be written. Nor was he a bookkeeper of any standing. His qualifications for the role could be summed up in the phrase, "He's a good Party member and the brother-in-law of somebody important."

The lack of abilities in no way prevented him from doing his job. The buck had to stop somewhere, and he was the perfect man to stop it. He made endless arbitrary decisions based, apparently, upon how to upset the fewest of his superiors. His favorite words were *bo dai,* which naturally meant "no."

"*Bo dai,*" he said having listened intently to the inspector's request. It was no less than Phosy expected. But Phosy was no two-left-footer when it came to circle-dancing with administrators.

"Yes, that was my first reaction too," he said. "Why rile the military? Who really cares that their soldiers kidnapped an innocent civilian on the street in front of witnesses? He probably deserved it. Why, the two young soldiers are probably downstairs right now putting in an official complaint about whatever it was he'd done. Because we all know this is not a country run by a military junta, but a democratic republic with a fully functioning police force charged with the responsibility of keeping the peace."

"I'm not—"

"In fact that's what I reminded Corporal Suwit on Friday."

"Who?"

"Corporal Suwit at the Armed Forces Ministry. Oh, sorry. I assumed you two were acquainted. He knows everything there is to know about you down to your shoe size."

"What in blazes does this Suwit have to do with me?"

"He's the head of the military—national police liaison department. You do know that exists, right?"

"There is no such thing."

Phosy had gambled on his boss having no more knowledge of the department than Phosy himself before he stumbled across it.

"With all due respect, sir, I was sitting in that office just a few days ago. Suwit seemed to have a lot of information about me and my cases. He had a file on my department as thick as a temple lintel."

"But that's . . . that's atrocious."

"Couldn't agree more, sir. Especially given some of his comments about . . . No, doesn't matter."

"Phosy!"

"No, really. I shouldn't say."

"I order you to tell me."

"There was nothing direct. Just comments about . . . about your suitability for this position. What they called 'a poor track record.'"

"Bastards."

"I know, sir. I told him I didn't want to hear any more."

"How dare the army keep files on us?"

"How dare they, indeed?"

The director was a broad man, brawny, easily angered. His cheeks reddened to signal he'd passed his limit, but commendably he didn't raise his voice. He placed his big hands flat on the desk and practiced his breathing. Phosy sat patiently. Finally, the director nodded.

"These witnesses," he said.

"Yes, sir?"

"Would they be prepared to give evidence?"

"I believe so."

"All right. Bring 'em in."

"Are you sure it's—?"

"Just do it."

Phosy stopped outside the director's door. He should have been sitting in that chair. He'd fought and spied bravely for the Pathet Lao during the resistance years. He'd agreed to join the police to convert men of war into peacekeepers. He'd been integral in the writing of most of the temporary regulations they were using as their flimsy legal base. But it seemed that for every competent man or woman there was an incompetent man above. It was the law of trickle-up irresponsibility. And the competent man and woman spent so much time manipulating the incompetent men they had neither the time nor the motivation to do their jobs properly.

Phosy took a police jeep out to the kiosk of the cordial seller. He had a young sergeant by his side. He'd omitted to mention that the innocent civilian was not Lao. And there was, of course, just the one eyewitness, and she had no idea who the kidnappers were. All she had was an instinct, and that wouldn't carry any weight in the court of law—if in fact they had such things. But Phosy had people who owed him favors. He was certain one or two of them could be diverted retrospectively to the scene of the crime. And with backup, who knew what the cordial seller might recall?

She wasn't sitting behind the bottles when they arrived. He drove off the road and down the track that led to her bamboo hut. The pile of empties still dominated the yard. The hut wasn't a complicated structure: A single room on stilts with barely enough space for a pig below. A ladder up to an unfenced balcony.

Phosy stood on the middle step and banged on the banana-leaf door. There was no answer. The balcony was caked in dust from the road, but out of courtesy he kicked off his sandals and climbed up.

"Anybody there?" he called.

No answer. Even before he pushed the flimsy door a familiar smell hit him. He knew what to expect. The room was buzzing with flies. They seemed to congregate mostly around the far side of the room where a window shape was cut out of the panel. There was a dark, dry puddle. There had been a lot of blood, although much of it would have seeped down through the gaps in the bamboo flooring. He sighed and looked through the window. The scenery was beautiful: white terns on the backs of buffalo, lush green paddies, and verdant trees that looked like they could defy the advance of development forever. The only nature that ever disappointed him was of the human variety.

◙ ◙ ◙

It was an odd breakfast. Captain Gumron had been dragged out of his bed at two to investigate yet another murder at Sawan Village. As there was no phone line to Nam Som, Yuth, the headman's slow-witted son, had taken the village motorcycle to alert the police. The captain, having talked to some peculiar Lao coroner and his wife—both apparently in the country illegally—had interviewed the eyewitness to the crime. She was riddled with cataracts in both eyes, but he really had no choice but to re-arrest Abbot Rayron. The sun was up, and he and his constable were tired and in need of a feed. As the alms at Sawan village were legendary, they decided to accept the offer of breakfast before dragging the suspect off to jail. The only other good news was that this was court day. They would have had to come anyway to cart the monk off to hear the judge's decision on the previous month's hearings. So, in a way, they were killing two birds with one stone.

As Abbot Rayron was accused of multiple homicides, the Sangharaj had graciously agreed to take on the abbot's alms that morning. He returned with a feast worthy of a five-star hotel. Abbot Rayron sat a few meters behind the Supreme Patriarch, eating meagerly.

"Well, if you didn't do it, brother," said Captain Gumron, slurping up spoonfuls of delicious rice porridge, "you must have really pissed somebody off. Because it means there's a character out there pretending to be you killing folk and defiling corpses. Anybody hate you that much?"

"Not to my knowledge," said the abbot.

"It might not be personal," said Siri.

The captain had long since tired of the old Lao man's theories. He was on the verge of making this a double arrest.

"What do you mean, Siri?" asked the Sangharaj.

"Well, think about it," said Siri. "An anonymous monk committing crimes that mirror the revelations of the Buddha. This isn't a murderer who hates Abbot Rayron. It's a murderer who hates the religion."

"I'd like to remind you all this is an ongoing investigation," said the captain. "And I am not at liberty to discuss theories or wild accusations."

"Then don't say anything," said Madam Daeng. "Just listen."

The captain laughed. "One more comment like that, young lady, and I'll have you in handcuffs," said the captain.

Siri's haunches rose. The policeman was clearly flirting with his wife. The Thais had no scruples. The doctor had no choice but to lock horns with this rival.

"Whilst doing my rounds of the elderly and infirm of the village," he said, "I noticed how few villagers had hair above their collars. I think it's something the Thai police should have taken into consideration."

"What?" said the captain. "Hair fashion? Isn't that more the role of your morals police up in Laos? Length of hair. Length of hem. We've got better things to do."

"I'm talking, of course, about beginning the search for the man who's impersonating Abbot Rayron. Something you should have been doing months ago."

He stared at the Thai policeman, who was stuffing his face with food meant for the monks. He was in his fifties, and, despite the restrictive qualities of the Thai police uniform, he had a considerable paunch. He walked as if he expected a wild boar to run between his legs. He wasn't at all Madam Daeng's type, yet she fluttered her eyelids every time he looked her way.

"In fact," Siri continued, "if I were a Thai policeman I'd be looking at the elders of the village. One or two of them are losing their hair. I'd be focusing on men over forty."

"Mr. Coroner," said Gumron, using the derogatory term, "ghost doctor," suggesting Siri's role was more a vocation than a profession, "from getting out of bed this morning to my arrival here took thirty minutes. Anyone with a motorcycle or car can come here. Why would I concentrate my efforts on the village when anyone from the town could have done it?"

Siri smiled. "Because," he said, "this is a crime of hate. You have so many more splendid temples around Nam Som with many more monks to abuse. Much more explosive points to be made. But he chooses a small temple in the jungle. No. Whatever inspired these murders has its roots here."

"Of course," said the captain. "A man of science. You'd be delighted if the murderer was a shaman or an exorcist or any one of the weird characters who practice pagan rituals here. You're prejudiced."

Daeng wiped a tissue over her lips, smiled and left the men to their duel. Siri would have loved to race after her, lift her tail and shout, "Is this prejudice?"

He would gladly have disappeared right then and reappeared five minutes later to see the look of amazement on the man's face. But there was something about the captain. His ease around the villagers. His willingness to come to Sawan alone when other townies dared not unless they were in a tour group. Siri understood.

"You're from here," he said.

"What?"

"You're a Sawan lad. A child of the sages. These are your people."

"Grandfather, I think you've done enough amateur detective work, don't you?" He turned away from Siri's satisfied smile and addressed the abbot. "The constable and me came on two motorcycles. Do you want the boy to go back to bring a van, or . . . ?"

"I'm fine on the back of a motorcycle," said the abbot.

"I thought so," said the captain. "I don't suppose you have much in the way of belongings?"

The abbot held up his small saffron shoulder bag.

"When will the judge hear the abbot's case?" asked the Sangharaj.

"Well, sir, it's not exactly something you could set a clock to," said the captain. "We're on what they call the judicial circuit. Prosecutor Suthon is here once a month. When he's in town he gets through as many cases as he can in three days. He got here yesterday. Now, the more serious the case, the higher the priority. He'll be expecting to pass down a verdict on last month's murder. He won't be prepared at all for what happened last night. I'll have to type up the report of my findings here and that takes time. I don't know if he'll want to make a judgment without looking at the new evidence. So I'm guessing he'll not say a lot today."

"The abbot doesn't have the right to have witnesses speak on his behalf?" asked Siri.

"Usually not," said the captain. "All that stuff will be in my report."

"Doesn't that make you the judge?" said Siri.

"I don't write down opinions, Grandfather. I just make a note of what I see and what people tell me."

"That's what most of the newspapers in the world claim to be doing, but you'd be surprised how slanted the finished text turns out."

"Yeah, and you'd really know something about the world's newspapers."

"A bit."

"Nobody's ever questioned my reports," said the policeman. "I spend a lot of time getting them accurate."

His defensiveness was turning to annoyance, his tolerance taut as a piano wire. But still Siri pushed. "And meanwhile the accused rots away in a cell for a month waiting for the next judicial visit," he said.

The Sangharaj cut in like a boxing referee. "I too am concerned with the amount of time the abbot will have to wait before the next hearing."

"That's the system," said the captain. "We have cases ongoing for four or five years. We have witnesses and suspects die of old age before they hear a judgment."

"Isn't there any way to expedite the process?" asked the Sangharaj.

"In this country I'm sure money would speed things up," said Siri in the background.

Gumron ignored him. "Only one that I know," he said.

"And what would that be?" asked the Sangharaj.

"Publicity," said the captain. "If for some reason the press picks up on a story, especially if some celebrity's involved, and the TV people hop on board and the public weighs in on the side of the accused, then you'd be amazed how a case can speed up. Pressure from Bangkok to be seen doing its job. Good exposure overseas. But, then again it could all be over today."

"How so?" said Siri.

"Well, the judge has had time to go over the reports of the first three incidents. After the first two he said there wasn't enough evidence. But since then we had another murder, and now this. He might just recommend the death penalty this very day, and your abbot will be shipped off to Udon."

Siri looked at Abbot Rayron, whose expression hadn't changed since the doctor arrived. There had been no delight, no shock, no horror registered there. The doctor couldn't tell whether it was the look of enlightenment or resignation.

"And this all based on a couple of informal chats with villagers and scribbled notes and circumstantial evidence," said Siri. "No cross-examination. No research. No appeal. And I thought our system at home was barbaric."

The policeman had reached his limit. "Listen, you hick, Commie senior citizen, we do what we can on a low budget. We're swamped out here. It wasn't that long ago that all these cases were settled by village headmen with vested interests. You upset some old idiot today, and you find yourself in his court tomorrow. We've come a long way since then. You get your own house in order before you start throwing rocks at ours."

◙ ◙ ◙

Madam Nong had traveled back to Vientiane with the driver. Civilai was at the council office at exactly opening time. The officials of the district council office arrived between twenty and forty minutes later. Civilai continued to sit on a concrete bench in the garden where brown vines strangled the few surviving flowers and the grass was too high to walk through. Nobody asked him who he was or what he wanted. He noted how Communist bureaucracies constantly shifting cadres had created an impersonal, non-caring system.

He wasn't absolutely sure what he was doing there. Perhaps it was just that there had been nobody to complain to in the village, and the desire to vent one's frustrations could be a powerful thing. But there was something else. He'd felt ill at ease in Ban Toop. It wasn't a normal Lao village. He hoped that the government administrators could explain what was going on there.

At last he walked inside, where a greasy-faced girl was filing. "Where's your director?" he asked.

"Just sit down, Granddad," she said. "We'll get to you."

"I don't want to be got to," he said. "I want to speak to your director."

She sighed as if she'd had her fill of grumpy old people. Then she ignored him. She just carried on with her filing as if he didn't exist. Civilai hated being ignored almost as much as he hated the Chinese. He walked up behind her.

"What's in those files?" he asked.

"Oh, just sit down," she said.

"I wouldn't be surprised if one of your cabinet drawers was labeled something like . . . ooh, I don't know. Politburo? Am I right?"

She disregarded him, but she was clearly feeling uncomfortable. He walked along the bank of cabinets calling out the labels alphabetically until he reached the drawer he'd been looking for. He'd pulled it open and thumbed through the files before she could react. As he expected, the photographs of politburo members who had been retired from both the cabinet and the frames on the wall had been placed in the drawer. There was an expanding number of pictures of those who had passed away. He found the photo of himself just as the girl reached him. She made a lunge for it but his backward step was too quick for her.

"Well, look at this," he said. "I wonder who this vibrant young character is. He was a little thinner back then before the kitchen gods possessed him, but I think he's filled out quite nicely now, don't you?"

She looked at the photo, looked at the man who held it, then looked at the photo again. And her legs seemed to give way beneath her.

8

A Living Skeleton in the Closet

Civilai stood in the office of Comrade Luangrat, director of the local council, having refused water, juice, Coca-Cola, tea, coffee, snacks, cigarettes and "something a little stronger." He refused to sit as he listed the failings of the office. It was then that he added the debacle of his own official visit to the region and the absence of pomp and ceremony. The director was not the dynamic type. He looked like an old cinema usher who'd spent his life in the dark showing people to their seats. Even his embarrassment was subdued.

"We got the notification from Vientiane," he said.

"And threw it in the bin?"

"No, comrade," he said. "Naturally we informed the headman at Ban Toop. He insisted on making the arrangements for your visit himself."

"But it's the responsibility of you and your office to follow up on that. At the very least you should have been there to greet my wife and me. That's protocol."

"I know," said the director, timidly.

"So why weren't you?"

"It's . . . it's a little difficult to explain."

"Good. I have until my heart finally gives out to hear that difficult explanation."

Civilai sat behind the desk. The director was silent for the longest time.

"Well?" barked Civilai.

"The headman at Ban Toop is a very well-respected and powerful man."

"More respected and powerful than your office? More powerful than the administration you represent?"

"At the local level, I suppose one could say yes."

"You're afraid of him."

"Goodness, no. But my role here is to maintain cordial and productive relations with village communities that have been established for generations."

"Did he tell you not to send anyone to meet me?"

"Not in those words."

"Then, give me the words."

"He said they would welcome the esteemed visitor according to the traditions of the village."

Which means not welcoming him at all, thought Civilai, but he said nothing. He'd had enough. It was clear he was talking to the wrong man.

"I need a car," he said.

"We . . ."

"Yes?"

"We only have the one."

"That should be enough."

"There's no driver available."

"I've been driving since 1921. I think I remember how."

"But . . ."

"You really have a 'but' after all this?"

"No."

"I assume you have a fax machine?"

"Yes."

"Then I want you to contact my office in Vientiane. I'll give you the number. Tell them we have a village that could use a little discipline. You can use your own words. Explain to them what's happened and tell them to send out a team immediately. I'll stay until they get here. I'll come by this office tomorrow to collect the reply."

"You won't . . . I mean, this won't endanger my position here, will it?"

"Honestly, Comrade Luangrat," said Civilai, "I'm surprised you *have* a position here. Now, where's my car?"

◘ ◘ ◘

Nurse Dtui and Mr. Geung had been sitting in the reception area of the Ministry of Justice for forty-four minutes. There were only four hours between the lunch and dinner shifts at the noodle restaurant, so time was precious. Manivon, the chief clerk and secretary to Judge Haeng, had apologized every ten of those minutes. Apologizing took up a large chunk of her time most days. Dtui and Manivon had known and liked each other for a long time, so if strings could have been pulled to get Dtui into the judge's office they would have been. But her boss reminded everybody that these were particularly hectic times. The republic was a week away from formalizing diplomatic relations with Bulgaria. The Thai prime minister had visited, which had entailed setting up a number of impromptu meetings. The Soviet Development Commission had been touring the disastrous cooperative farming projects in the south, and there were moves afoot to recognize a Vietnamese puppet government in Cambodia led by an ex-officer of the Khmer Rouge.

In fact, Judge Haeng had been involved in none of these political matters but he used them as an excuse to hide out in his office with the blinds closed. Whenever Manivon knocked on his door he would jump out of his skin. He flinched at any loud sound and had stopped eating. Rumors were circulating in the ministry that he'd become an opium addict.

Dtui tapped Mr. Geung on the knee. "Let's go," she said.

"Go wh-where?" asked Geung.

"To disturb a rude judge," she told him.

"Poor judge," he said but followed her along the open corridor. If anyone had cause to hate the little judge—and many did—Mr. Geung should have been at the front of the queue. Haeng had gone to great pains to remove Geung from his position of morgue assistant at Mahosot Hospital. He'd called him a freak, said there was no budget to employ morons. Yet even though he understood all of these terms, honest, sweet Mr. Geung hadn't been able to find hatred in his heart.

They arrived at the unmarked door and Dtui knocked lightly before barging inside. She was just in time to see the judge drop to the floor behind his desk.

"Ha, ha. I spy you," said Geung.

"Judge Haeng," said Dtui, "it's me, Nurse Dtui."

"What do you want?" he asked.

She got on her knees. "Why are you under the desk?" she asked.

"Paper clip," he said. "Dropped one."

"Can I help you?" she asked.

"No." He banged his head on the underside of the desk when he tried to return to his chair. When he was finally seated he noticed Geung standing in the doorway.

"What's that doing here?" he asked.

"He's with me," said Dtui.

"I can see that," said the judge, slowly regaining his composure.

To Dtui, Haeng looked like a roll of moldy flannel.

"Are you all right?" she asked.

He was twiddling a pencil between his fingers to disguise his trembles.

"What gives you the right to inquire about my mind?" he asked.

"Err, I wasn't," she said. "I was asking after your health."

"Then don't," he said. "I'm perfectly well. Now, I don't believe you have an appointment." He looked menacingly at Geung, who waved his fingers in reply.

"In a way we do," said Dtui. "The doctor thinks he can help you with your little ghost problem. So he sent us."

"Siri?" said the judge. "Where the hell is he? I've been sending messages for two days."

"The doctor and Madam Daeng had to go . . . away on business."

"Damn. And what do you suppose a chubby girl can do for somebody like me?"

Dtui took one last gulp of her pride. She had promised Siri, after all. She remembered one of her mother's sayings. *When you're removing a splinter from a bear's paw, expect a few scratches.* Judge Haeng was a hard man to help.

"Look," she said. "Everything Dr. Siri knows about you—medically, politically, mentally and morally—I know about you too. The doctor and I have no secrets. So don't play the tough judge with me. I don't have to be here. I have noodles to boil and nurses to teach and a daughter to play with."

"Me too," said Geung with a grin.

"And, in fact, I'd be happier digging up beets in the communal garden than helping you. So either show a little humility, or we're leaving and you can spend the rest of your life haunted by a dwarf." She headed for the door.

"No, wait," he called.

Before heading to Comrade Koomki's apartment, they stopped off at the market for some supplies the doctor had recommended. At first they couldn't get Haeng to walk through the communal front doorway of the old colonial house.

"Tell me why we're here," he said.

"We're following up on a Dr. Siri hypothesis," Dtui told him. "Do you have the keys?"

She knew he did because she could hear them rattling in his shaky hand. She took them from him, walked along the corridor to Koomki's room and opened the door. The apartment smelled of excrement but not death. Dtui considered that a good sign.

"We might be in time," she said.

"What for?" shouted the judge.

"To prevent a loss of life."

"Whose?" asked the judge, slowly edging along the dark corridor toward the room.

"Let's see."

Dtui went immediately to the wardrobe and unlocked it. The stench from inside was horrendous. She put her hand over her mouth and nose and looked inside. The contents appeared to have been attacked by a madman with a machete. Clothes were ripped to shreds, the wooden shelves where split and scratched, and there were bloodstains around the lock. She took down a metal coat hanger and used it to poke around in the debris. It was on the bottom shelf beneath the folds of a nylon bedcover that she found it, as good as dead. Its claws were caked in dried blood from its attempts to escape. Some teeth were broken. Hair was shedding in clumps and it was as skinny as a lattice of toothpicks. But it was alive.

"Not dead yet!" shouted Dtui.

Haeng came tentatively into the room. "What is it?" he asked.

"A cat," said Dtui.

"A what?"

"Koomki kept a cat," said Dtui. "When you came to inspect the apartment, you locked her in the wardrobe."

He looked over her shoulder. "Are we too late?" he asked.

"Might be."

Mr. Geung gently lifted the body. She weighed no more than a lightbulb.

"But that was a month ago," said the judge. "This is impossible."

"You'd think so," said Dtui. "Defies all logic. But here it is."

She opened the bags they'd brought from the market and unwound the rubber band that fastened a plastic pouch of coconut water. Mr. Geung dipped his finger in the liquid and rubbed it over the cat's lips. There was no reaction. He tried again.

"Coconut water," she said. "Lot of nutrients and easy to digest. In a pinch it can be used in place of a saline drip.

I'd sooner she took it by mouth though if she's got the strength."

"But how?" said the judge. "How did Siri know it was in there?"

"Intelligent guess," she said. "Instinct. A whisper from the beyond. Who knows? But the doctor figured even a man like Koomki needed company, and cats don't really care about body odor or bad personalities as long as you feed them. Siri put two and two together. Saucer and towel on the floor, animal comics, the sound of crying. And he decided Comrade Koomki wasn't as tough as he pretended to be. He loved his cat and he couldn't move on as long as it was suffering."

"And that's why he's . . . he's . . ."

"Haunting you? Probably. We'll know for sure if we can't bring this little fellow back from the edge."

"Little girl," said Geung.

"I imagine if you killed his cat Comrade Koomki would dedicate the rest of his afterlife to making you miserable."

Geung put the cat on the table and tried again with drips of coconut water. Judge Haeng stood over her like a grieving parent.

"Will she . . . ?" asked the judge.

"She can't find her swallowing instinct," said Dtui. "Let's give her a hose job."

Dtui bit a corner off the plastic bag and squirted the juice into the cat's mouth through the hole. Most of it ended up on the table but some found its way down the throat and made her cough.

"I reckon that got through, don't you?" said Dtui.

A little tongue appeared between the cat's lips and licked at her wet whiskers.

"There you go," said Geung.

He left the cat with Dtui and went to take a look in the wardrobe.

"In-in-instant noodle packets," he said thumbing through the contents of the shelves, "leather boots chewed down to-to-to the soles. Shreds of p-p-paper."

He knelt down to look on the bottom of the cupboard and let out a victorious cheer.

"Here we, here we are," he said.

He pulled out a twenty-five liter water bottle that lay on its side. It was made of heavy duty plastic. The top was screwed on tightly and still had the water distributor's tape stretched over it.

"It must have been a frustrating obstacle for a cat dying of thirst," said Dtui. "But it's not full, so she got in there somehow. See anything, pal?"

"Here on the side," said Mr. Geung. "She scratched her w-w-w-way in."

"And wore her claws down to the stubs," said Dtui holding up one front paw.

The cat was lapping weakly at the puddle of coconut water in Dtui's palm, still with no strength to stand. Her eyes were closed, and her body shuddered from time to time.

"Lucky she wasn't a dog," said Dtui. "Cats originated in warmer climates. They don't drink as much as dogs. Just as well. It isn't exactly flowing out of the bottle, is it?"

"Only one drip so far," said Geung.

"Right," said Dtui. "One drip every ten minutes. She'd have to be one patient cat."

"She's a survi-vi-vivor," said Geung.

"She sure is," said Dtui. "I think we should take her home and fatten her up."

"No," said the judge.

"No, what?" said Dtui, about to get on her high horse.

"I mean, I'll take her."

"That's all right," said Dtui. "It'll be a burden for you. We can—"

"Seriously," said Haeng. "Give her to me. I'm responsible for what's happened to her."

"If you insist. But there are any of a hundred reasons why she might not make it through the night."

"I know."

And so, Dtui handed over the cat to a person she'd never imagined to have any compassion for man or beast.

◙ ◙ ◙

Civilai found himself at the wheel of a Renault that could easily have been the one he first drove back in 1921. Admittedly, some parts were held together with tape, but she was much tougher than she looked. She bounced along over rocks and ruts as if she were designed for such a terrain. There wasn't much to see on the forty-minute journey. The rice farmers had deserted the fields sooner than join cooperatives, so the paddies sat crusty and dry in the midday sun. In the far distance a storm was gathering as if Mother Nature had made a mistake with the sky design and tried to scribble it out. The only other vehicle he saw was a homemade tractor powered by a two-stroke diesel engine carrying twenty or so workers in straw hats. Civilai waved and smiled, but they all looked at him sourly.

Nor were there smiles upon his return to Ban Toop. He cruised slowly down the dusty main street with an elbow on the window ledge. He called out "Hey, you" to one child he saw there, but the boy looked away, pretending not to have heard. Despite the car's lack of speed, a suicidal chicken threw itself under the front wheel of the Renault. There was an almighty scream before the bird expired. In a normal world this would have resulted in the chicken's owner rushing from her house to claim compensation for the dead bird. But in Ban Toop, nobody reacted. Not a face peeked from a doorway.

"What if I strip off and do a jig on the roof?" Civilai shouted. "Would that get your attention?"

He continued to drive at the pace of a government committee meeting. He passed the old colonial building and once again noted its abnormal state of conservation. He parked in front of the headman's house. From recent experience he wasn't expecting the man to be home, and he wasn't disappointed. Even the wife was absent. But there was suddenly a flurry of activity. He went to the side of the house in time to see a lanky youth run out the back door and across the field. It was the fastest he'd seen anyone move in the village. Then, as he was walking back to the car he caught sight of a pedestrian. A crooked old lady with a gnarly staff was edging her way along the far side of the road. He calculated she'd reach the other end of the street sometime in the next millennium, which made her something of a captive audience.

"Any idea where the headman is?" he shouted.

She ignored him. Goodness knows how Civilai loved to be ignored. He decided there and then that he'd wrestle her to the ground sooner than have her take no notice. But all it took was for him to cross the road and stand in front of her.

"Get out of my way, baldy," she said.

"Oh, good," said Civilai. "You can see me."

"'Course I can. I'm not blind."

"Deaf, perhaps?"

"What?"

"I asked you if you knew where the headman was."

She was in a quandary. She wanted to keep going but her way was blocked, and it would take several minutes to go around the annoying man.

"Move!" she said.

"Not until you tell me where the headman is," he said.

"I don't know."

"I don't believe you."

Her face was parched and grooved like a terraced rice field left fallow for a hundred years. Little beads peered out from between the furrows.

"Let us be," she said. "We've found some kind of peace at last. Don't stir it all up again."

She shuffled a foot forward, and Civilai stepped out of her way. He didn't know what she meant, but he felt an overwhelming despair in her. He didn't want to add to her suffering, whatever it was.

He drove to the only other place he knew in Ban Toop, but the Tasitu mechanic's yard was also deserted. The scattered debris looked even more ancient. There was no jolly topless mechanic running out to meet the Renault. Civilai parked and walked to the brick building and called out.

"Maitreya, are you there?"

There was no answer, so Civilai walked in to the workshop. It smelled of old grease and flat petrol. Even the smells were odd in this odd village. In a working mechanic's shop the scents were fresh: oil bled from an engine, grease newly slapped on axles. But this shop had only lingering ghosts of the work once done there. Civilai doubted Maitreya had worked on a car engine since the turnover. So how did he make a living? How did anyone here make a living? Before he left Vientiane he'd checked the roster and found Ban Toop had rejected an offer to join a cooperative, citing a lack of able-bodied workers. That usually meant the rice farmers were doing very nicely, had access to the black market and would make a lot more money by going it alone. But in this area the fields were deserted and unloved.

Civilai walked to an alcove behind a cloth curtain in the back of the workshop. The space was barely broad enough for a workbench with a vice and an acetylene tank with a blowtorch. And on the bench was the oddest thing he'd seen in a very long—

"This how you do it in Vientiane?" came a booming voice from directly behind him.

Civilai's old heart missed a short run of beats. He looked over his shoulder to see Maitreya with a large rusting wrench in his hand. The old man gathered himself.

"Do what, young fellow?" he asked.

"Walk into people's places without an invite."

"It's just a workshop," said Civilai. "In fact I was hoping you might have a toilet back here."

The mechanic frowned. "Plenty of trees and bushes outside," he said.

"Ah, young Maitreya," said Civilai pushing past the younger man and back into the garage where there was space to avoid a swinging wrench, "my crouching tiger days are over. If I can't find a French *toilette* with a comfortable seat I'd sooner let it back up for a week. That's what I fear will be the death of me."

"You thought you'd find a French toilet in a workshop?"

"Why not? Judging from that fine old French villa back in the village, you had foreign influence here in Ban Toop. And the froggies always put in the bathroom before the walls and roof. It's a known fact."

The mechanic smiled and dropped the wrench onto the dirty floor, which surprised Civilai.

"You should be careful," said Maitreya. "I come back to find a strange car in the yard and someone nosing through my things. A man might act rashly, if you know what I mean. One of the boys just told me there was a stranger rooting around."

"I didn't hear you come back," said Civilai.

"Bicycle. Great weapon of war. The Japs used them a lot against the British. Whole units sneaking up on a garrison without a sound. Slit their throats before they knew what had hit 'em."

"I've never heard that."

The two stared at each other for a while.

"Tea?" said the mechanic.

"Thank you."

They sat on old Shell oil drums drinking their tea under a lush American iron filings tree. The fig tree beside it hadn't faired so well. Someone had used it as a notice board. There were hundreds of nails hammered into the trunk. It stood leafless and riddled with disease, its only fruit a truck tire hanging from a rope. The tree's demise probably paralleled that of the mechanic's business.

"I thought I made it clear I wasn't interested in any of this Buddha nonsense," said Maitreya.

"You did," said Civilai.

"Then why didn't you go back with your wife?"

Civilai smiled. "Well, you're right," he said, "you're not the next Buddha. I have no doubt about that. But I have a report to write, and just as we were about to leave something peculiar happened. I'm the type who can't sleep when there's a mystery left unsolved."

"I hope I can help," said Maitreya.

"An old woman came to see us at the guesthouse. She claimed to be your mother."

Maitreya laughed. "Spindly? Hair like an old carpet? Shaking hands?"

"That's her."

The mechanic took an unnecessarily slow draft of tea. "Wan's her name," he said. "They call her the fruit bat. She should have been locked up a long time ago."

"She's not your mother?"

"She's nobody's mother. Mad woman. Did she pull the virgin birth routine on you?"

"She had a note from the hospital."

"And did you notice there wasn't a name on the note? Every time there's a stranger in town she comes up with the same story claiming to have given birth to whoever it is the visitors have come to see. I don't know who wrote the note for her. I know for a fact she can't read or write. She just memorized the words. It's sad, Uncle, but it's hardly a mystery. But if you're into unanswered questions I imagine you're wondering why the village is empty."

"That had crossed my mind."

"Simple. We're preparing for our village festival. Everyone's off in the hills gathering wood and hunting for meat. It's a big deal for us. It was very bad luck that your visit coincided with it. The headman would have liked to meet you."

Maitreya tuned the Renault before he'd let Civilai leave. It was strange that a car mechanic wouldn't recognize the only car within fifty kilometers of the village. But as Civilai drove back to Pak Xan, he put together a long list of bizarre points. Strange it was that the village would be celebrating a festival that wasn't on any calendars. Strange that the town's only guesthouse should claim they'd never seen the fruit-bat woman before. Where else would she stalk strangers? Strange that a villager would call a government official "uncle" rather than "comrade." Strange that a man in an isolated village should know Madam Nong had already left. Strange that a poor village would reject the opportunity to join a rice cooperative. Strange that a mechanic would show such little respect for his tools.

But, as he drove back into a shocking pink sunset, Civilai couldn't make head or tail of the strangest thing of all. On the bench in the alcove behind the workshop was a Buddha image some sixty centimeters tall. But the top of its head was flat. For some reason, somebody had sliced off part of its skull and placed it on the bench beside the Buddha like half an unexploded bomb.

◙ ◙ ◙

Inspector Phosy had made an appointment by telephone, a rare occurrence in the People's Democratic Republic. It was often simpler to turn up at the place, ask whether the person you wish to see is there, announce your arrival and wait. But there was something ceremonial about a meeting at the Armed Forces Ministry. The telephone operator at police headquarters called the telephone operator at the ministry to make an appointment. Twenty minutes later, the telephone operator at the ministry called back and said the appointment was as soon as the inspector could get there.

Upon his arrival Phosy felt a little like royalty. He was met at the gate by a high ranking official and escorted to the police liaison office. The official knocked, opened the door and left. There were three men in the room. Corporal Suwit sat at his desk and two more officers sat on the plastic couch. They were wearing green uniforms that fit, another rare occurrence in Laos.

Phosy toured the room shaking hands, first with the two officers he didn't know. They stood (reluctantly, to Phosy's mind) to return the handshake.

"These are Colonels Viboun and Vinai," said Suwit. "I've asked them to join us because we're all concerned about this misunderstanding. The officers are keen to clear it up as soon as possible."

"Well, a big 'yes' to that," said the policeman. He sat not on the lone wooden chair in the middle of the room but at the end of the couch. Its two occupants had to shuffle along to give him room.

"I can't tell you how many nightmares this case has given me," said Phosy.

"We hope you've made some progress," said the man directly beside him. He spoke without turning his head in the inspector's direction.

"Oh, comrade," said Phosy, "you wouldn't believe how many wrong turns we've made and how much bad luck we're having."

He thought somebody might ask a question, but nobody did.

"Look, I know this will probably turn out to be totally unrelated to you fellows, but I'd really appreciate it if you'd allow me to just get it all off my chest."

"Feel free," said the farthest colonel.

"Well, first," said Phosy, "we discovered that the cyclist who was kidnapped isn't even a Lao citizen. He's Thai."

"How did you learn that?" asked Suwit.

"We found his ID at the guesthouse he'd been staying at," said Phosy. "So naturally, we had to contact the Thais and they insisted on sending some of their people to assist with the inquiry. We told them we're perfectly capable of finding him ourselves. They said there'd be an international incident if we didn't, so we assumed he was connected . . . if you know what I mean. They wouldn't kick up such a dust storm if he was just a tourist. So that raised the profile of the investigation, and, I tell you, that's all I needed because I'm dealing with some nervous witnesses already."

"Witnesses?" said the nearest colonel.

"Right," said Phosy. "Our main witness, the one who saw the actual abduction directly in front of her, she got cold feet because her sister was killed by—we suspect—a jealous boyfriend and she—the witness, that is—she came home to find blood everywhere and her sister buried under a pile of empty bottles. It took us an age to calm the witness down. Am I going too fast for you? No? Good."

He took the opportunity to help himself to one of the unchilled soft drinks on the coffee table in front of him. The couch soldiers were being oddly quiet.

"I hope you found somewhere secure to house the witnesses," said Suwit.

"Not sure I'd call it safe," said Phosy. "And I'm trusting you boys to keep this to yourselves, but we've got the main witness above a friend's noodle shop on Fa Ngum. We doubt the death of her sister is connected to this case but you can never be too sure. Am I right? Of course I am. But if the boyfriend does turn up we'll know he did it because we have his fingerprints from the crime scene."

"His fingerprints?" said the nearest colonel.

"One or two sets still unidentified," said Phosy.

The other colonel laughed. "This isn't some American thriller," said the farthest colonel. "Are you sure you aren't overestimating the capabilities of your department?"

"I know what you mean," said Phosy. "A few months ago I was just as skeptical as you. But this—I don't know what to call him—this forensic-evidence genius shows up, trained overseas, and suddenly we're not only keeping up with our neighboring countries, we're leaping ahead of them. Things we wouldn't have noticed before, like the motorcycle tracks."

"What about them?" asked Suwit.

"We've made a plaster cast of the tracks of the motorcycle that the kidnappers were riding. And now we've got the tire tracks of the man who killed our witness's sister. Of course, they aren't connected, but if they were we'd know it soon enough."

There followed another silence.

"You mentioned witnesses, plural," said the nearest colonel.

"Yes, it's astounding how many people have nothing better to do than sit and observe," said the policeman. "I personally think we're being too generous to the elderly. They should be put to work on the drains or digging ditches. But that's just me. Once we had a witness who could describe the kidnappers it wasn't so hard to work backward along the route they'd taken. We found people who'd seen the cyclist and others who remembered him being tailed slowly by two young military types on a motorcycle."

"That's speculation," said the farthest colonel.

"You're quite right," Phosy agreed. "But we should know exactly what they look like soon enough. The Thais came up with a police portrait artist and the witnesses are really excited about the results. But listen to me. Here I am going on and on and not giving anyone else a chance to speak. I really do apologize for taking up your valuable time. I know you have a country to protect. I just wanted to keep you informed. Keep that old Armed Forces–National Police Force channel open. I'm so excited about the potential of us all working together in the future. Thank you."

He stood and had completed another round of handshakes before anyone realized the meeting was closed. He went to the door, opened it and stopped in the doorway.

"Really, thank you," he said. "I'll see myself out."

He sighed heavily on his way down the echoing staircase. Of course it was all fiction. Lies. His only witness was dead. There were no plaster casts or fingerprints or sketch artists. The police department didn't even have enough whistles to go around. Two muggings over the course of a week would have been considered a crime spree. The slick police force he'd described to the soldiers was one he'd learned about from the stories of Dr. Siri. They had no forensics department. His only reason for exaggerating the progress on Noo's kidnapping case was to poke a very short stick into a very scary hornet's nest. Now all he could do was stand back and see if they'd bite.

But first he had to return to headquarters and arrange protection for his wife. Nurse Dtui looked passably like the dead cordial seller. If the killer thought he'd murdered the wrong woman, there was a chance he'd try again. And Phosy had set up his wife, even given them a location. If the military was connected to this whole affair as he believed, there'd be a visit to Madam Daeng's noodle shop soon enough.

As he rode his lilac Vespa along Lan Xang Avenue, he reconsidered his actions. What was he doing? Could he be more irresponsible? What if the assassins shot first and asked questions after? And for what? For one man's life. For a man he hardly knew. After so many years of bloodshed, who really cared whether one trouble-making Thai monk vanished from the face of the earth? Or a cordial seller? Or his own wife and child? And that, of course, was the key. The victims could have been Dtui or Mali. The re-educators had pummeled it into him back in the seminars. In this new system even the poorest, most feeble rice farmer would have the same rights as the greatest general. That's what they'd said. That was the myth of socialism. It wasn't the army he was up against; it was the sagging ideology. It was the duty of the community to protect its weakest members. He never thought he'd hear himself say it but, damn, it was the principle of the thing. Dtui was a fighter. She'd take it well. That's why he'd chosen her as a wife.

◘ ◘ ◘

Before returning the Renault to its owner, Civilai filled the tank at one hard-to-find rusty pump and asked for directions to the high school. When he arrived he was too late for classes, but he hoped there might still be staff around. The school looked new and dilapidated at the same time. Unlike the French colonists, who weren't huge on wasting education on the locals, the Americans veritably vomited schools all over the place. Their policy was to use local tradesmen and materials wherever possible, which explained why the buildings had already started to fall down.

As it turned out, there were a number of teachers engaged in after-school activities: the band, the vegetable allotments, after-hours political classes for the remedial and, although the light was fading fast, a football match was in progress. The two teams playing shirts against skins were just about to start the second half. Despite all his years of rhetoric in favor of women's rights, he found himself surprised and disoriented to see that the referee was a young woman.

"Good game?" Civilai asked her.

"A bit one-sided," she told him.

"Are you a teacher here?" he asked.

"Yes, comrade."

"I'm looking for someone who might have been teaching in Pak Xan back in the old regime."

"Then you're looking for Teacher Grit," she said.

Teacher Grit taught math and had been doing so, he said, since before the birth of Pythagoras. For all its lines and wrinkles his was a face anyone would want to nuzzle. He'd been at the school since it was built by the Americans, whom he remembered fondly. He dropped one or two English words into his reminiscences. In fact, they'd leveled his family compound in order to build the school and had relocated his family to a sturdy but cultureless home just opposite.

"We teach upon the hallowed ground of my ancestors," said Grit. "I wouldn't be surprised if we were sitting here above the potted ashes of my great-grandmother. They didn't mark graves back then."

"You'd remember the French then," said Civilai.

"Bien sûr," said Grit. "Those bastards wouldn't let me go to school. They reminded my mother I was Lao and the French and Vietnamese were the elite classes. We were laborers."

"Then how did you become a teacher?" asked Civilai.

"We crossed the river. My mother convinced the administrators over there we were Thai so my three siblings and I all studied in Beun Kan. I went on to the teachers college in Chiang Mai. Came back here and labored for the bastard French until the Americans turned up. Damned fine colonists, the Americans."

"What do you remember about the French administration here?"

"Bastards."

"Apart from that."

"Pig ignorant. Arrogant."

"I'm thinking specifically about the owner of a colonial home out in Ban Toop," said Civilai.

"Ah, yes. Now you're talking about the most arrogant and ignorant of them all, Administrateur Marche. He was based here for almost ten years."

"And what was his connection to Ban Toop?"

"He *was* Ban Toop. He established the village. Nobody

knew why he chose the place. Not beautiful at all. He had a fine house here in Pak Xan. He was like an emperor here. He was in charge of everything. When I returned from Thailand everyone was afraid of him. I offered to teach at the temple, and he laughed in my face and put me in a quarry."

"Who built his house at Ban Toop?"

"He had a team of Vietnamese builders there for three months. When it was finished they returned to Vietnam and Marche had a fine house in the middle of nowhere. Really, there was nothing there. We assumed he wanted a country home like they do in Europe. Somewhere to escape. He'd drive out there on weekends with his assorted concubine whores."

"What did he do there?"

"Heaven knows. He was a very secretive man. And there was something . . . dark about him. There were many rumors, but rumors are our national pastime."

"Do you remember any of them?"

"There was talk of children disappearing. Never children from the town. Always the daughters of travelers."

"You think he had something to do with that?"

"Who can say? When you dislike someone enough you will the gossip to be true. But I do know for certain he was removed from his post very suddenly by the French Protectorate. One day he was gone, and there were parties in the streets. But by then a small community had grown around his house in Ban Toop. It continued to grow even after he left."

"And what do you know about the place now?"

"You know? I'm not really the person to ask. I haven't been there for ages."

"You're probably more trustworthy than anyone I'm likely to meet in an official capacity."

The old teacher got to his feet and started to wipe the equations from the blackboard with a damp rag. "There are those who say Ban Toop is a law unto itself," said Grit. "The local government cadres are afraid of the place. But in a way I can see why. After decades of minimal help from Vientiane, a community learns to fend for itself to survive. It builds walls. The next leader comes along and tells them, 'We're in charge now. You have to do what we say.' But who knows who'll be running the country next year, or next month even? So the local communities put on their armor."

"You're not shy about being an anarchist, are you?"

"When I came back from Thailand I was hotheaded and angry," said Grit. "But I soon learned to keep my mind open and my mouth shut. Then you get to an age where your mind's shut, and you can't stop your mouth from running off. But by then everybody's stopped listening."

"You're not wrong there, comrade. Do you know the headman at Ban Toop?"

"I've met him. He seems harmless enough. Why are you interested?"

"Just curiosity really. I went there on an official visit and he was too busy cockfighting to see me."

"Yes, I've heard he's not that sociable when it comes to Party activities."

"It sounds like exactly the type of place for the government to be running back-to-back political seminars. Somebody needs to teach the Ban Toop leaders a lesson in good manners."

Civilai stood and shook the old teacher's hand warmly. "One last matter," he said. "Would there be some type of local repository of documents dating from the French administration days?"

"There would if your crowd hadn't marched into town and burned everything."

"I was afraid you'd say that."

"But . . ."

"Yes?"

"If you promise not to set fire to it, there's a . . . I wouldn't call it a repository exactly, more like a suitcase."

"A suitcase?"

"Two, if I remember right. I assume the last administrator had planned to take them with him when he left, but there wasn't enough room in the getaway car. They're in a cupboard in Sirimongkol Temple."

"Do you suppose they'd let me take a look at them?"

"I doubt anyone would care one way or another."

Civilai dropped off the Renault at the district council buildings, expecting the place to be deserted, but one lamp still burned inside. He went to the door to find the same greasy-faced clerk engaged in the endless pursuit of solving the world's filing problems.

"Comrade," she said, startled.

"Don't you have a husband to go home to?" he asked.

She smiled for the first time. Her teeth were all over the place. "Last-minute duty," she said.

"Do you know whether Vientiane got back to me about my fax?"

"Fax? Nothing as far as I know."

"Who operates the fax machine?"

"Me, usually. But I'm sure Comrade Luangrat took care of it personally if it was important," she said.

"Look," Civilai put on his charm voice. "I can see you're really busy, but I don't suppose you could dig out a photograph of all the regional headmen by any chance?"

"A photograph?"

"Yes, you know. Headman seminar, workshop, pep talk. They always take pictures at the end of those things. Give out certificates."

"Probably," she said and walked directly to the correct cabinet. Filing was her life. "Here, October last year. Cooperative Farm Training Programme for Village Leaders."

Civilai riffled through the photographs. A hundred men in three rows in front of the council office. None of them was smiling.

"Which one's Comrade Noulak, the headman at Ban Toop?" he asked.

"Oh, he wasn't here," she said.

"Why not?"

"He had a cold, or malaria. I can't remember which."

"Then, his deputy?"

"He wasn't here either."

"Must have been an epidemic. Lucky the whole village wasn't wiped out completely."

She looked blank.

"Any other meetings?" he asked.

She produced graduation photos for the July Workshop on Water Management and Sewage, and the February seminar on Fruit for a Healthy Future. Again, she was unable to pick out the headman.

"He isn't so enthusiastic about meetings," she said.

"I'm astounded he's still the headman," said Civilai. "He has no choice but to attend."

They looked at five more photographs of serious men at local government events, but the clerk was unable to point to anyone from Ban Toop.

"I'm beginning to believe he doesn't exist," said Civilai.

"Oh, he does," said the clerk. "I've met him. He's a very polite man. Perhaps . . ."

"Perhaps what?"

"They aren't official photographs so they're filed under 'unofficial photographs,' but I remember he was in town for the rocket festival last year."

"The rocket festival that was banned?"

"Yes, that's the one. Our official photographer wasn't around but one of the Soviet experts from the road survey project had a camera. He made copies and sent them to us. Here they are."

She pulled out a paper pouch with the name of the pharmacy that had developed them written on the front. It was in Thai. Only five months on, and the photos were already starting to fade.

"I'm sure he's in here somewhere," said the clerk, thumbing through the pictures.

Civilai was fatigued from the long day and the even longer life. Each evening reminded him he was no longer forty.

"Look, never mind," he said. "I'll probably never get to meet him anyway."

"No, I'm sure . . . Yes, here he is."

She handed Civilai the photograph. It depicted a typical Lao party scene. A lot of drunken men. Some equally drunken wives. In the background the words PAK XAN WELCOMES OUR SOVIET BROTHERS had been cut out of polystyrene and glued onto the wall. And standing beside a ridiculously large black music speaker with a glass in his hand was the elusive headman of Ban Toop. The shot was a little fuzzy, and Civilai couldn't tell whether the man was drunk or had merely blinked when the flash went off. He was wearing a traditional collarless Lao shirt that flattered his stomach, but there was no doubt in Civilai's mind: Comrade Noulak, the headman of Ban Toop, and Maitreya, the imminent reincarnation of the Buddha, were one and the same person.

9

The Case of the File in the Case

Everything looked normal. But when you're expecting trouble, when you have that voice in your gut that says, "Something's coming," even the smallest of abnormalities have to be checked out. They'd all seen the motorcycle earlier that evening. The rider stopped opposite Daeng's noodle restaurant and had pretended to be looking out over the river. He was about thirty, fit, and he wore a baseball cap, but you could tell his hair was cropped close to his scalp.

As arranged, Mr. Geung had carried a bucket of slops across the empty road to dump on the riverbank. They'd told him to act as if he had mental problems. He'd been practicing all afternoon. Crazy Rajhid was perched unseen in the tree overhead for backup.

"Hey, retard," said the man.

"Y-y-y-yes, comrade?" said Geung.

"That woman," said the man, nodding in Dtui's direction. She was wiping the tables. "How long's she worked here?"

"No noh, noh, noh, noh . . ."

"Oh shit."

"Noh, noh, not long," said Geung.

"What does that mean," said the man. "A month? A week? A day?"

"Yes," said Geung.

"Which?"

"I'm no, I'm no, I'm not very good with numbers."

"Was she here last week?"

"Ta, ta, ta"—he could tell the stutter annoyed the man intensely—"ta, ta . . ."

"I'm not here all week, you moron."

"Ta, ta, ta two or three days. Whaaaa why you asking?"

"I like the look of her," he said. "Think I'll ask her out." The man smiled. His teeth were neat and white as a row of coconut chunks.

"She, she, she, sheeee's sad," said Geung. "Her sister die-die-di—"

The man revved the engine on his bike and kicked down the stand.

"Don't worry, retard," he said. "I'll make her happy. She sleeping here?"

"Yes, comrade."

Geung was left in a cloud of exhaust.

Agent Geung had been able to recite the conversation verbatim, which is why they were expecting a late night return from the motorcycle rider and his cohorts. Upon his arrival at police headquarters after the ministry bluff it had occurred to Phosy that he had no legitimate reason to request a squad of men to protect his wife. So he'd been left with his old friend and colleague,

Sergeant Sihot, who was rarely busy in the evening, and Tumsin the butcher, who was so backed up on favors for the detective he'd need another lifetime to repay him. At the end of the evening noodle shift they'd sat around the restaurant with warm tea and Chinese donuts and weighed the odds.

"Hand grenade," said Sergeant Sihot.

"That's how I'd do it if I wanted to teach the restaurant owner a lesson," said Phosy. "But this is an assassination. I'd need to confirm my target had been taken out. A hand grenade's too random."

"Then they'll shoot me," said Dtui, surprisingly cheerful.

"Possible," said Phosy. "But they know I'm on the case, and I probably have backup."

"That's me," said Tumsin the butcher.

"They wouldn't want to risk a shootout or a fistfight," Phosy continued. "I guess a sniper on the riverbank or in a boat might work, but he'd be sitting there all night hoping Dtui walks past a window."

"And the military couldn't hit a buffalo from two meters," said Sergeant Sihot.

"Things have changed since you were in the army," Phosy told him. "They have time to train them now."

"Let's face it," said Dtui. "The motorcycle rider asked if I'm sleeping here. They'll go the ninja route. Wait till everyone's asleep, tippy-toe over the rooftops, drop down through an open window and garrote me before I have a chance to let out a scream."

"That's the way I'd do it," said Phosy.

"See why I married him?" said Dtui. "We have so much in common."

Mr. Geung turned to his fiancée, Tukta.

"I wo-won't let anyone garrote you, darling," he said, and they kissed. Everyone turned away.

With Sergeant Sihot on point on the riverbank and Rajhid still clinging to the upper branches of his tree, the front of the restaurant was taken care of. Mr. Geung with Tukta on pillion rode the restaurant bicycle in the direction of Siri's house just in case they were being watched. At the Lane Xang Hotel they dismounted and crept back through the shadows to take up their positions. The others pulled down the metal shutters, and turned out the lights. With butcher Tumsin on a stool in the small backyard clutching his favorite cleaver, Phosy and Dtui went upstairs confident that every eventuality was covered. Their inquisitive daughter was absent, and they weren't expecting to be slaughtered in their beds until after midnight, so for half an hour they took advantage of the comfortable mattress and the abundance of adrenalin before retiring to their respective rooms.

The motorcycle ninja was not spotted when he returned to the restaurant at 2 A.M. because he had hopped over the small wall into the backyard and not disturbed the sleeping butcher. The upstairs window shutters were open. His equipment was simple enough: a rope with a football sock tied to one end. Inside the sock was a metal *petong* ball. He aimed for a point between the shutters and tossed the rope. The ball arced and looped over the left shutter, pulling the rope back into the hands of the waiting ninja. And there it hung. He pulled on the ends to test the hinges then hoisted himself up with the agility of a gibbon.

It could not have been simpler. He perched on the window ledge looking down at the fat girl. She was alone. It was a dark, cloudy night, but she was burning a scented candle beside her sleeping mat. The flame flickered. She wore a figure-hugging nylon nightdress. Her hair fanned out across the pillow. He liked them big. It was almost a shame he had to kill her. But he'd screwed up once. He couldn't get it wrong again. His bare feet made no sound on the parquet floor. The blade was in a holster at his belt. It was a ballet he'd choreographed. Two steps forward, slash, two steps back to avoid the blood. He took the first step, except . . .

Some dark angular shape appeared in the window frame through which he'd just climbed. He turned his head and saw some half-naked Indian sitting on the ledge. And the naked half was not the top. Then, in an instant, someone was on him from the other side. One strong hand grabbed the wrist that held the blade in an unbreakable grip. The sleeping woman had been neither asleep nor a woman. The wig remained fanned out on the pillow bereft of a head. Crazy Rajhid leapt from the sill and positioned himself so he could kick the motorcycle ninja in the groin. No martial art on the planet can counter that. Then another man came, then a woman, and the ninja was pinned to the parquet tiles like a moth in a museum display cabinet.

"Bugger it," he said.

◙ ◙ ◙

An unused foreign language could fade as rapidly as the flowers in a wreath. For fifteen years in Paris, French had come more naturally to him than Lao. Now here was Civilai in a dusty temple office with stacks of mildewed papers on the table in front of him. Every one of the reports he read was a challenge to his eyesight and to his memory. Sirimongkol Temple was more functional than decorative. Its large events hall had become a community center with Vietnamese language classes, bomb disposal workshops and lessons in beekeeping. Hives were spaced out across a yard that was once gay with festivals. But early that morning when Civilai had arrived the only movement was from a flock of chickens being shooed out of the prayer hall.

There was just the one monk in residence, a feeble-minded young man more used to following orders than making decisions. He'd remembered the two old French suitcases and had led Civilai to a tall wooden cupboard where they'd remained untouched for decades. He hadn't asked Civilai his name or what his business was. He didn't tell the visitor to be careful with the old documents. He just laughed a little when Civilai said "thank you."

One suitcase contained paper spaghetti and droppings. There were several entrances and exits in the vinyl that were the shape of mouse holes in cartoons, which gave Civilai cause to chuckle. The contents had served the temple rats better than they would him. The other suitcase had proven too much of a challenge for the rodents. It was also almost beyond Civilai. He'd spent about half an hour with his penknife attempting to free the spring locks from their rusty shrouds. He'd feared the documents would be unreadable. When the lid finally lifted the stink of mold on the leather case overpowered him. But the lettering was so clear on most of the papers they might have been typed a week earlier.

From the dates Teacher Grit had provided, Civilai narrowed down the search to the period around 1942. He worked his way down the stack, wondering whether he might succumb to lung infection before he found what he was looking for. It had been a fruitless search so far. In fact the only personal communication he'd found referring to Administrateur Marche was a formal letter from Paris telling him the Vichy would honor its agreement to ship the administrator's luggage to France at the end of his truncated tenure. The phrase that Civilai found interesting in the letter was, ". . . despite the unfortunate circumstances." It went on to give details on how to itemize personal belongings but did not elaborate on what the unfortunate circumstances might be.

It was not until Civilai started to sift through the personal correspondence of Administrateur Lebouef, Marche's successor, that a plot began to unfurl. Shortly after he took over, Lebouef had been asked to host a Monsieur Gallas, a junior detective from the French Sûreté Nationale. He had been appointed to conduct inquiries into the activities of Administrateur Marche during his stay in Laos. Evidently, somebody of importance had curtailed Marche's contract and ordered an investigation. There were no copies of Monsieur Gallas's reports, but Administrateur Lebouef had included the original mission statement with his letter to the protectorate.

It appeared that Marche had been less than candid about his background when applying for a post in French Indochina, and the Paris police had been less than conscientious in their examination of the man's past. If they had been more thorough they would have found the records of his involvement in two court cases dealing with the disappearance of teenage girls. In both cases, the prosecution had failed to make a strong enough argument against

Marche, who was subsequently acquitted. Thus, Marche had had no legal obligation to disclose the arrests. The mission statement went on to say:

> *Our office became involved in this affair following M. Marche's written application for acquiescence to take up a government post in Paris upon his return. It is the guiding principle of the Vichy administration to thoroughly scrutinize applicants for official positions. Whilst examining the administrator's affairs prior to his appointment in Indochina we uncovered the court dealings and a number of other complaints which had, for some reason, not been investigated. There were also several grievances from French and Vietnamese citizens reported during his tenure in Pak Xan. We came upon one complaint, for example, from a French accountant, M. Charles Delon, who was employed by the Vichy throughout the region during that time. He claimed that Administrateur Marche had been integral in the procurement of teenage girls in Laos. The accountant had been made aware of this matter by his clerical assistant, a French citizen of Vietnamese origin, who was the mother of one of the girls concerned.*
>
> *As the procurement of teenage girls was not a rare occurrence in Laos and the arrangement was usually deemed to be consensual, the matter was not further pursued at the time. It was only when viewed in relation to the earlier cases that we began to see a pattern. Our department commenced an investigation into the actions of M. Marche with more vigor, and it was then that we uncovered suspicion of crimes far more nefarious than mere kidnapping. This is the rationale behind Marche's*

recall to France and Inspector Gallas's journey to Indochina and specifically to Pak Xan. It is hoped he will be able to gather sufficient data to support our suspicions and build a strong legal case against Marche. We appreciate your cooperation in this matter.

Yours sincerely,

Police Commissioner Alain Boyer

"Crimes far more nefarious than mere kidnapping," said Civilai aloud. "Damn, if that doesn't leave a reader on the edge of his seat."

He huffed and coughed his way through another half hour of administrative dross but found neither a word of the progress of Inspector Gallas nor reports on a trial nor further mention of the Vietnamese clerk's missing daughter. But Civilai persevered because, as Siri often said, "A story without an ending is like a tin of corned beef without a can opener."

The sun had reached its highest point by the time Civilai found another mention of the case. It was in a copy of a monthly report from Administrateur Lebouef to his desk officer in Paris. It was the seventeenth of forty-two asterisked items on issues pending. It was a short but tart reference—one that made the hairs stand up on Civilai's arms.

Six months on and still no news of the whereabouts of Inspector Gallas.

Civilai walked back to his guesthouse with no great urgency. He found it hard to walk fast and be brilliant at the same time. And this matter needed all the brilliance he could muster. He hoped the team he'd requested would be there soon. There was something eerie, threatening even, about the whole situation. Having some ministry people beside him would buoy his confidence. Initially his inquiries about the old colonial building had been unrelated to the reception he hadn't been given. It was just idle interest. But he'd been uncomfortable about the place since they'd first parked in front of it. Innocuous but imposing at the same time, it stood out like an Arc de Triomphe in the desert. There was no logical link between a reluctant would-be Buddha and a French child abuser more than thirty years earlier, but Civilai was certain a connection existed.

At the guesthouse a sweaty man in a dark grey shirt rose from the only chair in the reception area and nodded curtly. His haircut made him look like he'd run his head through the blades of a combine harvester.

"Civilai Songsawat?" he said.

"Yes."

"I'm Sergeant Savath of the Pak Xan police force."

"You're a policeman?" said Civilai, looking him up and down.

"Yes," he said.

"You're wearing rubber flip-flops."

"They're comfortable."

Until Civilai's visit to Pak Xan, anarchy had been just a theoretical concept. Perhaps he'd been sheltered as a high-ranking official because he'd never actually felt it. But this area was crawling with a tangible sense of disrespect. Pak Xan anarchy exposed itself through its bad attitude.

"Do you have official police business with me?" Civilai snapped.

"Yes."

"Then go home and come back appropriately dressed."

He tried to push past the solid man to get to the staircase, but the policeman grabbed his arm. Civilai pulled away and was about to play his "Do you know who I am?" card when the policeman beat him to the payoff.

"Early this morning a woman's body was found in the reeds a few meters from where you and your wife were getting drunk on Sunday night."

Civilai took a step back, and the policeman released his grip.

"She'd been dead about forty-eight hours," Savath continued. "She'd been beaten so bad we couldn't recognize her at first. When we found out who she was we learned something interesting. The evening she died, guess who the last person she was seen speaking to was?"

◙ ◙ ◙

Siri's experience with real judges was limited. In fact the only arbitrators he'd ever appeared in front of were either military officers appointed to settle disputes or Haeng, who everyone agreed was a poor excuse for a judge. Siri's idea of what a judge should look like had been fashioned from early Hollywood, where the man in the chair was always balding and had white muttonchops and wise, saggy eyes.

So when Suthon, the traveling public prosecutor of Udon Thani entered the temporary courtroom Siri looked behind him for the real judge. Nobody else came. In Siri's eyes, the prosecutor was a boy. He was pale with no chin and had an ill-fitting piggy nose. He didn't even have a robe and instead wore a white shirt with a tie and black trousers like a college student. Siri's first instinct was to shout out, "How old are you exactly?" But to Madam Daeng's relief he kept his mouth shut.

They'd arrived three hours earlier in the back of the Sawan truck that was only ever used on special occasions. The Sangharaj had climbed aboard the truck's flatbed without complaints. He'd pulled his robe over his head to protect himself from the sun and hummed some non-ecclesiastical tunes all the way to Nam Som.

Siri had stared at him and imagined himself as a supreme patriarch. He was certain he wouldn't be at all humble. He'd ride around the country on his Triumph in his American sunglasses rooting out sinners. He'd have *S.P.* stamped in gold lettering on the back of his leather jacket. Perhaps that was why nobody had asked him to be the supreme patriarch.

The young judge was going through cases at a cracking pace. Siri noticed he dispensed wisdom only when he thought the accused might appreciate and understand it. Otherwise he'd hand out punishments with no embellishments. He knew the law and the penalty for breaking it. He spoke well and not over the heads of the uneducated. Despite the fact that the man, perhaps in his forties but clean shaven, was far too young for his position, Siri found himself admiring him.

Some of the accused entered the room in leg shackles led by uniformed police officers. When they'd heard the verdict they'd be escorted either back to the cells or into the arms of freedom. In most cases the only words they spoke were, "I do," when the administrator asked whether they understood the judgment. There was no schedule posted, and the only list of cases to be dealt with was the one on the table in front of the judge. So it was a pleasant surprise when he looked up and said, "I see Abbot Rayron is in the room and unchained."

Captain Gumron had been sitting at the rear of the courtroom writing reports. He hurried to the front and *wai*'d the judge. To Siri's further surprise, the judge *wai*'d him back.

"The abbot has been under the supervision of the Sangharaj of Laos," said the captain.

"And that's gone well, has it?" asked the judge.

"Quite well, sir. That is . . . until this morning."

"Don't tell me there was another incident," said the judge.

"Murder. The report should be on your desk, sir," said the captain.

"Witnesses?"

"One."

"Reliability?"

"Blind as an earthworm, sir."

The young judge looked at the abbot. "It seems like I have a new accusation against you every time I come here," he said. "What are we going to do with you?"

It was undoubtedly a rhetorical question, but Siri felt an uncontrollable urge to answer it.

"Release him," said the doctor.

Daeng pinched his arm.

"What was that?" said the judge. "Somebody have something to say?"

"It was me," said Siri.

Daeng sighed loudly.

"And you are . . . ?" said the judge.

"Sir, he's just . . ." began the captain, but the judge waved him off.

"Just an old student of the process of law," said Siri.

The judge smiled. "Your name, sir?"

"Dr. Siri Paiboun."

"And what is your assessment of this case, old student?" asked the judge.

Siri stood. "That the evidence is scant and largely circumstantial, the witnesses are unreliable and above all there is no motive."

Siri saw what he hoped was a smile of admiration on the young judge's face.

"I can tell from your accent that you hail from a country that currently has no laws," said the judge.

"Which is why I admire a legal system that has such clearly defined parameters," said Siri.

"Good response, old fellow," said the judge. "I don't often find men in my courtroom who can put together such long, grammatically correct sentences. Perhaps someday we can sit down over a beer and discuss the relative values of law versus lawlessness. But in the meantime I think I'll have to run with the premise that if enough circumstantial evidence falls repeatedly on the same suspect we cross the line of coincidence and enter the realm of probability."

"But you haven't even read the latest report," said Siri.

"Indeed I haven't, comrade counsel for the defense," said the judge, still with a pleasant smile on his face. "But it seems whenever I fail to put the abbot in a cell somebody else ends up dead. And being a coincidence doesn't make them any less dead. So, Abbot Rayron, I am ordering your detention here in a lockup at the Nam Som police station until we can transfer you to Udon Thani provincial court to face the charge of three counts of premeditated murder."

"But that's not—" began Siri.

"Quiet," said Captain Gumron.

Ugly began to kick up a fuss in front of the courtroom.

"I take it that's your dog outside?" said the judge. "I believe I saw you arrive together."

"I apologize," said Siri. "He's not that fond of police."

"Apology accepted and understood," said the judge, still smiling. "Now if you'd perhaps allow me a few minutes to take back control of my court, I was planning to mention that there's a month before that initial hearing in Udon. I'm sure if someone contributed a little brilliant detective work to the case before then and came up with a new suspect, we could also apologize to the abbot and pursue proceedings against a more likely murderer."

Interestingly, he looked not at the police captain during this speech, but at the abbot's entourage, specifically Siri.

"Your Honor," said Abbot Rayron.

It was the first time the monk had spoken, so everyone was surprised to hear his voice.

"Yes?" said the judge.

"I also apologize," said the abbot.

"For what?" asked the judge.

"For forcing you to make such a difficult choice."

Everyone looked on in amazement. The abbot had apologized to the judge for the inconvenience he'd caused. Even the unflappable judge was stunned. He stared at the monk mystified for a few seconds before waving him away.

Very few suspects sent to Udon had returned to tell the

tale. The provincial justice department frowned upon paying for two-way tickets, so only non-returnable certainties made it to the central courthouse. Yet the judge had given them hope. A uniformed officer *wai*'d the abbot before handcuffing himself to him. He nodded when the lock was secure and led the monk outside. Siri and the team followed with their heads bowed. By the time they reached the door, the next case was already being heard. For once, Siri and Daeng could think of nothing to say. They followed the Sangharaj out through the double doors into the glare of a late afternoon filled with shouts.

"How many have you killed, Abbot?"

"Are there other bodies we don't know about?"

"Is this the temple's way of clearing out the shamans?"

The abbot, chained to his grinning guard, was surrounded by reporters. There were the whirrs of cameras and the orders to "Look this way, Abbot."

They pushed rudely against him. One prodded a cassette recorder into his face. He had no chance to respond between the questions. The police guard enjoyed the attention and had no intention of hurrying the abbot to the cell. It wasn't until Siri, Daeng and Yuth, the headman's son, forced their way into the crowd and hustled both abbot and guard out of the forecourt that the madness abated. Most of the reporters were local, but there were one or two from Bangkok.

Someone had blabbed.

10

The Devil You Don't Know

Phosy had been sitting for an hour on an uncomfortable wooden bench one floor below his superior's office. With every minute he waited, his overactive policeman's instinct nipped at his nerves. He shuffled through the possible courses of action. Sergeant Sihot had said immediately after the ninja's capture that they should rope and gag the guy and throw him in the Mekhong. Show the enemy what they were up against. Half the detectives at headquarters would, at the very least, have beaten a confession out of the man. There on the itchy seat in the cold light of day neither of those scenarios seemed so bad. Even when the cocky ninja had stared Phosy in the face and mocked him, the detective had kept his hands to himself.

"You know it doesn't matter, don't you?" was what he'd said.

"What doesn't?" Phosy asked.

"Whatever you do to me, whatever information you extract from me by, whatever means—it's not going to make any difference."

"Beating you up would make a difference," Phosy had said, although he wasn't the type to hit a man in ropes.

"Only to you, Cop. Not to your case."

"Oh, I don't know. Tomorrow I file criminal charges against you. Then we see who attempts to bail you out. Then we'll know who your boss is at the armed forces ministry. And he'll find out that the police force has come a long way since the old regime."

"You have no idea, do you?"

"Tell me what I don't have any idea about."

"No idea who we are," said the man. "No idea how deep you are in something you should have kept out of. No idea how small and pathetic you are. How unimportant."

"Oh, kid," said Phosy, "when will you learn? There's no 'we.' You're a hired thug and not a very good one at that. Even if you're on a salary you're still a hired ruffian. You just do what your boss tells you. People like you are never let into the inner circle. You're a soldier ant, pal, and you just got squashed tonight."

"You should have let me kill her."

"What?"

"A killing would have given you something to charge me with. But what have you got? Breaking and entering? A petty thief. They won't even bother to charge me. I'll be out of there before lunch. Really, Constable. You should have let me slice open that ugly fat bitch."

Phosy reached in his shoulder bag.

"Bang," said the ninja.

But Phosy produced a Brownie Instamatic camera. The police department had three of them.

"Souvenir?"

"Kind of. I want to take a picture of you before you have your accident."

One of the few benefits of being a policeman in the People's Democratic Republic was that nobody cared about brutality in police custody. So that morning he'd merely had to tell the desk sergeant his prisoner got those two black eyes by dancing with a tall Ukrainian woman with a reinforced brassier. The sergeant almost fell off his chair laughing. But now on that hard wooden bench with his instincts twitching, Phosy was starting to believe he should have fed his ninja to the giant catfish.

Most of the government buildings had open-air corridors, so Phosy heard the voice from the floor above clearly enough.

"Phosy? You down there?"

"Yes."

"Come up."

It was the Lao version of the intercom.

The supervisor was leaning against the wall in front of his office smoking a Marlboro.

"Smoke?" he said.

"No, thanks," said Phosy when he arrived. "You have something to tell me?"

The supervisor puffed on his cigarette. Four years on and they were still finding stashes of them. It was as if the royalists had planted them before they fled the city to wipe out the enemy one lung at a time.

"Bo dai," said the supervisor.

"*Bo dai,* what?" as if he didn't know.

"You have to drop your investigation."

"I thought it was *our* investigation."

"It's not going anywhere. It's time to stop."

"We have a military hit man downstairs and seven witnesses prepared to state—"

"He's out," said the supervisor.

Phosy accepted one of the cigarettes. He didn't smoke, but he wanted to crush something in his fist.

"Had visitors, did you?" he asked.

"Phosy, don't—"

"You know we could save a lot of money on rent by moving into the armed forces ministry. They even have a lady who delivers tea and biscuits right to your office."

"Phosy!"

"Of course we'd be answerable to the general, but that's not much different than . . ."

"Phosy. It's not them."

"Not who?"

"The army didn't do it."

"Rubbish."

"It's true. They weren't responsible for the kidnapping. You were wrong."

◘ ◘ ◘

From the roof of his guesthouse Civilai could see Thailand. The Thais had long-distance telephones and faxes and even courier services where you'd give a man a letter and he'd speed off on his motorcycle and hand it over in person. So close—just across the river—but so far. In Pak Xan, the public phone at the post office wasn't active. A line was down somewhere. The postal worker even had the nerve to say, "But we do have a fax machine."

Two buses passed through town every day on their way to Vientiane. Civilai had entrusted notes to the drivers of both and handed over generous tips for the trouble of delivering the messages to the ministry. The odds of that working were as narrow as Laos winning a medal in the next Olympics. Like so many times before, he was being held prisoner by his country's non-communication system.

He went to the council office to see whether they'd had any luck with their own phone. But the greasy clerk was nowhere to be found, the director was off "in the field," and the telephone had a padlock that prevented unauthorized users from dialing. The second-in-command assured Civilai they'd bring him a message whenever they had a response from Vientiane. The only response Civilai wanted was a pickup truck with half a dozen embassy officials on board. The director had taken the Renault, so the assistant suggested in a most condescending fashion that the old man take advantage of this quiet period and relax. If he was lonely the man said he knew of a pretty young lady who was a most competent masseuse. This suggestion was punctuated with a wink.

Civilai had reluctantly agreed to stop at the police station to pay a courtesy call on the rude flip-flopped police officer. He was eating sweet suet balls at his desk and didn't offer one to his visitor.

"How did you know the dead woman?" he asked, dribbling sauce down his chin.

"I assume you have a remarkable memory," said Civilai, helping himself to a seat.

"Why?"

"Because you're beginning an interview without a pad or a pen. Unless you're planning to bite my replies into your suet balls in Morse code I'm assuming you'll be memorizing everything," said Civilai.

That entire speech was apparently meaningless to the policeman. "I asked you a question," he said.

Civilai sighed. "My wife and I encountered her on Sunday evening for the first time," he said. "We'd never seen her before."

"But she knew you," said the policeman.

"Knew of us, more like. She knew we'd been to Ban Toop."

At this point, one of the five framed black-and-white photos of senior Party members that lined the wall behind him came unscrewed. To prevent warping, very common of wooden frames in the tropics, a second screw anchored the frame at the bottom. This screw held, so the president now hung upside down and out of alignment. To his credit, the policeman barely reacted to this decoration malfunction and continued his interview. Civilai, on the other hand, found the sight of this upside-down ex-royal, now with a single eyebrow above his nose, rather hilarious. His replies to the policeman's questions were seasoned liberally with giggles. This riled the policeman, who took it as a personal insult. From that moment on any pretense at détente was canceled.

But all at once the dangling photograph took on entirely different characteristics in Civilai's mind. The fall from alignment was symbolic rather than accidental. And as he went through the motion of replying to the policeman's questions he rummaged through the clutter of his memory in search of a story. Scary tales around a campfire as a teenager. Gossip and rumors that had become folklore. He searched desperately for a connection.

"What have we here?" he said.

"I found three castaways on the coastal shelf," Friday said proudly.

"Welcome, castaways," Ishmael said. "Forgive me for remaining seated, but my feet are quite sore today, so I'm making use of our healing clay. It's very nice to meet you."

"It's nice to meet you, Ishmael," said Violet, who thought healing clay was of dubious scientific efficacy, a phrase which here means "unlikely to heal sore feet."

"Call me Ish," said Ishmael, leaning down to scratch the heads of one of the sheep. "And what shall I call you?"

"Violet, Klaus, and Sunny Baudelaire," Friday chimed in, before the siblings could introduce themselves.

"Baudelaire?" Ishmael repeated, and raised his eyebrows. He gazed at the three children in silence as he took a long sip of cordial from his seashell, and for just one moment his smile seemed to disappear. But then he gazed down at the siblings and grinned heartily. "We haven't had new islanders in quite some time. You're welcome to stay as long as you'd like, unless you're unkind, of course."

"Thank you," Klaus said, as kindly as he could. "Friday has told us a few things about the island. It sounds quite interesting."

"It depends on how you look at it," Ishmael said. "Even if you want to leave, you'll only have the opportunity once a year. In the meantime, Friday, why don't you show them to a tent, so they can change their clothes? We should have some new woolen robes that fit you nicely."

"We would appreciate that," Violet said. "Our concierge uniforms are quite soaked from the storm."

"I'm sure they are," Ishmael said, twisting a strand of beard in his fingers. "Besides, our custom is to wear nothing but white, to match the sand of the islands, the healing clay of the pool, and the wool of the wild sheep. Friday, I'm surprised you are choosing to break with tradition."

Friday blushed, and her hand rose to the sunglasses she was wearing. "I found these in the wreckage," she said. "The sun is so bright on the island, I thought they might come in handy."

"I won't force you," Ishmael said calmly, "but it seems to me you might prefer to dress according to custom, rather than showing off your new eyewear."

"You're right, Ishmael," Friday said quietly, and removed her sunglasses with one hand while the other hand darted into one of her robe's deep pockets.

"That's better," Ishmael said, and smiled at the Baudelaires. "I hope you will enjoy living on this island," he said. "We're all castaways here, from one storm or another, and rather than trying to return to the world, we've built a colony safe from the world's treachery."

"There was a treacherous person with them," Friday piped up eagerly. "His name was Count Olaf, but he was so nasty that I didn't let him come with us."

"Olaf?" Ishmael said, and his eyebrows raised again. "Is this man a friend of yours?"

"Fat chance," Sunny said.

"No, he isn't," Violet translated quickly. "To tell you the truth, we've been trying to escape from Count Olaf for quite some time."

"He's a dreadful man," Klaus said.

"Same boat," Sunny said.

"Hmmm," Ishmael said thoughtfully. "Is that the whole story, Baudelaires?"

The children looked at one another. Of course, the few sentences they'd uttered were not the whole story. There was much, much more to the story of the Baudelaires and Count Olaf, and if the children had recited all of it Ishmael probably would have wept until the tears melted away the clay so his feet were bare and he had nothing to sit on. The Baudelaires could have told the island's facilitator about all of Count Olaf's schemes, from his vicious murder of Uncle Monty to his betrayal of Madame Lulu at the Caligari Carnival. They could have told him about his disguises, from his false peg leg when he was pretending to be Captain Sham, to his running shoes and turban when he was calling himself Coach Genghis. They could have told Ishmael about Olaf's many comrades, from his girlfriend Esmé Squalor to the two white-faced women who had disappeared in the Mortmain Mountains, and they could have told Ishmael about all of the unsolved mysteries that still kept the Baudelaires awake at night, from the disappearance of Captain Widdershins from an underwater cavern to the strange taxi driver who had approached the children outside the Hotel Denouement, and of course they could have told Ishmael about that ghastly day at Briny Beach, when they first heard the news of their parents' deaths. But if the Baudelaires had told Ishmael the whole story, they would have had to tell the parts that put the Baudelaires in an unfavorable light, a phrase which here means "the things the Baudelaires had done that were perhaps as treacherous as Olaf." They would have talked about their own schemes, from digging a pit to trap Esmé to starting the fire that destroyed the Hotel Denouement. They would have mentioned their own disguises, from Sunny pretending to be Chabo the Wolf Baby to Violet and Klaus pretending to be Snow Scouts, and their own comrades, from Justice Strauss, who turned out to be more useful than they had first thought, to Fiona, who turned out to be more treacherous than they had imagined. If the Baudelaire orphans had told Ishmael the whole story, they might have looked as villainous as Count Olaf. The Baudelaires did not want to find themselves back on the coastal shelf, with all the detritus of the storm. They wanted to be safe from treachery and harm, even if the customs of the island colony were not exactly to their liking, and so, rather than telling Ishmael the whole story, the Baudelaires merely nodded, and said the safest thing they could think of.

"It depends on how you look at it," Violet

said, and her siblings nodded in agreement.

"Very well," Ishmael said. "Run along and find your robes, and once you've changed, please give all of your old things to Friday and we'll haul them off to the arboretum."

"Everything?" Klaus said.

Ishmael nodded. "That's our custom."

"Occulaklaus?" Sunny asked, and her siblings quickly explained that she meant something like, "What about Klaus's glasses?"

"He can scarcely read without them," Violet added.

Ishmael raised his eyebrows again. "Well, there's no library here," he said quickly, with a nervous glance at Friday, "but I suppose your eyeglasses are of some use. Now, hurry along, Baudelaires, unless you'd like a sip of cordial before you go."

"No, thank you," Klaus said, wondering how many times he and his siblings would be offered this strange, sweet beverage. "My siblings and I tried some, and didn't care much for the taste."

"I won't force you," Ishmael said again, "but your initial opinion on just about anything may change over time. See you soon, Baudelaires."

He gave them a small wave, and the Baudelaires waved back as Friday led them out of the tent and farther uphill where more tents were fluttering in the morning breeze.

"Choose any tent you like," Friday said. "We all switch tents each day—except for Ishmael, because of his feet."

"Isn't it confusing to sleep in a different place each night?" Violet asked.

"It depends on how you look at it," Friday said, taking a sip from her seashell. "I've never slept any other way."

"Have you lived your whole life on this island?" Klaus said.

"Yes," Friday said. "My mother and father took an ocean cruise while she was pregnant, and ran into a terrible storm. My father was devoured by a manatee, and my mother was washed ashore when she was pregnant with me.

You'll meet her soon. Now please hurry up and change."

"Prompt," Sunny assured her, and Friday took her hand out of her pocket and shook Sunny's. The Baudelaires walked into the nearest tent, where a pile of robes lay folded in one corner. In moments, they changed into their new clothes, happy to discard their concierge uniforms, which were soaked and salty from the night's storm. When they were finished, however, they stood and stared for a moment at the pile of damp clothing. The Baudelaires felt strange to don the garments of shibboleth, a phrase which here means "wear the warm and somewhat unflattering clothing that was customary to people they hardly knew." It felt as if the three siblings were casting away everything that had happened to them prior to their arrival on the island. Their clothing, of course, was not the Baudelaires' whole story, as clothing is never anyone's whole story, except perhaps in the case of Esmé Squalor, whose villainous and fashionable clothing revealed just how villainous and fashionable she was. But the Baudelaires could not help but feel that they were abandoning their previous lives, in favor of new lives on an island of strange customs.

"I won't throw away this ribbon," Violet said, winding the slender piece of cloth through her fingertips. "I'm still going to invent things, no matter what Ishmael says."

"I'm not throwing away my commonplace book," Klaus said, holding the dark blue notebook. "I'll still research things, even if there's no library here."

"No throw this," Sunny said, and held up a small metal implement so her siblings could see. One end was a small, simple handle, perfect for Sunny's petite hands, and the other end branched into several sturdy wires that were meshed together like a small shrubbery.

"What is that?" Violet asked.

"Whisk," Sunny said, and she was exactly right. A whisk is a kitchen tool used to mix ingredients together rapidly, and the youngest Baudelaire was happy to have such a useful item in her possession.

"Yes," Klaus said. "I remember our father used to use it when he prepared scrambled eggs. But where did it come from?"

"Gal Friday," Sunny said.

"She knows Sunny can cook," Violet said, "but she must have thought Ishmael would make her throw the whisk away."

"I guess she's not so eager to follow all of the colony's customs," Klaus said.

"Guesso," Sunny agreed, and put the whisk in one of her robe's deep pockets. Klaus did the same with his commonplace book, and Violet did the same with her ribbon, and the three of them stood together for a moment, sharing their pocketed secrets. It felt strange to be keeping secrets from people who had taken them in so kindly, just as it felt strange not to tell Ishmael their whole story. The secrets of the ribbon, the commonplace book, and the whisk felt submerged, a word for "hidden" that usually applies to things underwater, such as a submarine submerged in the sea, or a boat's figurehead submerged in a coastal shelf, and with each step the Baudelaires took out of the tent, they felt their submerged secrets bumping up against them from within the pockets of their robes.

The word "ferment," like the words "bear," "yarn," and "hard," can mean two completely different things. One meaning is the chemical process by which the juice of certain fruits becomes sweeter and stronger, as Klaus explained to his siblings on the coastal shelf. But the other meaning of "ferment" refers to something building inside someone, like a secret that may be eventually found out, or a scheme that someone has been planning for quite some time. As the three Baudelaires exited the tent, and handed the detritus of their previous lives to Friday, they felt their own secrets fermenting inside them, and wondered what other secrets and schemes lay undiscovered. The Baudelaire orphans followed Friday back down the sloping beach, and wondered what else was fermenting on this strange island that was their new home.

CHAPTER
Four

By the time the Baudelaire orphans returned to Ishmael's tent, the joint was hopping, a phrase which here means "full of islanders in white robes, all holding items they had scavenged from the coastal shelf." The sheep were no longer napping but standing stiffly in two long lines, and the ropes tying them together led to a large wooden sleigh—an unusual form of transportation in such warm weather. Friday led the children through the colonists and sheep, who stepped aside and looked curiously at the three new castaways. Although this was the first time that the Baudelaires were castaways, they were accustomed to being strangers in a community, from their days at Prufrock Preparatory School to their time spent in the Village of Fowl Devotees, but they still did not enjoy being stared at. But it is one of the strange truths of life that practically nobody likes to be stared at and that practically nobody can stop themselves from staring, and as the three children made their way toward Ishmael, who was still sitting on his enormous clay chair, the Baudelaires could not help looking back at the islanders with the same curiosity, wondering how so many people could become castaways on the same island. It was as if the world was full of people with lives as unfortunate as that of the Baudelaires, all ending up in the very same place.

Friday led the Baudelaires to the base of Ishmael's chair, and the facilitator smiled down at the children as they sat at his clay-covered feet. "Those white robes look very handsome on you Baudelaires," he said. "Much better than those uniforms you were wearing earlier. You're going to be wonderful colonists, I am sure of it."

"Pyrrhonic?" Sunny said, which meant something along the lines of, "How can you be sure of such a thing based on our clothing?" But rather than translate, Violet remembered that the colony valued kindness and decided to say something kind.

"I can't tell you how much we appreciate this," Violet said, careful not to lean against the mounds of clay that hid Ishmael's toes. "We didn't know what would happen to us after the storm, and we're grateful to you, Ishmael, for taking us in."

"Everyone is taken in here," Ishmael said, apparently forgetting that Count Olaf had been abandoned. "And please, call me Ish. Would you like some cordial?"

"No, thank you," said Klaus, who could not bring himself to call the facilitator by his nickname. "We'd like to meet the other colonists, if that's all right."

"Of course," Ishmael said, and clapped his hands for attention. "Islanders!" he cried. "As I'm sure you've noticed, we have three new castaways with us today—Violet, Klaus, and Sunny, the only survivors of that terrible storm. I'm not going to force you, but as you bring up your storm scavenging items for my suggestions, why don't you introduce yourselves to our new colonists?"

"Good idea, Ishmael," said someone from the back of the tent.

"Call me Ish," said Ishmael, stroking his beard. "Now then, who's first?"

"I suppose I am," said a pleasant-looking man who was holding what looked like a large, metal flower. "It's nice to meet you three. My name is Alonso, and I've found the propeller of an airplane. The poor pilot must have flown straight into the storm."

"What a shame," Ishmael said. "Well, there's no airplane to be found on the island, so I don't think a propeller will be of much use."

"Excuse me," Violet said hesitantly, "but I know something about mechanical devices. If we rigged the propeller up to a simple hand-powered motor, we'd have a perfect fan for keeping cool on particularly hot days."

There was a murmur of appreciation from the crowd, and Alonso smiled at Violet. "It does get mighty hot around here," he said. "That's a good idea."

Ishmael took a sip of cordial from his seashell, and then frowned at the propeller. "It depends on how you look at it," he said. "If we only made one fan, then we'd all be arguing over who got to stand in front of it."

"We could take turns," Alonso said.

"Whose turn will it be on the hottest day of

the year?" Ishmael countered, a word which here means "said in a firm and sensible tone of voice, even though it was not necessarily a sensible thing to say." "I'm not going to force you, Alonso, but I don't think building a fan is worth all the fuss it might cause."

"I suppose you're right," Alonso said, with a shrug, and put the propeller on the wooden sleigh. "The sheep can take it to the arboretum."

"An excellent decision," Ishmael said, as a girl perhaps one or two years older than Violet stepped forward.

"I'm Ariel," she said, "and I found this in a particularly shallow part of the shelf. I think it's a dagger."

"A dagger?" Ishmael said. "You know we don't welcome weapons on the island."

Klaus was peering at the item Ariel was holding, which was made of carved wood rather than metal. "I don't think that's a dagger," Klaus said. "I believe it's an old tool used for cutting the pages of books. Nowadays most books are sold with their pages already separated, but some years ago each page was attached to the next, so you needed an implement to slice open the folds of paper and read the book."

"That's interesting," Ariel remarked.

"It depends on how you look at it," Ishmael said. "I fail to see how it could be of use here. We've never had a single book wash ashore—the storms simply tear the pages apart."

Klaus reached into his pocket and touched his hidden commonplace book. "You never know when a book might turn up," he pointed out. "In my opinion, that tool might be useful to keep around."

Ishmael sighed, looking first at Klaus and then at the girl who had found the item. "Well, I'm not going to force you, Ariel," he said, "but if I were you I would toss that silly thing onto the sleigh."

"I'm sure you're right," Ariel said, shrugging at Klaus, and she put the page cutter next to the propeller as a plump man with a sunburned face stepped forward.

"Sherman's the name," said Sherman, with a little bow to all three siblings. "And I found a cheese grater. I nearly lost a finger prying it away from a nest of crabs!"

"You shouldn't have gone to all that trouble," Ishmael said. "We're not going to have much use for a cheese grater without any cheese."

"Grate coconut," Sunny said. "Delicious cake."

"Cake?" Sherman said. "Egad, that would be delicious. We haven't had dessert since I've arrived here."

"Coconut cordial is sweeter than dessert," Ishmael said, raising his seashell to his lips. "I certainly wouldn't force you, Sherman, but I do think it would be best if that grater were thrown away."

Sherman took a sip from his own seashell, and then nodded, looking down at the sand.

"Very well," he said, and the rest of the morning proceeded in a similar manner. Islander after islander introduced themselves and presented the items they had found, and nearly every time the colony's facilitator discouraged them from keeping anything. A bearded man named Robinson found a pair of overalls, but Ishmael reminded him that the colony only wore the customary white robes, even though Violet could imagine herself wearing them while inventing some sort of mechanical device, so as not to get her robe dirty. An old woman named Erewhon held up a pair of skis that Ishmael dismissed as impractical, although Klaus had read of people who had used skis to cross mud and sand, and a red-haired woman named Weyden offered a salad spinner, but Ishmael reminded her that the island's only salads were to be made from the seaweed that was rinsed in the pool and dried out in the sun, rather than spun, even though Sunny could almost taste a dried coconut snack that such an appliance could have made. Ferdinand offered a brass cannon, which Ishmael was afraid would hurt someone, and Larsen held up a lawn mower only to have Ishmael remind her that the beach did not need to be trimmed regularly. A boy about Klaus's age introduced himself as Omeros, and held up a deck of playing cards he had found, but Ishmael convinced him that a deck of cards was likely to lead to gambling, and he dumped his item into the sleigh, as did a young girl named Finn, who'd found a typewriter that Ishmael had pronounced useless without paper. Brewster had found a window that had survived the storm without breaking, but Ishmael pointed out that you didn't need a window to admire the island's views, and Calypso had found a door that the facilitator had hinted could not be attached to any of the island's tents. Byam, whose mustache was unusually curly, discarded some batteries he had found, and Willa, whose head was unusually large, decided against a garden hose that was encrusted with barnacles. Mr. Pitcairn took the top of a chest of drawers to the arboretum, followed by Ms. Marlow, who had the bottom of a barrel. Dr. Kurtz threw out a silver tray, and Professor Fletcher ejected a chandelier, while Madame Nordoff denied the island a checkerboard and Rabbi Bligh agreed that the services of a large, ornate bird cage were not necessary on the island. The only items that the islanders ended up keeping were a few nets, which they would add to their supply of nets used to catch fish, and a few blankets, which Ishmael thought would eventually fade to white in the island sun. Finally, two siblings named Jonah and Sadie Bellamy displayed the boat on which the Baudelaires had arrived, with its figurehead still missing and its nameplate reading COUNT OLAF still taped to the back, but the colony was almost finished with its customary outrigger for Decision Day, and so the Bellamys lifted the boat onto the sleigh without much discussion. The sheep wearily dragged the sleigh out of the tent, up over the brae, and toward the far side of the island to dump the items in the arboretum, and the islanders excused themselves, at Ishmael's suggestion, to wash their hands for lunch. Within moments the only occupants of the tent were Ishmael, the Baudelaire orphans, and the girl who had first brought them to the tent, as if the siblings were merely another piece of wreckage to be picked over for approval.

"Quite a storm, wasn't it?" asked Ishmael, after a short silence. "We scavenged even more junk than usual."

"Were any other castaways found?" Violet asked.

"Do you mean Count Olaf?" Ishmael asked. "After Friday abandoned him, he'd never dare approach the island. He's either wandering around the coastal shelf, or he's trying to swim his way back to wherever he came from."

The Baudelaires looked at one another, knowing full well that Count Olaf was likely hatching some scheme, particularly as none of the islanders had found the boat's figurehead, where the deadly spores of the Medusoid Mycelium were hidden. "We weren't just thinking of Olaf," Klaus said. "We had some friends who may have been caught in the same storm—a pregnant woman named Kit Snicket who was in a submarine with some associates, and a group of people who were traveling by air."

Ishmael frowned, and drank some cordial from his seashell. "Those people haven't turned up," he said, "but don't despair, Baudelaires. It seems that everything eventually washes up on our shores. Perhaps their crafts were unharmed by the storm."

"Perhaps," Sunny agreed, trying not to think that they might not have been as lucky as that.

"They might turn up in the next day or so," Ishmael continued. "Another storm is heading this way."

"How do you know?" Violet asked. "Is there a barometer on the island?"

"There's no barometer," Ishmael said, referring to a device that measures the pressure in the atmosphere, which is one way of predicting the weather. "I just know there's one coming."

"How would you know such a thing?" Klaus asked, stopping himself from retrieving his commonplace book so he could take notes. "I've always heard that the weather is difficult to predict without advanced instruments."

"We don't need any advanced instruments on this colony," Ishmael said. "I predict the weather by using magic."

"Meledrub," Sunny said, which meant something along the lines of, "I find that very difficult to believe," and her siblings silently agreed. The Baudelaires, as a rule, did not believe in magic, although their mother had had a nifty card trick she could occasionally be persuaded to perform. Like all people who have seen something of the world, the children had come across plenty of things they had been unable to explain, from the diabolical hypnotism techniques of Dr. Orwell to the way a girl named Fiona had broken Klaus's heart, but they had never been tempted to solve these mysteries with a supernatural explanation like magic. Late at night, of course, when one is sitting upright in bed, having been woken up by a sudden loud noise, one believes in all sorts of supernatural things, but it was early afternoon, and the Baudelaires simply could not imagine that Ishmael was some sort of magical weatherman. Their doubt must have shown on their faces, for the facilitator immediately did what many people do when they are not believed, and hurriedly changed the subject.

"What about you, Friday?" Ishmael asked. "Did you find anything else besides the castaways and those awful sunglasses?"

Friday looked quickly at Sunny, but then shook her head firmly. "No," she said.

"Then please go help your mother with lunch," he said, "while I talk to our new colonists."

"Do I have to?" Friday asked. "I'd rather stay here, with the Baudelaires."

"I'm not going to force you," Ishmael said gently, "but I'm sure your mother could use some help."

Without another word, Friday turned and left the tent, walking up the sloping beach toward the other tents of the colony, and the Baudelaires were alone with their facilitator, who leaned down to speak quietly to the orphans.

"Baudelaires," he said, "as your facilitator, allow me to give you a piece of advice, as you begin your stay on this island."

"What might that be?" Violet asked.

Ishmael looked around the tent, as if spies were lurking behind the white, fluttering fabric. He took another sip from his seashell, and cracked his knuckles. "Don't rock the boat," he said, using an expression which here means "Don't upset people by doing something that is not customary." His tone was very cordial, but the children could hear something less cordial almost hidden in his voice, the way a coastal shelf is almost hidden by water. "We've been living by our customs for quite some time. Most of us can scarcely remember our lives before we became castaways, and there is a whole generation of islanders who have never lived anywhere else. My advice to you is not to ask so many questions or meddle around too much with our customs. We have taken you in, Baudelaires, which is a kindness, and we expect kindness in return. If you keep prying into the affairs of the island, people are going to think you're unkind—just like Friday thought Olaf was unkind. So don't rock the boat. After all, rocking the boat is what got you here in the first place."

Ishmael smiled at his little joke, and although they found nothing funny about poking fun at a shipwreck that had nearly killed them, the children gave Ishmael a nervous smile in return, and said no more. The tent was silent for a few minutes, until a pleasant-looking woman with a freckly face walked into the tent carrying an enormous clay jar.

"You must be the Baudelaires," she said, as Friday followed her into the tent carrying a stack of bowls fashioned from coconut shells, "and you must be starving, too. I'm Mrs. Caliban, Friday's mother, and I do most of the cooking around here. Why don't you have some lunch?"

"That would be wonderful," Klaus said. "We're quite hungry."

"Whatya fixin?" asked Sunny.

Mrs. Caliban smiled, and opened the jar so the children could peek inside. "Ceviche," she said. "It's a South American dish of chopped raw seafood."

"Oh," Violet said, with as much enthusiasm as she could muster. Ceviche is an acquired taste, a phrase which here means "something you don't like the first few times you eat it," and although the Baudelaires had eaten ceviche before—their mother used to make it in the Baudelaire kitchen, to celebrate the beginning of crab season—it was none of the children's favorite food, and not precisely what they had in mind as a first meal after being shipwrecked. When I was shipwrecked recently, for instance, I had the fortune to wash aboard a barge where I enjoyed a late supper of roast leg of lamb with creamed polenta and a fricassee of baby artichokes, followed by some aged Gouda served with roasted figs, and finished up with some fresh strawberries dipped in milk chocolate and crushed honeycomb, and I found this to be a wonderful antidote to being tossed like a rag doll in the turbulent waters of a particularly stormy creek. But the Baudelaires accepted their bowls of ceviche, as well as the strange utensils Friday handed them, which were made of wood and looked like a combination of a fork and a spoon.

"They're runcible spoons," Friday explained. "We don't have forks or knives in the colony, as they can be used as weapons."

"I suppose that's sensible," Klaus said,

although he couldn't help but think that nearly anything could be used as a weapon, if one were in a weaponry mood.

"I hope you like it," Mrs. Caliban said. "There's not much else you can cook with raw seafood."

"Negihama," Sunny said.

"My sister is something of a chef," Violet explained, "and was suggesting that she could prepare some Japanese dishes for the colony, if there were any wasabi to be had."

The younger Baudelaires gave their sister a brief nod, realizing that Violet was asking about wasabi not only because it might allow Sunny to make something palatable—a word which here means "that wasn't ceviche"—but because wasabi, which is a sort of horseradish often used in Japanese food, was one of the few defenses against the Medusoid Mycelium, and with Count Olaf lurking about, she wanted to think about possible strategies should the deadly fungus be let loose from the helmet.

"We don't have any wasabi," Mrs. Caliban said. "We don't have any spices at all, in fact. No spices have washed up on the coastal shelf."

"Even if they did," Ishmael added quickly, "I think we'd just throw them in the arboretum. The stomachs of the colonists are used to spiceless ceviche, and we wouldn't want to rock the boat."

Klaus took a bite of ceviche from his runcible spoon, and grimaced at the taste. Traditionally a ceviche is marinated in spices, which gives it an unusual but often delicious flavor, but without such seasoning, Mrs. Caliban's ceviche tasted like whatever you might find in a fish's mouth while it was eating. "Do you eat ceviche for every meal?" he asked.

"Certainly not," Mrs. Caliban said with a little laugh. "That would get tiresome, wouldn't it? No, we only have ceviche for lunch. Every morning we have seaweed salad for breakfast, and for dinner we have a mild onion soup served with a handful of wild grass. You might get tired of such bland food, but it tastes better if you wash it down with coconut cordial." Friday's mother reached into a deep pocket in her white robe, and brought out three large seashells that had been fashioned into canteens, and handed one to each Baudelaire.

"Let's drink a toast," Friday suggested, holding up her own seashell. Mrs. Caliban raised hers, and Ishmael wiggled in his clay chair and opened the stopper of his seashell once more.

"An excellent idea," the facilitator said, with a wide, wide smile. "Let's drink a toast to the Baudelaire orphans!"

"To the Baudelaires!" agreed Mrs. Caliban, raising her seashell. "Welcome to the island!"

"I hope you stay here forever and ever!" Friday cried.

The Baudelaires looked at the three islanders grinning at them, and tried their best to grin back, although they had so much on their minds that their grins were not very enthusiastic. The

Baudelaires wondered if they really had to eat spiceless ceviche, not only for this particular lunch, but for future lunches on the island. The Baudelaires wondered if they had to drink more of the coconut cordial, and if refusing to do so would be considered rocking the boat. They wondered why the figurehead of the boat had not been found, and they wondered where Count Olaf was, and what he was up to, and they wondered about their friends and associates who were somewhere at sea, and about all of the people they had left behind in the Hotel Denouement. But at this moment, the Baudelaires wondered one thing most of all, and that was why Ishmael had called them orphans, when they hadn't told him their whole story. Violet, Klaus, and Sunny looked first at their bowls of ceviche, and then at Friday and her mother, and then at their seashells, and finally up at Ishmael, who was smiling down at them from his enormous chair, and the castaways wondered if they really had reached a place that was far from the world's treachery or if the world's treachery was just hidden someplace, the way Count Olaf was hidden somewhere very nearby at that very moment. They looked up at their facilitator, uncertain if they were safe after all, and wondering what they could do about it if they weren't.

"I won't force you," Ishmael said quietly to the children, and the Baudelaire orphans wondered if that were true after all.

C H A P T E R

Five

Unless you are unusually insouciant—which is merely a fancy way of saying "the opposite of curious"—or one of the Baudelaire orphans yourself, you are probably wondering whether or not the three children drank the coconut cordial that was offered them rather forcefully by Ishmael. Perhaps you have been in situations yourself, where you have been offered a beverage or food you would rather not consume by someone you would rather not refuse, or perhaps you have been warned about people who will offer such things and told to avoid succumbing, a word which here means "accepting, rather than refusing, what you are given." Such situations are often referred to as incidents of "peer pressure," as "peer" is a word for someone with whom you are associating and "pressure" is a word for the influence such people often have. If you are a braeman or braewoman—a term for someone who lives all alone on a hill—then peer pressure is fairly easy to avoid, as you have no peers except for the occasional wild sheep who may wander near your cave and try to pressure you into growing a woolly coat. But if you live among people, whether they are people in your family, in your school, or in your secret organization, then every moment of your life is an incident of peer pressure, and you cannot avoid it any more than a boat at sea can avoid a surrounding storm. If you wake up in the morning at a particular time, when you would rather hide your head under your pillow until you are too hungry to stand it any longer, then you are succumbing to the peer pressure of your warden or morning butler. If you eat a breakfast that someone prepares for you, or prepare your own breakfast from food you have purchased, when you would rather stomp your feet and demand delicacies from faraway lands, then you are succumbing to the peer pressure of your grocer or breakfast chef. All day long, everyone in the world is succumbing to peer pressure, whether it is the pressure of their fourth grade peers to play dodge ball during recess or the pressure of their fellow circus performers to balance rubber balls on their noses, and if you try to avoid every instance of peer pressure you will end up without any peers whatsoever, and the trick is to succumb to enough pressure that you do not drive your peers away, but not so much that you end up in a situation in which you are dead or otherwise uncomfortable. This is a difficult trick, and most people never master it, and end up dead or uncomfortable at least once during their lives.

The Baudelaire orphans had been uncomfortable more than enough times over the course of their misadventures, and having found themselves on a distant island with only one set of peers to choose from, they succumbed to the pressure of Ishmael, and Friday, and Mrs. Caliban, and all of the other islanders who lived with the children in their new home. They sat in Ishmael's tent, and drank a bit of coconut cordial as they ate their lunch of spice-free ceviche, even though the drink left them feeling a bit dizzy and the food left them feeling a bit slimy, rather than leaving the colony and finding their own food and drink. They wore their white robes, even though they were a bit heavy for the warm weather, rather than trying to fashion garments of their own. And they kept quiet about the discouraged items they were keeping in their pockets—Violet's hair ribbon, Klaus's commonplace book, and Sunny's whisk—rather than rocking the boat, as the colony's facilitator had warned them, not even daring to ask Friday why she had given Sunny the kitchen implement in the first place.

But despite the strong taste of cordial, the bland taste of the food, the unflattering robes, and the secret items, the Baudelaires still felt more at home than they had in quite some time. Although the children had always managed to find a companion or two no matter where they wandered, the Baudelaires had not really been accepted by any sort of community since Count Olaf had framed the children for murder, forcing them to hide and disguise themselves countless times. The Baudelaires felt safe living with the colony, knowing that Count Olaf was not allowed near them, and that their associates, if they, too, ended up as castaways, would be welcomed into the tent as long as they, too, succumbed to the islanders' peer pressure.

Spiceless food, unflattering clothing, and suspicious beverages seemed a fair price to pay for a safe place to call home, and for a group of people who, if not exactly friends, were at least companions for as long as they wished to stay.

The days passed, and the island remained a safe if bland place for the siblings. Violet would have liked to spend her days assisting the islanders in the building of the enormous outrigger, but at Ishmael's suggestion she assisted Friday, Robinson, and Professor Fletcher with the colony's laundry, and spent most of her time at the saltwater falls, washing everyone's robes and laying them out on rocks to dry in the sun. Klaus would have enjoyed walking over the brae to catalog all of the detritus the colonists had collected while storm scavenging, but everyone had agreed with the facilitator's idea that the middle Baudelaire would stay at Ishmael's side at all times, so he spent his days piling clay on the old man's feet, and running to refill his seashell with cordial.

Only Sunny was allowed to do something in her area of expertise, but assisting Mrs. Caliban with the cooking was not very interesting, as the colony's three meals were very easy to prepare. Every morning, the youngest Baudelaire would retrieve the seaweed that Alonso and Ariel had harvested from the sea, after it had been rinsed by Sherman and Robinson and laid out to dry by Erewhon and Weyden, and simply throw it into a bowl for breakfast. In the afternoon, Ferdinand and Larsen would bring an enormous pile of fish they had captured in the colony's nets, so Sunny and Mrs. Caliban could mush it into ceviche with their runcible spoons, and in the evening the two chefs would light a fire and slowly simmer a pot of wild onions Omeros and Finn had picked, along with wild grasses reaped by Brewster and Calypso that served as dinner's only spice, and serve the soup alongside seashells full of the coconut cordial Byam and Willa had fermented from coconuts Mr. Pitcairn and Ms. Marlow had gathered from the island's coconut trees. None of these recipes was very challenging to prepare, and Sunny ended up spending much of her day in idleness, a word which here means "lounging around with Mrs. Caliban, sipping coconut cordial and staring at the sea."

After so many frantic encounters and tragic experiences, the children were not accustomed to leading such a calm life, and for the first few days they felt a bit restless without the treachery of Count Olaf and his sinister mysteries, and the integrity of V.F.D. and its noble deeds, but with every good night's sleep in the breezy comfort of a tent, and every day's work at easy tasks, and every sip of the sweet coconut cordial, the strife and treachery of the children's lives felt farther and farther away. After a few days, another storm arrived, just as Ishmael had predicted, and as the sky blackened and the island was covered in wind and rain, the Baudelaires huddled with the other islanders in the facilitator's tent, and they were grateful for their uneventful life on the colony, rather than the stormy existence they had endured since their parents had died.

"Janiceps," Sunny said to her siblings the next morning, as the Baudelaires walked along the coastal shelf. According to custom, the islanders were all storm scavenging, and here and there on the flat horizon, poking at the detritus of the storm. By "Janiceps," the youngest Baudelaire meant "I'm of two minds about living here," an expression which means that she couldn't decide if she liked the island colony or not.

"I know what you mean," Klaus said, who was carrying Sunny on his shoulders. "Life isn't very exciting here, but at least we're not in any danger."

"I suppose we should be grateful for that," Violet said, "even though life in the colony seems quite strict."

"Ishmael keeps saying he won't force us to do anything," Klaus said, "but everything feels a bit forced anyway."

"At least they forced Olaf away," Violet pointed out, "which is more than V.F.D. ever accomplished."

"Diaspora," Sunny said, which meant something like, "We live in such a distant place that the battle between V.F.D. and their enemies seems very far away."

"The only V.F.D. around here," Klaus said, leaning down to peer into a pool of water, "is our Very Flavorless Diet."

Violet smiled. "Not so long ago," she said, "we were desperate to reach the last safe place by Thursday. Now, everywhere we look is safe, and we have no idea what day it is."

"I still miss home," Sunny said.

"Me too," Klaus said. "For some reason I keep missing the library at Lucky Smells Lumbermill."

"Charles's library?" Violet asked, with an amazed smile. "It was a beautiful room, but it only had three books. Why on earth do you miss that place?"

"Three books are better than none," Klaus said. "The only thing I've read since we arrived here is my own commonplace book. I suggested to Ishmael that he could dictate a history of the colony to me, and that I'd write it down so the islanders would know about how this place came to be. Other colonists could write down their own stories, and eventually this island would have its own library. But Ishmael said that he wouldn't force me, but he didn't think it would be a good idea to write a book that would upset people with its descriptions of storms and castaways. I don't want to rock the boat, but I miss my research."

"I know what you mean," Violet said. "I keep missing Madame Lulu's fortune-telling tent."

"With all those phony magic tricks?" Klaus said.

"Her inventions were pretty ridiculous," Violet admitted, "but if I had those simple mechanical materials, I think I could make a simple water filtration system. If we could manufacture fresh water, the islanders wouldn't have to drink coconut cordial all day long. But Friday said that the drinking of the cordial was inveterate."

"Nospine?" Sunny asked.

"She meant people had been drinking it for so long that they wouldn't want to stop," Violet said. "I don't want to rock the boat, but I miss working on inventions. What about you, Sunny? What do you miss?"

"Fountain," Sunny said.

"The Fowl Fountain, at the Village of Fowl Devotees?" Klaus asked.

"No," Sunny said, shaking her head. "In city."

"The Fountain of Victorious Finance?" Violet asked. "Why on earth would you miss that?"

"First swim," Sunny said, and her siblings gasped.

"You can't remember that," Klaus said.

"You were just a few weeks old," Violet said.

"I remember," Sunny said firmly, and the elder Baudelaires shook their heads in wonder. Sunny was talking about an afternoon long ago, during an unusually hot autumn in the city. The Baudelaire parents had some business to attend to, and brought along the children, promising to stop at the ice cream store on the way home. The family had arrived at the banking district, pausing to rest at the Fountain of Victorious Finance, and the Baudelaires' mother had hurried into a building with tall, curved towers poking out in all directions, while their father waited outside with the children. The hot weather made Sunny very cranky, and she began to fuss. To quiet her, the Baudelaires' father dipped her bare feet in the water, and Sunny had smiled so enthusiastically that he had begun to dunk Sunny's body, clothes and all, into the fountain, until the youngest Baudelaire was screaming with laughter. As you may know, the laughter of babies is often very contagious, and before long not only were Violet and Klaus also jumping into the fountain, but the Baudelaires' father, too, all of them laughing and laughing as Sunny grew more and more delighted. Soon the Baudelaires' mother came out of the building, and looked in astonishment for a moment at her soaking and giggling family, before putting down her pocketbook, kicking off her shoes, and joining them in the refreshing water. They laughed all the way home, each footstep a wet *squish*, and sat out on their front steps to dry in the sun. It was a wonderful day, but very long ago—so long ago Violet and Klaus had almost forgotten it themselves. But as Sunny reminded them, they could almost hear her newborn laughter, and see the incredulous looks of the bankers who were passing by.

"It's hard to believe," Violet said, "that our parents could laugh like that, when they were already involved with V.F.D. and all its troubles."

"The schism must have seemed a world away that day," Klaus said.

"And now," Sunny said, and her siblings

nodded in agreement. With the morning sun blazing overhead, and the sea sparkling at the edge of the coastal shelf, their surroundings seemed as far from trouble and treachery as that afternoon in the Fountain of Victorious Finance. But trouble and treachery are rarely as far away as one thinks they are on the clearest of days. On that faraway afternoon in the banking district, for instance, trouble could be found in the corridors of the towered building, where the Baudelaires' mother was handed a weather report and a naval map that would reveal, when she studied them by candlelight that evening, far greater trouble than she had imagined, and treachery could be found just past the fountain, where a woman disguised as a pretzel vendor took a photograph of the laughing family, and slipped her camera into the coat pocket of a financial expert who was hurrying to a restaurant, where the coat-check boy would remove the camera and hide it in an enormous parfait glass of fruit that a certain playwright would order for dessert, only to have a quick-thinking waitress pretend that the cream in the zabaglione sauce had gone sour and dump the entire dish into a garbage can in the alley, where I had been sitting for hours, pretending to look for a lost puppy who was actually scurrying into the back entrance of the towered building, removing her disguise, and folding it into her handbag, and this morning on the coastal shelf was no different. The Baudelaires took a few more steps in silence, squinting into the sun, and then Sunny knocked gently on her brother's head and pointed out at the horizon. The three children looked carefully, and saw an object resting unevenly on the edge of the shelf, and this was trouble, even though it didn't look like trouble at the time. It was hard to say what it looked like, only that it was large, and square, and ragged, and the children hurried closer to get a better view. Violet led the way, stepping carefully around a few crabs snapping along the shelf, and Klaus followed behind, with Sunny still on his shoulders, and even when they reached the object they found it difficult to identify.

At first glance, the large, square, ragged object looked like a combination of everything the Baudelaires missed. It looked like a library, because the object seemed to be nothing more than stacks and stacks of books, piled neatly on top of one another in a huge cube. But it also looked like an invention, because wrapped around the cube of books, the way string is wrapped around a package, were thick straps that appeared to be made out of rubber, in varying shades of green, and on one side of the cube was affixed a large flap of battered wood. And it also looked like a fountain, as water was trickling out of it from all sides, leaking through the bloated pages of the books and splashing down to the sand of the coastal shelf. But although this was a very unusual sight, the children stared not at the cube but at something at the top of this strange contraption. It was a bare foot, hanging over the side of the cube as if there were someone sleeping on the top of all those books, and the Baudelaires could see, right on the ankle, a tattoo of an eye.

"Olaf?" Sunny asked, but her siblings shook their heads. They had seen Count Olaf's foot more times than they would like to count, and this foot was much narrower and cleaner than the villain's.

"Climb onto my back," Violet said to her brother. "Maybe we can hoist Sunny to the top."

Klaus nodded, climbed carefully onto his sister's back, and then, very slowly, stood on Violet's shoulders. The three Baudelaires stood in a trembling tower, and Sunny reached out her little hands and pulled herself up, as she had pulled herself out of the elevator shaft at 667 Dark Avenue not so long ago, and saw the woman who was lying unconscious on top of the stack of books. She was dressed in a dress of dark red velvet, which was streaked and soaked from the rain, and her hair lay sprawled behind her like a wide, tangled fan. The foot that was hanging over the side of the cube was bent a strange, wrong way, but she looked otherwise unharmed. Her eyes were closed, and her mouth was frowning, but her belly, full and round from her pregnancy, rose and fell with calm, deep breaths, and her hands, covered in long, white gloves, lay gently on her chest, as if she were comforting herself, or her child.

"Kit Snicket," Sunny called down to her siblings, her voice hushed with amazement.

"Yes?" replied a voice that was high-pitched and grating, a word which here means "irritating, and sadly familiar." From behind the cube of books, a figure stepped out to greet the children, and Sunny looked down and frowned as the tower of elder Baudelaires turned to face the person who was confronting them. This person was also wearing a talaric—a word which here means "just reaching the ankles"—dress that was streaked and soaked, although the dress was not just red but orange and yellow as well, the colors melting together as the person walked closer and closer to the children. This person was not wearing gloves, but a pile of seaweed had been arranged to resemble long hair, which cascaded hideously down this person's back, and although this person's belly was also full and round, it was full and round in an odd and unconvincing way. It would have been very unusual if the belly were genuine, because it was obvious from looking at the person's face that the person was not a woman, and pregnancy occurs very rarely in males, although the male seahorse is a creature that becomes pregnant from time to time.

But this person, stepping closer and closer to the towered elder Baudelaires and gazing angrily up at the youngest, was no seahorse, of course. If the odd cube of books was trouble, then this man was treachery, and as is so often the case with treachery, his name was Count Olaf. Violet and Klaus stared at the villain, and

Sunny stared at Kit, and then the three children looked out at the horizon, where other islanders who had spotted the strange object were heading toward them. Lastly, the Baudelaire orphans looked at one another, and wondered if a schism were so very far away after all, or if they had traveled a world away only to find all the trouble and treachery of the world staring them right in the face.

CHAPTER SIX

At this point, you may find yourself recognizing all of the sad hallmarks of the Baudelaire orphans' sad history. The word "hallmarks" refers to something's distinguishing characteristics, such as the frothy foam and loud fizz that are the hallmarks of a root beer float, or the tearstained photographs and the loud fizz that are the hallmarks of a broken heart. Certainly the Baudelaires themselves, who as far as I know have not read their own sad history, but of course are its primary participants, had a queasy feeling in their stomachs as the islanders approached them, holding various items they had found while storm scavenging. It appeared that once again, after arriving in a strange new home, Count Olaf would fool everyone with his latest disguise, and the Baudelaires would once again be in grave danger. In fact, Count Olaf's talaric disguise did not even cover the tattoo of an eye he wore on his ankle, as the islanders, living so far from the world, would not know about this notorious mark and so could be fooled even more easily. But as the colonists drew close to the cube of books where Kit Snicket lay unconscious, suddenly the Baudelaires' history went contrary to expectations, a phrase which here means "The young girl they had first met on the coastal shelf recognized Count Olaf immediately."

"That's Olaf!" Friday cried, pointing an accusatory finger at the villain. "Why is he dressed as a pregnant woman?"

"I'm dressed as a pregnant woman because I am a pregnant woman," Count Olaf replied, in his high-pitched, disguised voice. "My name is Kit Snicket, and I've been looking everywhere for these children."

"You're not Kit Snicket!" Mrs. Caliban cried.

"Kit Snicket is up on this pile of books," Violet said indignantly, helping Sunny down from the top of the cube. "She's a friend of ours, and she may be hurt, or ill. But this is Count Olaf, who is no friend of ours."

"He's no friend of ours, either," Friday said, and there was a murmur of agreement from the islanders. "Just because you've put something inside your dress to look pregnant, and thrown a clump of seaweed on your hair to make a wig, doesn't mean you won't be recognized." She turned to face the three children, who noticed for the first time that the islander had a suspicious bump under her robe, as if she, too, had hidden something under her clothing. "I hope he hasn't been bothering you. I told him specifically to go away."

Count Olaf glared at Friday, but then turned

to try his treachery on the other islanders. "You primitive people won't tell a pregnant woman to go away, will you?" he asked. "I'm in a very delicate condition."

"You're not in a very delicate condition," said Larsen firmly. "You're in a very transparent disguise. If Friday says you're this Olaf person, then I'm sure you are, and you're not welcome here, due to your unkindness."

"I've never been unkind in my life," Olaf said, running a bony hand through his seaweed. "I'm nothing but a fairly innocent maiden with my belly full of baby. It is the Baudelaires who have been unkind, along with this impostor sleeping on top of this damp library."

"Library?" Fletcher said with a gasp. "We've never had a library on the island."

"Ishmael said that a library was bound to lead to trouble," said Brewster, "so we were lucky that a book has never ended up on our shores."

"You see?" Olaf said, his orange and yellow

dress rustling in the morning breeze. "That treacherous woman up there has dragged these books to your colony, just to be unkind to you poor primitive people. And the Baudelaires are friends with her! They're the ones you should abandon here, and I should be welcomed to Olaf-Land and given gifts."

"This island is not called Olaf-Land!" cried Friday. "And you're the one we abandoned!"

"This is confusing!" cried Omeros. "We need a facilitator to sort this out!"

"Omeros is right," said Calypso. "We shouldn't decide anything until we've talked to Ishmael. Come on, let's take all this detritus to Ishmael's tent."

The colonists nodded, and a few villagers walked together to the cube of books and began to push it along the shelf. It was difficult work, and the cube shuddered as it was dragged along the bumpy surface. The Baudelaires saw Kit's foot bob violently up and down and feared that their friend would fall.

"Stop," Klaus said. "It's not safe to move someone who may be seriously injured, particularly if she's pregnant."

"Klaus is right," said Dr. Kurtz. "I remember that from my days in veterinary school."

"If Muhammad will not come to the mountain," Rabbi Bligh said, using an expression that the islanders understood at once, "the mountain will come to Muhammad."

"But how can Ishmael come here?" asked Erewhon. "He couldn't walk all this way with his injured feet."

"The sheep can drag him here," said Sherman. "We can put his chair on the sleigh. Friday, you guard Olaf and the Baudelaires, while the rest of us will go fetch our facilitator."

"And some more coconut cordial," said Madame Nordoff. "I'm thirsty and my seashell is almost empty."

There was a murmur of agreement from the islanders, and they began to make their way back toward the island, still carrying all of the items they had found while scavenging. In a few minutes, the colonists were nothing more than faint shapes on the misty horizon, and the Baudelaires were alone with Count Olaf and with Friday, who took a big sip from her seashell and then smiled at the children.

"Don't worry, Baudelaires," the girl said, holding one hand over the bulge in her robe. "We'll sort this out. I promise you that this terrible man will be abandoned once and for all."

"I'm not a man," Olaf insisted in his disguised voice. "I'm a lady with a baby inside her."

"Pellucid theatrics," Sunny said.

"My sister's right," Violet said. "Your disguise isn't working."

"Oh, I don't think you'd want me to stop pretending," the villain said. He was still talking in his ridiculous high-pitched voice, but his eyes shone brightly from behind his seaweed bangs. He reached behind him and revealed the harpoon gun, with its bright red trigger and one last harpoon ready to be fired. "If I were to say that I was Count Olaf, instead of Kit Snicket, I might begin behaving like a villain, rather than a noble person."

"You've never behaved like a noble person," Klaus said, "no matter what name you've been using. And that weapon doesn't scare us. You only have one harpoon, and this island is full of people who know how wicked and unkind you are."

"Klaus is right," Friday said. "You might as well put your weapon down. It's useless in a place like this."

Count Olaf looked first at Friday, and then at the three Baudelaires, and he opened his mouth as if to say another treacherous thing in his disguised voice. But then he shut his mouth again, and glared down at the puddles of the coastal shelf. "I'm tired of wandering around here," he muttered. "There's nothing to eat but seaweed and raw fish, and everything valuable has been taken by all those fools in robes."

"If you didn't behave so horridly," Friday

said, "you could live on the island."

The Baudelaires looked at one another nervously. Although it seemed a bit cruel to abandon Olaf on the shelf, they did not like the idea that he might be welcomed into the colony. Friday, of course, did not know the whole story of Count Olaf, and had only experienced his unkindness once, on the day she first encountered him, but the Baudelaires could not tell Friday the whole story of Olaf without telling the whole story of themselves, and they did not know what Friday would think of their own unkindnesses and treachery.

Count Olaf looked at Friday as if thinking something over. Then, with a suspicious smile, he turned to the Baudelaires and held out the harpoon gun. "I suppose you're right," he said. "The harpoon gun is useless in a place like this." He was still talking in his disguised voice, and his hand caressed his false pregnancy as if there were actually a baby growing inside him.

The Baudelaires looked at Olaf and then at

the weapon. The last time the children had touched the harpoon gun, the penultimate harpoon had fired and a noble man by the name of Dewey had been killed. Violet, Klaus, and Sunny would never forget the sight of Dewey sinking into the waters of the pond as he died, and looking at the villain offering them the weapon only reminded them of how dangerous and terrible the weapon was.

"We don't want that," Violet said.

"Obviously this is some trick of yours," Klaus said.

"It's no trick," Olaf said in his high-pitched voice. "I'm giving up my villainous ways, and I want to live with you on the island. I'm sorry to hear that you don't believe me."

His face was very serious, as if he *were* very sorry to hear that, but his eyes were shiny and bright, the way they are when someone is telling a joke. "Fibber," Sunny said.

"You insult me, madam," Olaf said. "I'm as honest as the day is long."

The villain was using an expression that is used by many people despite the fact that it scarcely means anything at all. Some days are long, such as at the height of summer, when the sun shines for a very long time, or Halloween day, which always seems to last forever until it is finally time to put on one's costume and demand candy from strangers, and some days are short, particularly during the wintertime or when one is doing something enjoyable, such as reading a good book or following random people on the street to see where they will go, and so if someone is as honest as the day is long, they may not be honest at all. The children were relieved to see that Friday was not fooled by Olaf's use of a vague expression, and she frowned at the villain sternly.

"The Baudelaires told me you were not to be trusted," the young girl said, "and I can see that they spoke the truth. You'll stay right here, Olaf, until the others arrive and we decide what to do with you."

"I'm not Count Olaf," Count Olaf said, "but in the meantime, could I have a sip of this coconut cordial I heard mentioned?"

"No," Friday said, and turned her back on the villain to gaze wistfully at the cube of books. "I've never seen a book before," she confessed to the Baudelaires. "I hope Ishmael thinks it's O.K. to keep them here."

"You've never seen a book?" Violet said in amazement. "Do you know how to read?"

Friday took a quick look around the coastal shelf, and then nodded her head quickly. "Yes," she said. "Ishmael didn't think it was a good idea to teach us, but Professor Fletcher disagreed, and held secret classes on the coastal shelf for those of us who were born on the island. From time to time, I keep in practice by sketching the alphabet in the sand with a stick, but without a library there's not much I can do. I hope Ishmael won't suggest that we let the sheep drag all these books to the arboretum."

"Even if he does, you won't have to throw

them away," Klaus reminded her. "He won't force you."

"I know," Friday said with a sigh. "But when Ishmael suggests something, everybody agrees, and it's hard not to succumb to that kind of peer pressure."

"Whisk," Sunny reminded her, and took the kitchen implement out of her pocket.

Friday smiled at the youngest Baudelaire, but quickly put the item back in Sunny's pocket. "I gave you that whisk because you said you were interested in cooking," she said. "It seemed a shame to deny your interests just because Ishmael might not think a kitchen implement was appropriate. You'll keep my secret, won't you?"

"Of course," Violet said, "but it's also a shame to deny your interest in reading."

"Maybe Ishmael won't object," Friday said.

"Maybe," Klaus said, "or maybe we could try a little peer pressure of our own."

"I don't want to rock the boat," Friday said

with a frown. "Ever since my father's death, my mother has wanted me to be safe, which is why we left the world far behind and decided to stay here on the island. But the older I get, it seems the more secrets I have. Professor Fletcher taught me secretly to read. Omeros taught me secretly to skip rocks, even though Ishmael says it's dangerous. I secretly gave Sunny a whisk." She reached into her robe, and smiled. "And now I have another secret, just for me. Look what I found curled up in a broken wooden crate."

Count Olaf had been glaring silently at the children, but as Friday revealed her secret he let out a shriek even more high-pitched than his fake voice. But the Baudelaire orphans did not shriek, even though Friday was holding a frightening-looking thing, as dark as a coal mine and as thick as a sewer pipe, that uncurled itself and quickly darted toward the three children. Even as the creature opened its mouth, the morning sun glinting on its sharp teeth, the Baudelaires did not shriek, but marveled that once again their history was going contrary to expectations.

"Incredi!" Sunny cried, and it was true, for the enormous snake that was wrapping itself around the Baudelaires was, incredibly, a creature they had not seen for quite some time and never thought they would see again in their lives.

"It's the Incredibly Deadly Viper!" Klaus said in amazement. "How in the world did it end up here?"

"Ishmael said that everything eventually washes up on the shores of this island," Violet said, "but I never thought I'd see this reptile again."

"Deadly?" Friday asked nervously. "Is it poisonous? It seemed friendly to me."

"It *is* friendly," Klaus reassured her. "It's one of the least deadly and most friendly creatures in the animal kingdom. Its name is a misnomer."

"How can you be sure?" Friday asked.

"We knew the man who discovered it," Violet said. "His name was Dr. Montgomery Montgomery, and he was a brilliant herpetologist."

"He was a wonderful man," Klaus said. "We miss him very much."

The Baudelaires hugged the snake, particularly Sunny, who'd had a special attachment to the playful reptile, and thought for a moment of kind Uncle Monty and the days the children had spent with him. Then, slowly, they remembered how those days had ended, and they turned to look at Count Olaf, who had slaughtered Monty as part of a treacherous plot. Count Olaf frowned, and looked back at them. It was strange to see the villain just sitting there, shuddering at a snake, after his murderous scheme to get the orphans in his clutches. Now, so far from the world, it was as if Olaf no longer had clutches, and his murderous schemes were as useless as the harpoon gun that lay in his hands.

"I've always wanted to meet a herpetologist," said Friday, who of course did not know the whole story of Monty and his murder. "The island doesn't have an expert on snakes. There's so much of the world I'm missing by living here."

"The world is a wicked place," Count Olaf said quietly, and now it was the Baudelaires who shuddered. Even with the hot sun beating down on them, and the weight of the Incredibly Deadly Viper in their laps, the children felt a chill at the villain's words, and everyone was silent, watching the islanders approach along with the sheep, who had Ishmael in tow, a phrase which here means "dragged along on the sleigh behind them, sitting on his white chair as if he were a king, with his feet still covered in hunks of clay and his woolly beard billowing in the wind." As the colonists and sheep walked closer and closer, the children could see that the sheep had something else in tow, too, which sat on the sleigh behind the facilitator's chair. It was the large, ornate bird cage that had been found after the previous storm, shining in the sunlight like a small fire.

"Count Olaf," Ishmael said in a booming voice, as soon as his chair arrived. He stared down at the villain scornfully but also carefully, as if memorizing his face.

"Ishmael," Count Olaf said, in his disguised tone.

"Call me Ish," Ishmael said.

"Call me Kit Snicket," Olaf said.

"I'm not going to call you anything," Ishmael growled. "Your reign of treachery is over, Olaf." In one swift motion, the facilitator leaned down and snatched the seaweed wig off Olaf's head. "I've been told of your schemes and disguises, and we won't stand for it. You'll be locked up immediately."

Jonah and Sadie lifted the bird cage from the sleigh, set it on the ground, and pushed open its door, glaring meaningfully at Count Olaf. With a nod from Ishmael, Weyden and Ms. Marlow stepped toward the villain, wrestled the harpoon gun from his hands, and dragged him toward the bird cage, as the Baudelaire orphans looked at one another, unsure exactly how they felt. On one hand, it seemed as if the children had been waiting their entire lives for someone to utter precisely the words Ishmael had uttered, and they were eager for Olaf to finally be punished for his dreadful acts, from his recent kidnapping of Justice Strauss to the time, long ago, when he had thrown Sunny into a bird cage and dangled her from his tower window. But they weren't convinced that Count Olaf should be locked in a cage himself, even a cage as large as the one that had washed ashore. It wasn't clear to the children if what was happening now, on the coastal shelf, was the arrival of justice at last, or just another unfortunate event. Throughout their history the Baudelaires had always hoped that Count Olaf would end up in the hands of the authorities, and would be punished by the High Court after a trial. But members of the High Court had turned out to be as corrupt and sinister as Olaf himself, and the authorities were far, far away from the island, and looking for the Baudelaires in order to charge them with arson and murder. It was difficult to say, so far from the world, how the three children felt about Count Olaf being dragged into a bird cage, but as was so often the case, it did not matter how the three children felt about it, because it happened anyway. Weyden and Ms. Marlow dragged the struggling villain to the door of the bird cage and forced him to duck inside. He snarled, and wrapped his arms around his false pregnancy, and rested his head against his knees, and hunched his back, and the Bellamy siblings shut the door of the cage and latched it securely. The villain fit in the cage, but just barely, and you had to look closely to see that the mess of limbs and hair and orange and yellow cloth was a person at all.

"This isn't fair," Olaf said. His voice was muffled from inside the cage, although the children noticed that he was still using a high-pitched tone, as if he could not help pretending

to be Kit Snicket. "I'm an innocent pregnant woman, and these children are the real villains. You haven't heard the whole story."

"It depends on how you look at it," Ishmael said firmly. "Friday told me you were unkind, and that's all we need to hear. And this seaweed wig is all we need to see!"

"Ishmael's right," Mrs. Caliban said firmly. "You've been nothing but treacherous, Olaf, and the Baudelaires have been nothing but good!"

"'Nothing but good,'" Olaf repeated. "Ha! Why don't you look in the baby's pockets if you think she's so good. She's hiding a kitchen implement that one of your precious islanders gave her!"

Ishmael peered down at the youngest Baudelaire from his vantage point, a phrase which here means "chair perched on a sleigh dragged by sheep." "Is that true, Sunny?" he asked. "Are you keeping a secret from us?"

Sunny looked up at the facilitator, and then

at the bird cage, remembering how uncomfortable it was to be locked up. "Yes," she admitted, and took the whisk out of her pocket as the islanders gasped.

"Who gave this to you?" Ishmael demanded.

"Nobody gave it to her," Klaus said quickly, not daring to look at Friday. "It's just something that survived the storm along with us." He reached into his pocket and brought out his commonplace book. "Each of us has something, Ishmael. I have this notebook, and my sister has a ribbon she likes to use to tie up her hair."

There was another gasp from the assembled colonists, and Violet took the ribbon out of her pocket. "We didn't mean any harm," she said.

"You were told of the island's customs," the facilitator said sternly, "and you chose to ignore them. We were very kind to you, giving you food and clothing and shelter, and even letting you keep your glasses. And in turn, you were unkind to us."

"They made a mistake," Friday said, swiftly gathering the forbidden items from the Baudelaires and giving Sunny a brief and grateful look. "We'll let the sheep take these things away, and forget all about it."

"That seems fair," said Sherman.

"I agree," Professor Fletcher said.

"Me too," Omeros said, who had picked up the harpoon gun.

Ishmael frowned, but as more and more islanders expressed their agreement, he succumbed to peer pressure and gave the orphans a small smile. "I suppose they can stay," he said, "if they don't rock the boat any further." He sighed, and then suddenly frowned down at a puddle. During the conversation, the Incredibly Deadly Viper had decided to take a brief swim, and was now staring up at the facilitator from a pool of seawater.

"What is that?" Mr. Pitcairn asked, with a frightened gasp.

"It's a friendly snake we found," Friday said.

"Who told you it was friendly?" demanded Ferdinand.

Friday shared a quick dismayed look with the Baudelaires. After all that had happened, they knew there was no hope of convincing Ishmael that keeping the snake was a good idea. "Nobody told me," Friday said quietly. "It just seems friendly."

"It looks incredibly deadly," Erewhon said with a frown. "I say we dump it in the arboretum."

"We don't want a snake slithering around the arboretum," Ishmael said, stroking his beard quickly. "It might hurt the sheep. I won't force you, but I think we should abandon it here with Count Olaf. Come along now, it's almost lunchtime. Baudelaires, please push that cube of books to the arboretum, and—"

"Our friend shouldn't be moved," Violet interrupted, with a gesture to Kit's unconscious figure. "We need to help her."

"I didn't realize there was a castaway up

there," Mr. Pitcairn said, peering at the bare foot that was still hanging over the side of the cube. "Look, she has the same tattoo as the villain!"

"She's my girlfriend," said Olaf from the bird cage. "You should either punish us both or set us both free."

"She's not your girlfriend!" Klaus cried. "She's our friend, and she's in trouble!"

"It seems that from the moment you joined us, the island is threatened with secrecy and treachery," Ishmael said, with a weary sigh. "We've never had to punish anyone here before you arrived, and now there's another suspicious person lurking around the island."

"Dreyfuss?" Sunny said, which meant "What precisely are you accusing us of?" but the facilitator kept talking as if she had not said a word.

"I won't force you," Ishmael said, "but if you want to be a part of the safe place we've constructed, I think you should abandon this Kit

Snicket person, too, even though I've never heard of her."

"We won't abandon her," Violet said. "She needs our help."

"As I said, I won't force you," Ishmael said, with one last tug on his beard. "Good-bye, Baudelaires. You can stay here on the coastal shelf with your friend and your books, if those things are so important to you."

"But what will happen to them?" asked Willa. "Decision Day is approaching, and the coastal shelf will flood with water."

"That's their problem," Ishmael said, and gave the islanders an imperious—the word "imperious," as you probably know, means "mighty and a bit snobbish"—shrug. As his shoulders raised, a small object rolled out of the sleeve of his robe and landed with a small *plop!* in a puddle, narrowly missing the bird cage where Olaf was prisoner. The Baudelaires could not identify the object, but whatever it was, it was enough to make Ishmael hurriedly clap his hands to distract anyone who might be wondering about it.

"Let's go!" he cried, and the sheep began to drag him back toward his tent. A few islanders gave the Baudelaires apologetic looks, as if they disagreed with Ishmael's suggestions but did not dare to resist the peer pressure of their fellow colonists. Professor Fletcher and Omeros, who had secrets of their own, looked particularly regretful, and Friday looked as if she might cry. She even started to say something to the Baudelaires, but Mrs. Caliban stepped forward and put her arm firmly around the girl's shoulders, and she merely gave the siblings a sad wave and walked away with her mother. The Baudelaires were too stunned for a moment to say anything. Contrary to expectations, Count Olaf had not fooled the inhabitants of this place so far from the world, and had instead been captured and punished. But still the Baudelaires were not safe, and certainly not happy to find themselves abandoned on the coastal shelf like so much detritus.

"This isn't fair," Klaus said finally, but he said it so quietly that the departing islanders probably did not hear. Only his sisters heard him, and the snake the Baudelaires thought they would never see again, and of course Count Olaf, who was huddled in the large, ornate bird cage like an imprisoned beast, and who was the only person to answer him.

"Life isn't fair," he said, in his undisguised voice, and for once the Baudelaire orphans agreed with every word the man said.

CHAPTER
Seven

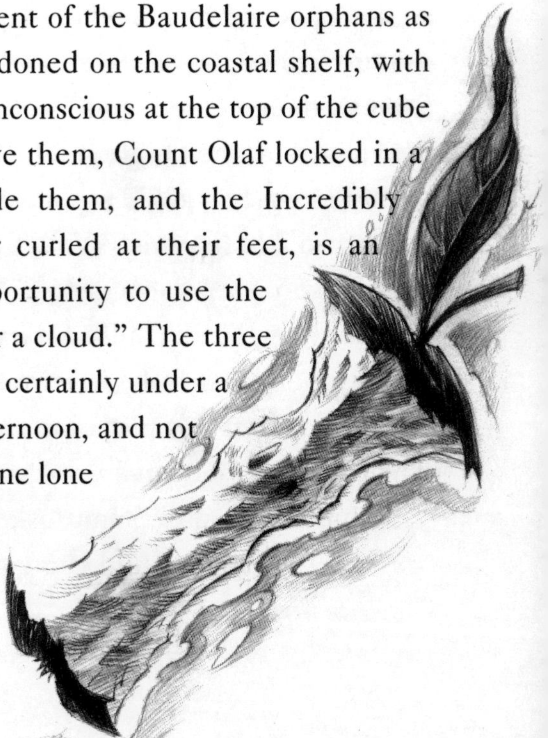

The predicament of the Baudelaire orphans as they sat abandoned on the coastal shelf, with Kit Snicket unconscious at the top of the cube of books above them, Count Olaf locked in a cage alongside them, and the Incredibly Deadly Viper curled at their feet, is an excellent opportunity to use the phrase "under a cloud." The three children were certainly under a cloud that afternoon, and not just because one lone mass of condensed water vapor, which Klaus was able to identify as being of the cumulus variety, was hanging over them in the sky like another castaway from the previous night's storm. The expression "under a cloud" refers to people who are out of favor in a particular community, the way most classrooms have at least one child who is quite unpopular, or most secret organizations have at least one rhetorical analyst who is under suspicion. The island's only community had certainly placed Violet, Klaus, and Sunny under a cloud, and even in the blazing afternoon sun the children felt the chill of the colony's suspicion and disapproval.

"I can't believe it," Violet said. "I can't believe we've been abandoned."

"We thought we could cast away everything that happened to us before we arrived here," Klaus said, "but this place is no safer than anywhere else we've been."

"But what to do?" Sunny asked.

Violet looked around the coastal shelf. "I

suppose we can catch fish and harvest seaweed to eat," she said. "Our meals won't be much different from those on the island."

"If fire," Sunny said thoughtfully, "then saltbake carp."

"We can't live here," Klaus pointed out. "Decision Day is approaching, and the coastal shelf will be underwater. We either have to live on the island, or figure out a way to get back to where we came from."

"We'll never survive a journey at sea without a boat," Violet said, wishing she had her ribbon back so she could tie up her hair.

"Kit did," Sunny pointed out.

"The library must have served as a sort of raft," Klaus said, running his hand along the books, "but she couldn't have come far on a boat of paper."

"I hope she met up with the Quagmires," Violet said.

"I hope she'll wake up and tell us what happened," Klaus said.

"Do you think she's seriously hurt?" Violet asked.

"There's no way to tell without a complete medical examination," Klaus said, "but except for her ankle, she looks all right. She's probably just exhausted from the storm."

"Worried," Sunny said sadly, wishing there was a dry, warm blanket on the coastal shelf that the Baudelaires might have used to cover their unconscious friend.

"We can't just worry about Kit," Klaus said. "We need to worry about ourselves."

"We have to think of a plan," Violet said wearily, and all three Baudelaires sighed. Even the Incredibly Deadly Viper seemed to sigh, and laid its head sympathetically on Sunny's foot. The Baudelaires stood on the coastal shelf and thought of all their previous predicaments, and all the plans they'd thought up to make themselves safe, only to end up in the midst of another unfortunate event. The cloud they were under seemed to get bigger and darker, and the children might have sat there for quite some time had not the silence been broken by the voice of the man who was locked in a bird cage.

"I have a plan," Count Olaf said. "Let me out and I'll tell you what it is."

Although Olaf was no longer using his high-pitched voice, he still sounded muffled from within the cage, and when the Baudelaires turned to look at him it was as if he were in one of his disguises. The yellow and orange dress he had been wearing covered most of him up, and the children could not see the curve of his false pregnancy or the tattoo of an eye he had on his ankle. Only a few toes and fingers extended from between the bird cage's bars, and if the siblings peered closely they could see the wet curve of his mouth, and one blinking eye staring out from his captivity.

"We're not letting you out," Violet said. "We have enough trouble without you wandering around loose."

"Suit yourself," Olaf said, and his dress rustled as he attempted to shrug. "But you'll drown as surely as I will when the coastal shelf floods. You can't build a boat, because the islanders have scavenged everything from the storm. And you can't live on the island, because the colonists have abandoned you. Even though we're shipwrecked, we're still in the same boat."

"We don't need your help, Olaf," Klaus said. "If it weren't for you, we wouldn't be here in the first place."

"Don't be so sure of that," Count Olaf said, and his mouth curled into a smile. "Everything eventually washes up on these shores, to be judged by that idiot in the robe. Do you think you're the first Baudelaires to find yourselves here?"

"What you mean?" Sunny demanded.

"Let me out," Olaf said, with a muffled chuckle, "and I'll tell you."

The Baudelaires looked at one another

doubtfully. "You're trying to trick us," Violet said.

"Of course I'm trying to trick you!" Olaf cried. "That's the way of the world, Baudelaires. Everybody runs around with their secrets and their schemes, trying to outwit everyone else. Ishmael outwitted me, and put me in this cage. But I know how to outwit him and all his islander friends. If you let me out, I can be king of Olaf-Land, and you three can be my new henchfolk."

"We don't want to be your henchfolk," Klaus said. "We just want to be safe."

"Nowhere in the world is safe," Count Olaf said.

"Not with you around," Violet agreed.

"I'm no worse than anyone else," Count Olaf said. "Ishmael is just as treacherous as I am."

"Fustianed," Sunny said.

"It's true!" Olaf insisted, although he probably did not understand what Sunny had said.

"Look at me! I'm stuffed into a cage for no good reason! Does that sound familiar, you stupid baby?"

"My sister is not a baby," Violet said firmly, "and Ishmael is not treacherous. He may be misguided, but he's only trying to make the island a safe place."

"Is that so?" Olaf said, and the cage shook as he chuckled. "Why don't you reach into that pool, and see what Ishmael dropped into the puddle?"

The Baudelaires looked at one another. They had almost forgotten about the object that had rolled out of the facilitator's sleeve. The three children stared down into the water, but it was the Incredibly Deadly Viper who wriggled into the murky depths of the puddle and came back with a small object in its mouth, which it deposited into Sunny's waiting hand.

"Takk," Sunny said, thanking the snake by scratching it on the head.

"What is it?" Violet said, leaning in to look

at what the viper had retrieved.

"It's an apple core," Klaus said, and his sisters saw that it was so. Sunny was holding the core of an apple, which had been so thoroughly nibbled that scarcely anything remained.

"You see?" Olaf asked. "While the other islanders have to do all the work, Ishmael sneaks off to the arboretum on his perfectly healthy feet and eats all the apples for himself! Your beloved facilitator not only has clay on his feet, he has feet of clay!"

The bird cage shook with laughter, and the Baudelaire orphans looked first at the apple core and then at one another. "Feet of clay" is an expression which refers to a person who appears to be honest and true, but who turns out to have a hidden weakness or a treacherous secret. If someone turns out to have feet of clay, your opinion of them may topple, just as a statue will topple if its base turns out to be badly constructed. The Baudelaires had thought Ishmael was wrong to abandon them on the coastal shelf, of course, but they believed he had done it to keep the other islanders out of harm's way, just as Mrs. Caliban had not wanted Friday to upset herself by learning to read, and although they did not agree with much of the facilitator's philosophy, they at least respected the fact that he was trying to do the same thing the Baudelaires had been trying to do since that terrible day on the beach when they had first become orphans: to find or build a safe place to call home. But now, looking at the apple core, they realized what Count Olaf said was true. Ishmael had feet of clay. He was lying about his injuries, and he was selfish about the apples in the arboretum, and he was treacherous in pressuring everyone else on the island to do all the work. Gazing at the treacherous teeth marks the facilitator had left behind, they remembered his claim that he predicted the weather by magic, and the strange look in his eye when he insisted that the island had no library, and the Baudelaires wondered what other secrets the bearded facilitator was hiding. Violet, Klaus, and Sunny sank to a mound of damp sand, as if they had feet of clay themselves, and leaned against the cube of books, wondering how they could have traveled so far from the world only to find the same dishonesty and treachery they always had.

"What is your plan?" Violet asked Count Olaf, after a long silence.

"Let me out of this cage," Olaf said, "and I'll tell you."

"Tell us first," Klaus said, "and perhaps we'll let you out."

"Let me out first," Olaf insisted.

"Tell us first," Sunny insisted, just as firmly.

"I can argue with you all day," the villain growled. "Let me out, I tell you, or I'll take my plan to my grave!"

"We can think of a plan without you," Violet said, hoping she sounded more confident than she felt. "We've managed to escape plenty of difficult situations without your help."

"I have the only weapon that can threaten

Ishmael and his supporters," Count Olaf said.

"The harpoon gun?" Klaus said. "Omeros took that away."

"Not the harpoon gun, you scholarly moron," Count Olaf said contemptuously, a word which here means "while trying to scratch his nose within the confines of the bird cage." "I'm talking about the Medusoid Mycelium!"

"Fungus!" Sunny cried. Her siblings gasped, and even the Incredibly Deadly Viper looked astonished in its reptilian way as the villain told them what you may have already guessed.

"I'm not really pregnant," he confessed with a caged grin. "The diving helmet containing the spores of the Medusoid Mycelium is hidden in this dress I'm wearing. If you let me out, I can threaten the entire colony with these deadly mushrooms. All those robed fools will be my slaves!"

"What if they refuse?" Violet asked.

"Then I'll smash the helmet open," Olaf crowed, "and this whole island will be destroyed."

"But we'll be destroyed, too," Klaus said. "The spores will infect us, the same as everyone else."

"Yomhashoah," Sunny said, which meant "Never again." The youngest Baudelaire had already been infected by the Medusoid Mycelium not long ago, and the children did not like to think about what would have happened if they hadn't found some wasabi to dilute the poison.

"We'll escape on the outrigger, you fool," Olaf said. "The island imbeciles have been building it all year. It's perfect for leaving this place behind and heading back to where the action is."

"Maybe they'll just let us leave," Violet said. "Friday said that anyone who wishes to leave the colony can climb aboard the outrigger on Decision Day."

"That little girl hasn't been here long," sneered Count Olaf, "so she still believes Ishmael lets people do whatever they want. Don't be as dumb as she is, orphans."

Klaus wished desperately that his commonplace book was open in his lap, so he could take notes, instead of on the far side of the island, with all of the other forbidden items. "How do you know so much about this place, Olaf?" he demanded. "You've only been here a few days, just like us!"

"Just like you," the villain repeated mockingly, and the cage shook with laughter again. "Do you think your pathetic history is the only story in the world? Do you think this island has just sat here in the sea, waiting for you to wash up on its shores? Do you think that I just sat in my home in the city, waiting for you miserable orphans to stumble into my path?"

"Boswell," Sunny said. She meant something along the lines of, "Your life doesn't interest me," and the Incredibly Deadly Viper seemed to hiss in agreement.

"I could tell you stories, Baudelaires," Count Olaf said in a muffled wheeze. "I could tell you secrets about people and places that you'd never dream of. I could tell you about arguments and schisms that started before you were born. I could even tell you things about yourselves that you could never imagine. Just open the door of my cage, orphans, and I'll tell you things you could never discover on your own."

The Baudelaires looked at one another and shuddered. Even in broad daylight, trapped in a cage, Count Olaf was still frightening. It was as if there was something villainous that could threaten them even if it were locked up tight, far away from the rest of the world. The three siblings had always been curious children. Violet had been eager to unlock the mysteries of the mechanical world with her inventing mind since the first pair of pliers had been placed in her crib. Klaus had been keen to read everything he got his hands on since the alphabet was first printed on the wall of his bedroom by a visitor to the Baudelaire home. And Sunny was always exploring the universe through her mouth, first by biting anything that interested her, and later by tasting food carefully in order to improve her cooking skills. Curiosity was one of the Baudelaires' most important customs, and one might think that they would be very curious indeed to hear more about the mysteries the villain had mentioned. But there was something very, very sinister about Count Olaf's words. Listening to him talk felt like standing on the edge of a deep well, or walking on a high cliff in the dead of night, or listening to a strange rustling sound outside your bedroom window, knowing that at any moment something dangerous and enormous could happen. It made the Baudelaires think of that terrible question mark on the radar screen of the *Queequeg*—a secret so gigantic and important that it could not fit in their hearts or minds, something that had been hidden their entire lives and might destroy their entire lives once it was revealed. It was not a secret the Baudelaire orphans wanted to hear, from Count Olaf or from anyone else, and although it felt like a secret that could not be avoided, the children wanted to avoid it anyway, and without another word to the man in the cage the three siblings stood up and walked around the cube of books until they were at the far end, where Olaf and his bird cage could not be seen. Then, in silence, the three siblings sat back down, leaned against the strange raft, and stared out at the flat horizon of the sea, trying not to think about what Olaf had said. Occasionally they took sips of coconut cordial from the seashells that hung from their waists, hoping that the strong, strange drink would distract them from the strong, strange thoughts in their heads. All afternoon, until the sun set on the rippling horizon of the sea, the Baudelaire orphans sat and sipped, and wondered if they dared learn what lay at the heart of their sad lives, when every secret, every mystery, and every unfortunate event had been peeled away.

CHAPTER
Eight

Thinking about something is like picking up a stone when taking a walk, either while skipping rocks on the beach, for example, or looking for a way to shatter the glass doors of a museum. When you think about something, it adds a bit of weight to your walk, and as you think about more and more things you are liable to feel heavier and heavier, until you are so burdened you cannot take any further steps, and can only sit and stare at the gentle movements of the ocean waves or security guards, thinking too hard about too many things to do anything else. As the sun set, casting long shadows on the coastal shelf, the Baudelaire orphans felt so heavy from their thoughts they could scarcely move. They thought about the island, and the terrible storm that had brought them there, and the boat that had taken them through the storm, and their own treachery at the Hotel Denouement that had led them to escape in the boat with Count Olaf, who had stopped calling out to the Baudelaires and was now snoring loudly in the bird cage. They thought about the colony, and the cloud the islanders had put them under, and the peer pressure that had led the islanders to decide to abandon them, and the facilitator who started the peer pressure, and the secret apple core of the facilitator that seemed no different than the secret items that had gotten the Baudelaires in trouble in the first place. They thought about Kit Snicket, and the storm that had left her unconscious on top of the strange library raft, and their friends the Quagmire triplets, who may also have been caught in the same stormy sea, and Captain Widdershins's submarine that lay under the sea, and the mysterious schism that lay under everything like an enormous question mark. And the Baudelaires thought, as they did every time they saw the sky grow dark, of their parents. If you've ever lost someone, then you know that sometimes when you think of them you try to imagine where they might be, and the Baudelaires thought of how far away their mother and father seemed, while all the wickedness in the world felt so close, locked in a cage just a few feet from where the children sat. Violet thought, and Klaus thought, and Sunny thought, and as the afternoon drew to evening they felt so burdened by their thoughts that they felt they could scarcely hold another thought, and yet as the last rays of the sun disappeared on the horizon they found something else to think about, for in the darkness they heard a familiar voice, and they had to think of what to do.

"Where am I?" asked Kit Snicket, and the children heard her body rustle on the top layer of books over the snoring.

"Kit!" Violet said, standing up quickly. "You're awake!"

"It's the Baudelaires," Klaus said.

"Baudelaires?" Kit repeated faintly. "Is it really you?"

"Anais," Sunny said, which meant "In the flesh."

"Where are we?" Kit said.

The Baudelaires were silent for a moment, and realized for the first time that they did not even know the name of the place where they were. "We're on a coastal shelf," Violet said finally, although she decided not to add that they had been abandoned there.

"There's an island nearby," Klaus said. The middle Baudelaire did not explain that they were not welcome to set foot on it.

"Safe," Sunny said, but she did not mention that Decision Day was approaching, and that soon the entire area would be flooded with seawater. Without discussing the matter, the

Baudelaires decided not to tell Kit the whole story, not yet.

"Of course," Kit murmured. "I should have known I'd be here. Eventually, everything washes up on these shores."

"Have you been here before?" Violet asked.

"No," Kit said, "but I've heard about this place. My associates have told me stories of its mechanical wonders, its enormous library, and the gourmet meals the islanders prepare. Why, the day before I met you, Baudelaires, I shared Turkish coffee with an associate who was saying that he'd never had better Oysters Rockefeller than during his time on the island. You must be having a wonderful time here."

"Janiceps," Sunny said, restating an earlier opinion.

"I think this place has changed since your associate was here," said Klaus.

"That's probably true," Kit said thoughtfully. "Thursday did say that the colony had suffered a schism, just as V.F.D. did."

"Another schism?" Violet asked.

"Countless schisms have divided the world over the years," Kit replied in the darkness. "Do you think the history of V.F.D. is the only story in the world? But let's not talk of the past, Baudelaires. Tell me how you made your way to these shores."

"The same way you did," Violet said. "We were castaways. The only way we could leave the Hotel Denouement was by boat."

"I knew you ran into danger there," Kit said. "We were watching the skies. We saw the smoke and we knew you were signaling us that it wasn't safe to join you. Thank you, Baudelaires. I knew you wouldn't fail us. Tell me, is Dewey with you?"

Kit's words were almost more than the Baudelaires could stand. The smoke she had seen, of course, was from the fire the children had set in the hotel's laundry room, which had quickly spread to the entire building, interrupting Count Olaf's trial and endangering the lives of all the people inside, villains and volunteers alike. And Dewey, I'm sad to remind you, was not with the Baudelaires, but lying dead at the bottom of a pond, still clutching the harpoon that the three siblings had fired into his heart. But Violet, Klaus, and Sunny could not bring themselves to tell Kit the whole story, not now. They could not bear to tell her what had happened to Dewey, and to all the other noble people they had encountered, not yet. Not now, not yet, and perhaps not ever.

"No," Violet said. "Dewey isn't here."

"Count Olaf is with us," Klaus said, "but he's locked up."

"Viper," Sunny added.

"Oh, I'm glad Ink is safe," Kit said, and the Baudelaires thought they could almost hear her smile. "That's my special nickname for the Incredibly Deadly Viper. Ink kept me good company on this raft after we were separated from the others."

"The Quagmires?" Klaus asked. "You found them?"

"Yes," Kit said, and coughed a bit. "But they're not here."

"Maybe they'll wash up here, too," Violet said.

"Maybe," Kit said uncertainly. "And maybe Dewey will join us, too. We need as many associates as we can if we're going to return to the world and make sure that justice is served. But first, let's find this colony I've heard so much about. I need a shower and a hot meal, and then I want to hear the whole story of what happened to you." She started to lower herself down from the raft, but then stopped with a cry of pain.

"You shouldn't move," Violet said quickly, glad for an excuse to keep Kit on the coastal shelf. "Your foot's been injured."

"Both my feet have been injured," Kit corrected ruefully, lying back down on the raft. "The telegram device fell on my legs when the submarine was attacked. I need your help,

Baudelaires. I need to be someplace safe."

"We'll do everything we can," Klaus said.

"Maybe help is on the way," Kit said. "I can see someone coming."

The Baudelaires turned to look, and in the dark they saw a very tiny, very bright light, skittering toward them from the west. At first the light looked like nothing more than a firefly, darting here and there on the coastal shelf, but gradually the children could see it was a flashlight, around which several figures in white robes huddled, walking carefully among the puddles and debris. The shine of the flashlight reminded Klaus of all of the nights he spent reading under the covers in the Baudelaire mansion, while outside the night made mysterious noises his parents always insisted were nothing more than the wind, even on windless evenings. Some mornings, his father would come into Klaus's room to wake him up and find him asleep, still clutching his flashlight in one hand and his book in the other, and as the flashlight drew closer and closer, the middle Baudelaire could not help but think that it was his father, walking across the coastal shelf to come to his children's aid after all this time. But of course it was not the Baudelaires' father. The figures arrived at the cube of books, and the children could see the faces of two islanders: Finn, who was holding the flashlight, and Erewhon, who was carrying a large, covered basket.

"Good evening, Baudelaires," Finn said. In the dim light of the flashlight she looked even younger than she was.

"We brought you some supper," Erewhon said, and held out the basket to the children. "We were concerned that you might be quite hungry out here."

"We are," Violet admitted. The Baudelaires, of course, wished that the islanders had expressed their concern in front of Ishmael and the others, when the colony was deciding to abandon the children on the coastal shelf, but as Finn opened the basket and the children smelled the island's customary dinner of onion soup, the children did not want to look a gift horse in the mouth, a phrase which here means "turn down an offer of a hot meal, no matter how disappointed they were in the person who was offering it."

"Is there enough for our friend?" Klaus asked. "She's regained consciousness."

"I'm glad to hear it," Finn said. "There's enough food for everyone."

"As long as you keep the secret of our coming here," Erewhon said. "Ishmael might not think it was proper."

"I'm surprised he doesn't forbid the use of flashlights," Violet said, as Finn handed her a coconut shell full of steaming soup.

"Ishmael doesn't forbid anything," Finn said. "He'd never force me to throw this flashlight away. However, he did suggest that I let the sheep take it to the arboretum. Instead I slipped it into my robe, as a secret, and Madame Nordoff has been secretly supplying me with batteries in exchange for my secretly teaching her how to yodel, which Ishmael says might frighten the other islanders."

"And Mrs. Caliban secretly slipped me this picnic basket," Erewhon said, "in exchange for my secretly teaching her the backstroke, which Ishmael says is not the customary way to swim."

"Mrs. Caliban?" said Kit, in the darkness. "Miranda Caliban is here?"

"Yes," Finn said. "Do you know her?"

"I know her husband," Kit said. "He and I stood together in a time of great struggle, and we're still very good friends."

"Your friend must be a little confused after her difficult journey," Erewhon said to the Baudelaires, standing on tiptoes so she could hand Kit some soup. "Mrs. Caliban's husband perished many years ago in the storm that brought her here."

"That's impossible," Kit said, reaching down to take the bowl from the young girl. "I just had Turkish coffee with him."

"Mrs. Caliban is not the sort to keep secrets," Finn said. "That's why she lives on the island. It's a safe place, far from the treachery of the world."

"Enigmorama," Sunny said, putting her coconut shell of soup on the ground so she could share it with the Incredibly Deadly Viper.

"My sister means that it seems this island has plenty of secrets," Klaus said, thinking wistfully of his commonplace book and all the secrets its pages contained.

"I'm afraid we have one more secret to discuss," Erewhon said. "Turn the flashlight off, Finn. We don't want to be seen from the island."

Finn nodded, and turned the flashlight off. The Baudelaires had one last glimpse of each other before the darkness engulfed them, and for a moment everyone stood in silence, as if afraid to speak.

Many, many years ago, when even the great-great-grandparents of the oldest person you know were not even day-old infants, and when the city where the Baudelaires were born was nothing more than a handful of dirt huts, and the Hotel Denouement nothing but an architectural sketch, and the faraway island had a name, and was not considered very faraway at all, there was a group of people known as the Cimmerians. They were a nomadic people, which meant that they traveled constantly, and they often traveled at night, when the sun would not give them sunburn and when the coastal shelves in the area in which they lived were not flooded with water. Because they traveled in shadows, few people ever got a good look at the Cimmerians, and they were considered sneaky and mysterious people, and to this day things done in the dark tend to have a somewhat sinister reputation. A man digging a hole in his backyard during the afternoon, for instance, looks like a gardener, but a man digging a hole at night looks like he's burying some terrible secret, and a woman who gazes out of her window in the daytime appears to be enjoying the view, but looks more like a spy if she waits until nightfall. The nighttime digger may actually be planting a tree to surprise his niece while the niece giggles at him from the window, and the morning window watcher may actually be planning to blackmail the so-called gardener as he buries the evidence of his vicious crimes, but thanks to the Cimmerians, the darkness makes even the most innocent of activities seem suspicious, and so in the darkness of the coastal shelf, the Baudelaires suspected that the question Finn asked was a sinister one, even though it could have been something one of their teachers might have asked in the classroom.

"Do you know the meaning of the word 'mutiny'?" she asked, in a calm, quiet voice.

Violet and Sunny knew that Klaus would answer, although they were pretty sure themselves what the word meant. "A mutiny is when a group of people take action against a leader."

"Yes," Finn said. "Professor Fletcher taught me the word."

"We are here to tell you that a mutiny will take place at breakfast," said Erewhon. "More and more colonists are getting sick and tired of the way things are going on the island, and Ishmael is the root of the trouble."

"Tuber?" Sunny asked.

"'Root of the trouble' means 'the cause of the islanders' problems,'" Klaus explained.

"Exactly," Erewhon said, "and when Decision Day arrives we will finally have the opportunity to get rid of him."

"Rid of him?" Violet repeated, the phrase sounding sinister in the dark.

"We're going to force him aboard the outrigger right after breakfast," Erewhon said, "and push him out to sea as the coastal shelf floods."

"A man traveling the ocean alone is unlikely to survive," Klaus said.

"He won't be alone," Finn said. "A number

of islanders support Ishmael. If necessary, we'll force them to leave the island as well."

"How many?" Sunny asked.

"It's hard to know who supports Ishmael and who doesn't," Erewhon said, and the children heard the old woman sip from her seashell. "You've seen how he acts. He says he doesn't force anyone, but everyone ends up agreeing with him anyway. But no longer. At breakfast we'll find out who supports him and who doesn't."

"Erewhon says we'll fight all day and all night if we have to," Finn said. "Everyone will have to choose sides."

The children heard an enormous, sad sigh from the top of the raft of books. "A schism," Kit said quietly.

"Gesundheit," Erewhon said. "That's why we've come to you, Baudelaires. We need all the help we can get."

"After the way Ishmael abandoned you, we figured you'd be on our side," Finn said. "Don't you agree he's the root of the trouble?"

The Baudelaires stood together in the silence, thinking about Ishmael and all they knew about him. They thought of the way he had taken them in so kindly upon their arrival on the island, but also how quickly he had abandoned them on the coastal shelf. They thought about how eager he had been to keep the Baudelaires safe, but also how eager he was to lock Count Olaf in a bird cage. They thought about his dishonesty about his injured feet, and about his secret apple eating, but as the children thought of all they knew about the facilitator, they also thought about how much they didn't know, and after hearing both Count Olaf and Kit Snicket talk about the history of the island, the Baudelaire orphans realized they did not know the whole story. The children might agree that Ishmael was the root of the trouble, but they could not be sure.

"I don't know," Violet said.

"You don't know?" Erewhon repeated

incredulously. "We brought you supper, and Ishmael left you out here to starve, and you don't know whose side you're on?"

"We trusted you when you said Count Olaf was a terrible person," Finn said. "Why can't you trust us, Baudelaires?"

"Forcing Ishmael to leave the island seems a bit drastic," Klaus said.

"It's a bit drastic to put a man in a cage," Erewhon pointed out, "but I didn't hear you complaining then."

"Quid pro quo?" Sunny asked.

"If we help you," Violet translated, "will you help Kit?"

"Our friend is injured," Klaus said. "Injured and pregnant."

"And distraught," Kit added weakly, from the top of the raft.

"If you help us in our plan to defeat Ishmael," Finn promised, "we'll get her to a safe place."

"And if not?" Sunny asked.

"We won't force you, Baudelaires," Erewhon said, sounding like the facilitator she wanted to defeat, "but Decision Day is approaching, and the coastal shelf will flood. You need to make a choice."

The Baudelaires did not say anything, and for a moment everyone stood in a silence broken only by Count Olaf's snores. Violet, Klaus, and Sunny were not interested in being part of a schism, after witnessing all of the misery that followed the schism of V.F.D., but they did not see a way to avoid it. Finn had said that they needed to make a choice, but choosing between living alone on a coastal shelf, endangering themselves and their injured friend, and participating in the island's mutinous plan, did not feel like much of a choice at all, and they wondered how many other people had felt this way, during the countless schisms that had divided the world over the years.

"We'll help you," Violet said finally. "What do you want us to do?"

"We need you to sneak into the arboretum," Finn said. "You mentioned your mechanical abilities, Violet, and Klaus seems very well-read. All of the forbidden items we've scavenged over the years should come in very handy indeed."

"Even the baby should be able to cook something up," Erewhon said.

"But what do you mean?" Klaus asked. "What should we do with all the detritus?"

"We need weapons, of course," Erewhon said in the darkness.

"We hope to force Ishmael off the island peacefully," Finn said quickly, "but Erewhon says we'll need weapons, just in case. Ishmael will notice if we go to the far side of the island, but you three should be able to sneak over the brae, find or build some weapons in the arboretum, and bring them to us here before breakfast so we can begin the mutiny."

"Absolutely not!" cried Kit, from the top of the raft. "I won't hear of you putting your talents to such nefarious use, Baudelaires. I'm sure the island can solve its difficulties without resorting to violence."

"Did you solve your difficulties without resorting to violence?" Erewhon asked sharply. "Is that how you survived the great struggle you mentioned, and ended up shipwrecked on a raft of books?"

"My history is not important," Kit replied. "I'm worried about the Baudelaires."

"And we're worried about you, Kit," Violet said. "We need as many associates as we can if we're going to return to the world and make sure that justice is served."

"You need to be in a safe place to recuperate from your injury," Klaus said.

"And baby," said Sunny.

"That's no reason to engage in treachery," Kit said, but she did not sound so sure. Her voice was weak and faint, and the children heard the books rustling as she moved her injured feet uncomfortably.

"Please help us," Finn said, "and we'll help your friend."

"There must be a weapon that can threaten Ishmael and his supporters," Erewhon said, and now she did not sound like Ishmael. The Baudelaires had heard almost the exact same words from the imprisoned mouth of Count Olaf, and they shuddered to think of the weapon he was hiding in the bird cage.

Violet put down her empty soup bowl, and picked up her baby sister, while Klaus took the flashlight from the old woman. "We'll be back as soon as we can, Kit," the eldest Baudelaire promised. "Wish us luck."

The raft trembled as Kit uttered a long, sad sigh. "Good luck," she said finally. "I wish things were different, Baudelaires."

"So do we," Klaus replied, and the three children followed the narrow beam of the flashlight back toward the colony that had abandoned them. Their footsteps made small splashes on the coastal shelf, and the Baudelaires heard the quiet slither of the Incredibly Deadly Viper, loyally following them on their errand. There was no sign of a moon, and the stars were covered in clouds that remained from the passing storm, or perhaps were heralding a new one, so the entire world seemed to vanish outside the secret flashlight's forbidden light. With each damp and uncertain step, the children felt heavier, as if their thoughts were stones that they had to carry to the arboretum, where all the forbidden items lay waiting for them. They thought about the islanders, and the mutinous schism that would soon divide the colony in two. They thought about Ishmael, and wondered whether his secrets and deceptions meant that he deserved to be at sea. And they thought about the Medusoid Mycelium, fermenting in the helmet in Olaf's grasp, and wondered if the islanders would discover that weapon before the Baudelaires built another. The children traveled in the dark, just as so many other people had done before them, from the nomadic travels of the Cimmerians to the desperate voyages of the Quagmire triplets, who at that very moment were in circumstances just as dark although quite a bit damper than the Baudelaires', and as the children drew closer and closer to the island that had abandoned them, their thoughts made them heavier and heavier, and the Baudelaire orphans wished things were very different indeed.

CHAPTER
Nine

The phrase "in the dark," as I'm sure you know, can refer not only to one's shadowy surroundings, but also to the shadowy secrets of which one might be unaware. Every day, the sun goes down over all these secrets, and so everyone is in the dark in one way or another. If you are sunbathing in a park, for instance, but you do not know that a locked cabinet is buried fifty feet beneath your blanket, then you are in the dark even though you are not actually in the dark, whereas if you are on a midnight hike, knowing full well that several ballerinas are following close behind you, then you are not in the dark even if you are in fact in the dark. Of course, it is quite possible to be in the dark in the dark, as well as to be not in the dark not in the dark, but there are so many secrets in the world that it is likely that you are always in the dark about one thing or another, whether you are in the dark in the dark or in the dark not in the dark, although the sun can go down so quickly that you may be in the dark about being in the dark in the dark, only to look around and find yourself no longer in the dark about being in the dark in the dark, but in the dark in the dark nonetheless, not only because of the dark, but because of the ballerinas in the dark, who are not in the dark about the dark, but also not in the dark about the locked cabinet, and you may be in the dark about the ballerinas digging up the locked cabinet in the dark, even though you are no longer in the dark about being in the dark, and so you are in fact in the dark about being in the dark, even though you are not in the dark about being in the dark, and so you may fall into the hole that the ballerinas have dug, which is dark, in the dark, and in the park.

The Baudelaire orphans, of course, had been in the dark many times before they made their way in the dark over the brae to the far side of the island, where the arboretum guarded its many, many secrets. There was the darkness of Count Olaf's gloomy house, and the darkness of the movie theater where Uncle Monty had taken them to see a wonderful film called *Zombies in the Snow*. There were the dark clouds of Hurricane Herman as it roared across Lake Lachrymose, and the darkness of the Finite Forest as a train had taken the children to work at Lucky Smells Lumbermill. There were the dark nights the children spent at Prufrock Preparatory School, participating in Special Orphan Running Exercises, and the dark climbs up the elevator shaft of 667 Dark Avenue. There was the dark jail cell in which the children spent some time while living in the Village of Fowl Devotees, and the dark trunk of Count Olaf's car, which had carried them from Heimlich Hospital to the hinterlands, where the dark tents of the Caligari Carnival awaited them. There was the dark pit they had built high in the Mortmain Mountains, and the dark hatch they had climbed through in order to board the *Queequeg*, and the dark lobby of the Hotel Denouement, where they thought their dark days might be over. There were the dark eyes of Count Olaf and his associates, and the dark notebooks of the Quagmire triplets, and all of the dark passageways the children had discovered, that led to the Baudelaire mansion, and out of the Library of Records, and up to the V.F.D. Headquarters, and to the dark, dark depths of the sea, and all the dark passageways they hadn't discovered, where other people traveled on equally desperate errands. But most of all, the Baudelaire orphans had been in the dark about their own sad history. They did not understand how Count Olaf had entered their lives, or how he had managed to remain there, hatching scheme after scheme without anyone stopping him. They did not understand V.F.D., even when they had joined the organization themselves, or how the organization, with all of its codes, errands, and volunteers, had failed to defeat the wicked people who seemed to triumph again and again, leaving each safe place in ruins. And they did not understand how they could lose their parents and their home in a fire, and how this enormous injustice, this bad beginning to their sad history, was followed only by another injustice, and another, and another. The Baudelaire orphans did not understand how injustice and treachery could prosper, even this far from their home, on an island in the middle of a vast sea, and that happiness and innocence—the happiness and innocence of that day on Briny Beach, before Mr. Poe brought them the dreadful news—could always be so far out of reach. The Baudelaires were in the dark about the mystery of their own lives, which is why it was such a profound shock to think at last that these mysteries might be solved. The Baudelaire orphans blinked in the rising sun, and gazed at the expanse of the arboretum, and wondered if they might not be in the dark any longer.

"Library" is another word that can mean two different things, which means even in a library you cannot be safe from the confusion and mystery of the world. The most common use of the word "library," of course, refers to a collection of books or documents, such as the libraries the Baudelaires had encountered during their travels and troubles, from the legal library of Justice Strauss to the Hotel Denouement, which was itself an enormous library—with, it turned out, another library hidden nearby. But the word "library" can also refer to a mass of knowledge or a source of learning, just as Klaus Baudelaire is something of a library with the mass of knowledge stored in his brain, or Kit Snicket, who was a source of learning for the Baudelaires as she told them about V.F.D. and its noble errands. So when I write that the Baudelaire orphans had found themselves in the largest library they had ever seen, it is that definition of the word I am using, because the arboretum was an enormous mass of knowledge, and a source of learning, even without a single scrap of paper in sight. The items that had washed up on the shores of the island over the years could answer any question the Baudelaires had, and thousands more questions they'd never thought of. Stretched out as far as the eye could see were piles of objects, heaps of items, towers of evidence, bales of materials, clusters of details, stacks of substances, hordes of pieces, arrays of articles, constellations of details, galaxies of stuff, and universes of things—an accumulation, an aggregation, a compilation, a concentration, a crowd, a herd, a flock, and a register of seemingly everything on Earth. There was everything the alphabet could hold—automobiles and alarm clocks, bandages and beads, cables and chimneys, discs and dominos, earmuffs and emery boards, fiddles and fabric, garrotes and glassware, hangers and husks, icons and instruments, jewelry and jogging shoes, kites and kernels, levers and lawn chairs, machines and magnets, noisemakers and needles, orthodontics and ottomans, pull toys and pillars, quarters and quivers, race cars and rucksacks, saws and skulls, teaspoons and ties, urns and ukuleles, valentines and vines, wigs and wires, xeranthemums and xylorimbas, yachts and yokes, zithers and zabras, a word which here means "small boats usually used off the coasts of Spain and Portugal"—as well as everything that could hold the alphabet, from a cardboard box perfect for storing twenty-six wooden blocks, to a chalkboard perfect for writing twenty-six letters. There were any number of things, from a single motorcycle to countless chopsticks, and things with every number on them, from license plates to calculators. There were objects from every climate, from snowshoes to ceiling fans; and for every occasion, from menorahs to soccer balls; and there were things you could use on certain occasions in certain climates, such as a waterproof fondue set. There were inserts and outhouses, overpasses and underclothes, upholstery and down comforters, hotplates and cold creams and cradles and coffins, hopelessly destroyed, somewhat damaged, in slight disrepair, and brand-new. There were objects the Baudelaires recognized, including a triangular picture frame and a brass lamp in the shape of a fish, and there were objects the Baudelaires had never seen before, including the skeleton of an elephant and a glittering green mask one might wear as part of a dragonfly costume, and there were objects the Baudelaires did not know if they had seen before, such as a wooden rocking horse and a piece of rubber that looked like a fan belt. There were items that seemed to be part of the Baudelaires' story, such as a plastic replica of a clown and a broken telegraph pole, and there were items that seemed part of some other story, such as a carving of a black bird and a gem that shone like an Indian moon, and all the items, and all their stories, were scattered across the landscape in such a way that the Baudelaire orphans thought that the arboretum had either been organized according to principles so mysterious they could not be discovered, or it had not been organized at all. In short, the Baudelaire orphans had found themselves in the largest library they had ever seen, but they did not know where to begin their research. The children stood in awed silence and surveyed the endless landscape of objects and stories, and then looked up at the largest object of all, which towered over the arboretum and covered it in shade. It was the apple tree, with a trunk as enormous as a mansion and branches as long as a city street, which sheltered the library from the frequent storms and offered its bitter apples to anyone who dared to pick one.

"Words fail me," Sunny said in a hushed whisper.

"Me, too," Klaus agreed. "I can't believe what we're seeing. The islanders told us that everything eventually washes up on these shores, but I never imagined the arboretum would hold so many things."

Violet picked up an item that lay at her feet—a pink ribbon decorated with plastic daisies—and began to wind it around her hair. To those who hadn't been around Violet long, nothing would have seemed unusual, but those who knew her well knew that when she tied her hair up in a ribbon to keep it out of her eyes, it meant that the gears and levers of her inventing brain were whirring at top speed. "Think of what I could build here," she said. "I could build splints for Kit's feet, a boat to take us off the island, a filtration system so we could drink fresh water. . . ." Her voice trailed off, and she stared up at the branches of the tree. "I could invent anything and everything."

Klaus picked up the object at his feet—a cape made of scarlet silk—and held it in his hands. "There must be countless secrets in a place like this," he said. "Even without a book, I could investigate anything and everything."

Sunny looked around her. "Service à la Russe," she said, which meant something like, "Even with the simplest of ingredients, I could prepare an extremely elaborate meal."

"I don't know where to begin," Violet said, running a hand along a pile of broken white wood that looked like it had once been part of a gazebo.

"We begin with weapons," Klaus said grimly. "That's why we're here. Erewhon and Finn are waiting for us to help them mutiny against Ishmael."

The oldest Baudelaire shook her head. "It doesn't seem right," she said. "We can't use a place like this to start a schism."

"Maybe a schism is necessary," Klaus said. "There are millions of items here that could help the colony, but thanks to Ishmael, they've all been abandoned here."

"No one forced anyone to abandon anything," Violet said.

"Peer pressure," Sunny pointed out.

"We can try a little peer pressure of our own," Violet said firmly. "We've defeated worse people than Ishmael with far fewer materials."

"But do we really want to defeat Ishmael?" Klaus asked. "He's made the island a safe place, even if it is a little boring, and he kept Count Olaf away, even if he is a little cruel. He has feet of clay, but I'm not sure he's the root of the problem."

"What is the root of the problem?" Violet asked.

"Ink," Sunny said, but when her siblings turned to give her a quizzical look, they saw that the youngest Baudelaire was not answering their question, but pointing at the Incredibly Deadly Viper, who was slithering hurriedly away from the children with its eyes darting this way and that and its tongue extended to sniff the air.

"It appears to know where it's going," Violet said.

"Maybe it's been here before," Klaus said.

"Taylit," Sunny said, which meant "Let's follow the reptile and see where it heads." Without waiting to see whether her siblings agreed, she hurried after the snake, and Violet and Klaus hurried after her. The viper's path was as curved and twisted as the snake itself, and the Baudelaires found themselves scrambling over all sorts of discarded items, from a cardboard box, soaked through from the storm, that was full of something white and lacy, to a painted backdrop of a sunset, such as might be used in the performance of an opera. The children could tell that the path had been traveled before, as the ground was covered in footprints. The snake was slithering so quickly that the

Baudelaires could not keep up, but they could follow the footprints, which were dusted around the edges in white powder. It was dried clay, of course, and in moments the children reached the end of the path, following in Ishmael's footsteps, and they arrived at the base of the apple tree just in time to see the tail of the snake disappear into a gap in the tree's roots. If you've ever stood at the base of an old tree, then you know the roots are often close to the surface of the earth, and the curved angles of the roots can create a hollow space in the tree's trunk. It was into this hollow space that the Incredibly Deadly Viper disappeared, and after the tiniest of pauses, it was into this space that the Baudelaire orphans followed, wondering what secrets they would find at the root of the tree that sheltered such a mysterious place. First Violet, and then Klaus, and then Sunny stepped down through the gap into the secret space. It was dark underneath the roots of the tree, and for a moment the Baudelaires tried to adjust to the gloom and figure out what this place was, but then the middle Baudelaire remembered the flashlight, and turned it on so he and his siblings would no longer be in the dark in the dark.

The Baudelaire orphans were standing in a space much bigger than they would have imagined, and much better furnished. Along one wall was a large stone bench lined with simple, clean tools, including several sharp-looking razor-blades, a glass pot of paste, and several wooden brushes with narrow, fine tips. Next to the wall was an enormous bookcase, which was stuffed with books of all shapes and sizes, as well as assorted documents that were stacked, rolled, and stapled with extreme care. The shelves of the bookcase stretched away from the children past the beam of the flashlight and disappeared into the darkness, so there was no way of knowing how long the bookcase was, or the number of books and documents it contained. Opposite the bookcase stretched an elaborate kitchen, with a huge potbellied stove, several porcelain sinks, and a tall, humming refrigerator, as well as a square wooden table covered in appliances ranging from a blender to a fondue set. Over the table hung a rack from which dangled all manner of kitchen utensils and pots, as well as sprigs of dried herbs, a variety of whole dried fish, and even a few cured meats, such as salami and prosciutto, an Italian ham that the Baudelaire orphans had once enjoyed at a Sicilian picnic the family had attended. Nailed to the wall was an impressive spice rack filled with jars of herbs and bottles of condiments, and a cupboard with glass doors through which the children could see piles of plates, bowls, and mugs. Finally, in the center of this enormous space were two large, comfortable reading chairs, one with a gigantic book on the seat, much taller than an atlas and much thicker than even an unabridged dictionary, and the other just waiting for someone to sit down. Lastly, there was a curious device made of brass that looked like a large tube with a pair of binoculars at the bottom, which rose up into the thick canopy of roots that formed the ceiling. As the Incredibly Deadly Viper hissed proudly, the way a dog might wag its tail after performing a difficult trick, the three children stared around the room, each concentrating on their area of expertise, a phrase which here means "the part of the room in which each Baudelaire would most like to spend time."

Violet walked over to the brass device and peered into the eyes of the binoculars. "I can see the ocean," she said in surprise. "This is an enormous periscope, much bigger than the one in the *Queequeg*. It must run all the way up the trunk of the tree and jut out over the highest branch."

"But why would you want to look at the ocean from here?" Klaus asked.

"From this height," Violet explained, "you could see any storm clouds that might be heading this way. This is how Ishmael predicts the weather—not by magic, but with scientific equipment."

"And these tools are used to repair books," Klaus said. "Of course books wash up on the island—everything does, eventually. But the pages and bindings of the books are often damaged by the storm that brought them, so Ishmael repairs them and shelves them here." He picked up a dark blue notebook from the bench and held it up. "It's my commonplace book," he said. "He must have been making sure none of the pages were wet."

Sunny picked up a familiar object from the wooden table—her whisk—and held it to her nose. "Fritters," she said. "With cinnamon."

"Ishmael walks to the arboretum to watch for storms, read books, and cook spiced food," Violet said. "Why would he pretend to be an injured facilitator who predicts the weather through magic, claims that the island has no library, and prefers bland meals?"

Klaus walked to the two reading chairs and lifted the heavy, thick book. "Maybe this will tell us," he said, and shone the flashlight so his sisters could see the long, somewhat wordy title printed on the front cover.

"What does it mean?" Violet asked. "That title could mean anything."

Klaus noticed a thin piece of black cloth stuck in the book to mark someone's place, and opened the book to that page. The bookmark was Violet's hair ribbon, which the eldest Baudelaire quickly grabbed, as the pink ribbon with plastic daisies was not to her taste. "I think it's a history of the island," Klaus said, "written like a diary. Look, here's what the most recent entry says: 'Yet another figure from the shadowy past has washed ashore—Kit Snicket (see page 667). Convinced the others to abandon her, and the Baudelaires, who have already rocked the boat far too much, I fear. Also managed to have Count Olaf locked in a cage. Note to self: Why won't anyone call me Ish?'"

"Ishmael said he'd never heard of Kit Snicket," Violet said, "but here he writes that she's a figure from the shadowy past."

"Six six seven," Sunny said, and Klaus nodded. Handing the flashlight to his older sister, he quickly turned the pages of the book, flipping back in history until he reached the page Ishmael had mentioned.

"'Inky has learned to lasso sheep,'" Klaus read, "'and last night's storm washed up a postcard from Kit Snicket, addressed to Olivia Caliban. Kit, of course, is the sister of . . .'"

The middle Baudelaire's voice trailed off, and his sisters stared at him curiously. "What's wrong, Klaus?" Violet asked. "That entry doesn't seem particularly mysterious."

"It's not the entry," Klaus said, so quietly that Violet and Sunny could scarcely hear him. "It's the handwriting."

"Familia?" Sunny asked, and all three Baudelaires stepped as close as they could to one another. In silence, the children gathered around the beam of the flashlight, as if it were a warm campfire on a freezing night, and gazed down at the pages of the oddly titled book.

Even the Incredibly Deadly Viper crawled up to perch on Sunny's shoulders, as if it were as curious as the Baudelaire orphans to know who had written those words so long ago.

"Yes, Baudelaires," said a voice from the far end of the room. "That's your mother's handwriting."

C H A P T E R
Ten

Ishmael stepped out of the darkness, running a hand along the shelves of the bookcase, and walked slowly toward the Baudelaire orphans. In the dim glow of the flashlight, the children could not tell if the facilitator was smiling or frowning through his wild, woolly beard, and Violet was reminded of something she'd almost entirely forgotten. A long time ago, before Sunny

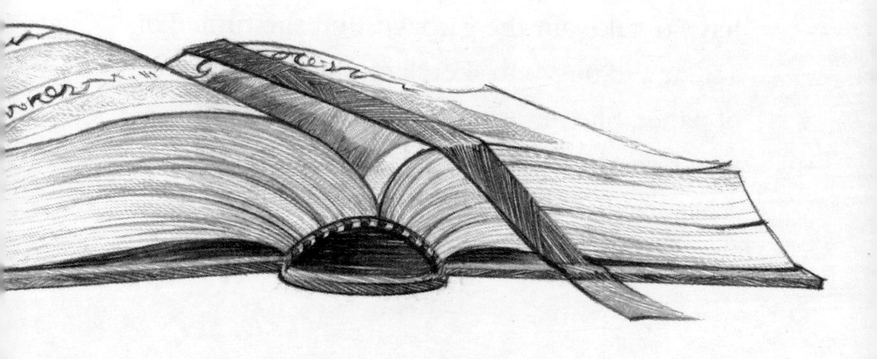

was born, Violet and Klaus had begun an argument at breakfast over whose turn it was to take out the garbage. It was a silly matter, but one of those occasions when the people arguing are having too much fun to stop, and all day, the two siblings had wandered around the house, doing their assigned chores and scarcely speaking to each other. Finally, after a long, silent meal, during which their parents tried to get them to reconcile—a word which here means "admit that it didn't matter in the slightest whose turn it was, and that the only important thing was to get the garbage out of the kitchen before the smell spread to the entire mansion"—Violet and Klaus were sent up to bed without dessert or even five minutes of reading. Suddenly, just as she was dropping off to sleep, Violet had an idea for an invention that meant no one would ever have to take out the garbage, and she turned on a light and began to sketch out her idea on a pad of paper. She became so interested in her invention that she did not listen for footsteps in the hallway outside, and so when her mother opened the door, she did not have time to turn out the light and pretend to be asleep. Violet stared at her mother, and her mother stared back, and in the dim light the eldest Baudelaire could not see if her mother was smiling or frowning—if she was angry at Violet for staying up past her bedtime, or if she didn't mind after all. But then finally, Violet saw that her mother was carrying a cup of hot tea. "Here you go, dear," she said gently. "I know how star anise tea helps you think." Violet took the steaming cup from her mother, and in that instant she suddenly realized that it had been her turn to take out the garbage after all.

Ishmael did not offer the Baudelaire orphans any tea, and when he flicked a switch on the wall, and lit up the secret space underneath the apple tree with electric lights, the children could see that he was neither smiling nor frowning, but exhibiting a strange combination of the two, as if he were as nervous about the Baudelaires as they were about him. "I knew you'd come here," he said finally, after a long silence. "It's in your blood. I've never known a Baudelaire who didn't rock the boat."

The Baudelaires felt all of their questions bump into each other in their heads, like frantic sailors deserting a sinking ship. "What is this place?" Violet asked. "How did you know our parents?"

"Why have you lied to us about so many things?" Klaus demanded. "Why are you keeping so many secrets?"

"Who are you?" Sunny asked.

Ishmael took another step closer to the Baudelaires and gazed down at Sunny, who gazed back at the facilitator, and then stared down at the clay still packed around his feet. "Did you know I used to be a schoolteacher?" he asked. "This was many years ago, in the city. There were always a few children in my chemistry classes who had the same gleam in their eyes that you Baudelaires have. Those students always turned in the most interesting assignments." He sighed, and sat down on one of the reading chairs in the center of the room. "They also always gave me the most trouble. I remember one child in particular, who had scraggly dark hair and just one eyebrow."

"Count Olaf," Violet said.

Ishmael frowned, and blinked at the eldest Baudelaire. "No," he said. "This was a little girl. She had one eyebrow and, thanks to an accident in her grandfather's laboratory, only one ear. She was an orphan, and she lived with her siblings in a house owned by a terrible woman, a violent drunkard who was famous for having killed a man in her youth with nothing but her bare hands and a very ripe cantaloupe. The cantaloupe was grown on a farm that is no longer in operation, the Lucky Smells Melon Farm, which was owned by—"

"Sir," Klaus said.

Ishmael frowned again. "No," he said. "The farm was owned by two brothers, one of whom was later murdered in a small village, where three innocent children were accused of the crime."

"Jacques," Sunny said.

"No," Ishmael said with another frown. "There was some argument about his name, actually, as he appeared to use several names depending on what he was wearing. In any case, the student in my class began to be very suspicious about the tea her guardian would pour for her when she got home from school. Rather than drink it, she would dump it into a houseplant that had been used to decorate a well-known stylish restaurant with a fish theme."

"Café Salmonella," Violet said.

"No," Ishmael said, and frowned once more. "The Bistro Smelt. Of course, my student realized she couldn't keep feeding tea to the houseplant, particularly after it withered away and the houseplant's owner was whisked off to Peru aboard a mysterious ship."

"The *Prospero*," Klaus said.

Ishmael offered the youngsters yet another frown. "Yes," he said, "although at the time the ship was called the *Pericles*. But my student didn't know that. She only wanted to avoid being poisoned, and I had an idea that an antidote might be hidden—"

"Yaw," Sunny interrupted, and her siblings nodded in agreement. By "yaw," the youngest Baudelaire meant "Ishmael's story is tangential," a word which here means "answering questions other than the ones the Baudelaires had asked."

"We want to know what's going on here on the island, at this very moment," Violet said, "not what happened in a classroom many years ago."

"But what is happening now and what happened then are part of the same story," Ishmael said. "If I don't tell you how I came to prefer tea that's as bitter as wormwood, then you won't know how I came to have a very important conversation with a waiter in a lakeside town. And if I don't tell you about that conversation, then you won't know how I ended up on a certain bathyscaphe, or how I ended up shipwrecked here, or how I came to meet your parents, or anything else contained in this book." He took the heavy volume from Klaus's hands and ran his fingers along the spine, where the long, somewhat wordy title was printed in gold block letters. "People have been writing stories in this book since the first castaways washed up on the island, and all the stories are connected in one way or another. If you ask one question, it will lead you to another, and another, and another. It's like peeling an onion."

"But you can't read every story, and answer every question," Klaus said, "even if you'd like to."

Ishmael smiled and tugged at his beard. "That's just what your parents told me," he said. "When I arrived here they'd been on the island a few months, but they'd become the colony's facilitators, and had suggested some new customs. Your father had suggested that a few castaway construction workers install the periscope in the tree, to search for storms, and your mother had suggested that a shipwrecked plumber devise a water filtration system, so the colony could have fresh water, right from the kitchen sink. Your parents had begun a library from all the documents that were here, and were adding hundreds of stories to the commonplace book. Gourmet meals were served, and your parents had convinced some of the other castaways to expand this underground space." He gestured to the long bookshelf, which disappeared into the darkness. "They wanted to dig a passageway that would lead to a marine research center and rhetorical advice service some miles away."

The Baudelaires exchanged amazed looks. Captain Widdershins had described such a place, and in fact the children had spent some desperate hours in its ruined basement. "You mean if we walk along the bookcase," Klaus said, "we'll reach Anwhistle Aquatics?"

Ishmael shook his head. "The passageway was never finished," he said, "and it's a good thing, too. The research center was destroyed in a fire, which might have spread through the passageway and reached the island. And it turned out that a very deadly fungus was contained in that place. I shudder to think what might happen if the Medusoid Mycelium ever reached these shores."

The Baudelaires looked at one another again, but said nothing, preferring to keep one of their secrets even as Ishmael told them some of his own. The story of the Baudelaire children may have connected with Ishmael's story of the spores contained in the diving helmet Count Olaf was hiding under his gown in the bird cage in which he was a prisoner, but the siblings saw no reason to volunteer this information.

"Some islanders thought the passage was a

wonderful idea," Ishmael continued. "Your parents wanted to carry all of the documents that had washed up here to Anwhistle Aquatics, where they might be sent to a sub-sub-librarian who had a secret library. Others wanted to keep the island safe, far from the treachery of the world. By the time I arrived, some islanders wanted to mutiny, and abandon your parents on the coastal shelf." The facilitator heaved a great sigh, and closed the heavy book in his lap. "I walked into the middle of this story," he said, "just as you walked into the middle of mine. Some of the islanders had found weapons in the detritus, and the situation might have become violent if I hadn't convinced the colony to simply abandon your parents. We allowed them to pack a few books into a fishing boat your father had built, and in the morning they left with a few of their comrades as the coastal shelf flooded. They left behind everything they'd created here, from the periscope I use to predict the weather to the commonplace book where I continue their research."

"You drove our parents away?" Violet asked in amazement.

"They were very sad to go," Ishmael said. "Your mother was pregnant with you, Violet, and after all of their years with V.F.D. your parents weren't sure they wanted their children exposed to the world's treachery. But they didn't understand that if the passageway had been completed, you would have been exposed to the world's treachery in any case. Sooner or later, everyone's story has an unfortunate event or two—a schism or a death, a fire or a mutiny, the loss of a home or the destruction of a tea set. The only solution, of course, is to stay as far away from the world as possible and lead a safe, simple life."

"That's why you keep so many items away from the others," Klaus said.

"It depends on how you look at it," Ishmael said. "I wanted this place to be as safe as possible, so when I became the island's facilitator, I suggested some new customs myself. I moved the colony to the other side of the island, and I trained the sheep to drag the weapons away, and then the books and mechanical devices, so none of the world's detritus would interfere with our safety. I suggested we all dress alike, and eat the same meals, to avoid any future schisms."

"Jojishoji," Sunny said, which meant something like, "I don't believe that abridging the freedom of expression and the free exercise thereof is the proper way to run a community."

"Sunny's right," Violet said. "The other islanders couldn't have agreed with these new customs."

"I didn't force them," Ishmael said, "but, of course, the coconut cordial helped. The fermented beverage is so strong that it serves as a sort of opiate for the people here."

"Lethe?" Sunny asked.

"An opiate is something that makes people drowsy and inactive," Klaus said, "or even forgetful."

"The more cordial the islanders drank," Ishmael explained, "the less they thought about the past, or complained about the things they were missing."

"That's why hardly anyone leaves this place," Violet said. "They're too drowsy to think about leaving."

"Occasionally someone leaves," Ishmael said, and looked down at the Incredibly Deadly Viper, who gave him a brief hiss. "Some time ago, two women sailed off with this very snake, and a few years later, a man named Thursday left with a few comrades."

"So Thursday is alive," Klaus said, "just like Kit said."

"Yes," Ishmael admitted, "but at my suggestion, Miranda told her daughter that he died in a storm, so she wouldn't worry about the schism that divided her parents."

"Electra," Sunny said, which meant "A family shouldn't keep such terrible secrets," but Ishmael did not ask for a translation.

"Except for those troublemakers," he said, "everyone has stayed here. And why shouldn't they? Most of the castaways are orphans, like me, and like you. I know your story, Baudelaires, from all the newspaper articles, police reports, financial newsletters, telegrams, private correspondence, and fortune cookies that have washed up here. You've been wandering this treacherous world since your story began, and you've never found a place as safe as this one. Why don't you stay? Give up your mechanical inventions and your reading and your cooking. Forget about Count Olaf and V.F.D. Leave your ribbon, and your commonplace book, and your whisk, and your raft library, and lead a simple, safe life on our shores."

"What about Kit?" Violet asked.

"In my experience, the Snickets are as much trouble as the Baudelaires," Ishmael said. "That's why I suggested you leave her on the coastal shelf, so she wouldn't make trouble for the colony. But if you can be convinced to choose a simpler life, I suppose she can, too."

The Baudelaires looked at one another doubtfully. They already knew that Kit wanted to return to the world and make sure justice was served, and as volunteers they should have been eager to join her. But Violet, Klaus, and Sunny were not sure they could abandon the first safe place they had found, even if it was a little dull. "Can't we stay here," Klaus asked, "and lead a more complicated life, with the items and documents here in the arboretum?"

"And spices?" Sunny added.

"And keep them a secret from the other islanders?" Ishmael said with a frown.

"That's what you're doing," Klaus couldn't help pointing out. "All day long you sit in your chair and make sure the island is safe from the detritus of the world, but then you sneak off to the arboretum on your perfectly healthy feet and write in a commonplace book while snacking on bitter apples. You want everyone to lead a simple, safe life—everyone except yourself."

"No one should lead the life I lead," Ishmael said, with a long, sad tug on his beard. "I've spent countless years cataloging all of the objects that have washed up on these shores and all the stories those objects tell. I've repaired all the documents that the storms have damaged, and taken notes on every detail. I've read more of the world's treacherous history than almost anyone, and as one of my colleagues once said, this history is indeed little more than the register of crimes, follies, and misfortunes of mankind."

"Gibbon," Sunny said. She meant something like, "We want to read this history, no matter how miserable it is," and her siblings were quick to translate. But Ishmael tugged at his beard again, and shook his head firmly at the three children.

"Don't you see?" he asked. "I'm not just the island's facilitator. I'm the island's parent. I keep this library far away from the people under my care, so that they will never be disturbed by the world's terrible secrets." The facilitator reached into a pocket of his robe and held out a small object. The Baudelaires saw that it was an ornate ring, emblazoned with the initial R, and stared at it, quite puzzled.

Ishmael opened the enormous volume in his lap, and turned a few pages to read from his notes. "This ring," he said, "once belonged to the Duchess of Winnipeg, who gave it to her daughter, who was also the Duchess of Winnipeg, who gave it to her daughter, and so on and so on and so on. Eventually, the last Duchess of Winnipeg joined V.F.D., and gave it to Kit Snicket's brother. He gave it to your mother. For reasons I still don't understand, she gave it back to him, and he gave it to Kit, and Kit gave it to your father, who gave it to your mother when they were married. She kept it locked in a wooden box that could only be opened by a key that was kept in a wooden box that could only be opened by a code that Kit Snicket learned from her grandfather. The wooden box turned to ashes in the fire that destroyed the Baudelaire mansion, and Captain Widdershins found the ring in the wreckage only to lose it in a storm at sea, which eventually washed it onto our shores."

"Neiklot?" Sunny asked, which meant "Why are you telling us about this ring?"

"The point of the story isn't the ring," Ishmael said. "It's the fact that you've never seen it until this moment. This ring, with its long secret history, was in your home for years, and your parents never mentioned it. Your parents never told you about the Duchess of Winnipeg, or Captain Widdershins, or the Snicket siblings, or V.F.D. Your parents never told you they'd lived here, or that they were forced to leave, or any other details of their own unfortunate history. They never told you their whole story."

"Then let us read that book," Klaus said, "so we can find out for ourselves."

Ishmael shook his head. "You don't understand," he said, which is something the middle

Baudelaire never liked to be told. "Your parents didn't tell you these things because they wanted to shelter you, just as this apple tree shelters the items in the arboretum from the island's frequent storms, and just as I shelter the colony from the complicated history of the world. No sensible parent would let their child read even the title of this dreadful, sad chronicle, when they could keep them far from the treachery of the world instead. Now that you've ended up here, don't you want to respect their wishes?" He closed the book again, and stood up, gazing at all three Baudelaires in turn. "Just because your parents have died," he said quietly, "doesn't mean they've failed you. Not if you stay here and lead the life they wanted you to lead."

Violet thought of her mother again, bringing the cup of star anise tea on that restless evening. "Are you sure this is what our parents would have wanted?" she asked, not knowing if she could trust his answer.

"If they didn't want to keep you safe," he said, "they would have told you everything, so you could add another chapter to this unfortunate history." He put the book down on the reading chair, and put the ring in Violet's hand. "You belong here, Baudelaires, on this island and under my care. I'll tell the islanders that you've changed your minds, and that you're abandoning your troublesome past."

"Will they support you?" Violet asked, thinking of Erewhon and Finn and their plan to mutiny at breakfast.

"Of course they will," Ishmael said. "The life we lead here on the island is better than the treachery of the world. Leave the arboretum with me, children, and you can join us for breakfast."

"And cordial," Klaus said.

"No apples," Sunny said.

Ishmael gave the children one last nod, and led the children up through the gap in the roots of the tree, turning off the lights as he went. The Baudelaires stepped out into the arboretum, and looked back one last time at the secret space. In the dim light they could just make out the shape of the Incredibly Deadly Viper, who slithered over Ishmael's commonplace book and followed the children into the morning air. The sun filtered through the shade of the enormous apple tree, and shone on the gold block letters on the spine of the book. The children wondered whether the letters had been printed there by their parents, or perhaps by the previous writer of the commonplace book, or the writer before that, or the writer before that. They wondered how many stories the oddly titled history contained, and how many people had gazed at the gold lettering before paging through the previous crimes, follies, and misfortunes and adding more of their own, like the thin layers of an onion. As they walked out of the arboretum, led by their clay-footed facilitator, the Baudelaire orphans wondered about their own unfortunate history, and that of their parents and all the other castaways who had washed up on the shores of the island, adding chapter upon chapter to *A Series of Unfortunate Events.*

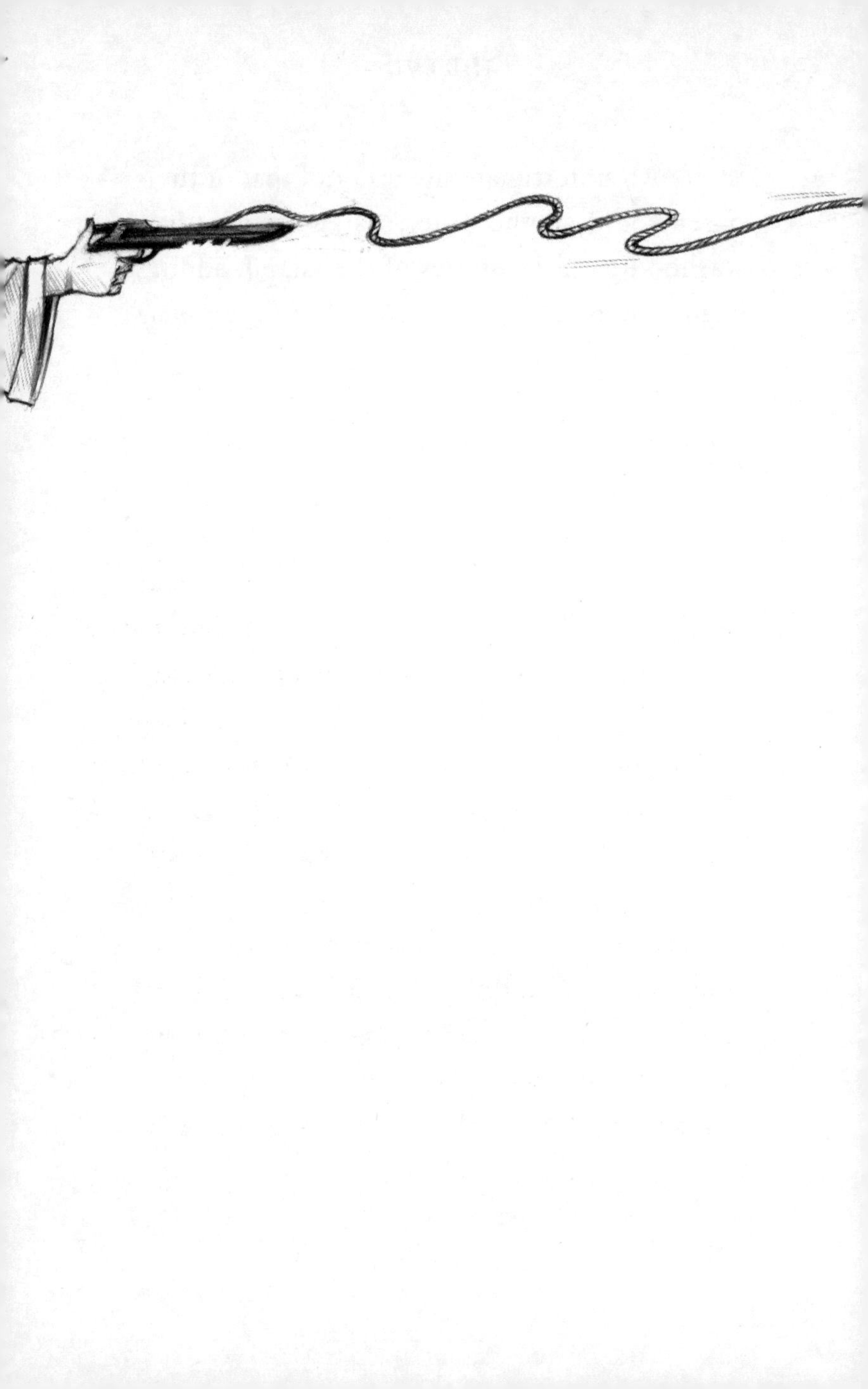

CHAPTER Eleven

Perhaps one night, when you were very small, someone tucked you into bed and read you a story called "The Little Engine That Could," and if so then you have my profound sympathies, as it is one of the most tedious stories on Earth. The story probably put you right to sleep, which is the reason it is read to children, so I will remind you that the story involves the engine of a train that for some reason has the ability to think and talk. Someone asks the Little Engine That Could to do a difficult task too dull for me to describe, and the engine isn't sure it can accomplish this, but it begins to mutter to itself, "I think I can, I think I can, I think I can," and before long it has muttered its way to success. The moral of the story is that if you tell yourself you can do something, then you can actually do it, a moral easily disproved if you tell yourself that you can eat nine pints of ice cream in a single sitting, or that you can shipwreck yourself on a distant island simply by setting off in a rented canoe with holes sawed in it.

I only mention the story of the Little Engine That Could so that when I say that the Baudelaire orphans, as they left the arboretum with Ishmael and headed back toward the island colony, were on board the Little Engine That Couldn't, you will understand what I mean. For one thing, the children were being dragged back to Ishmael's tent on the large wooden sleigh, helmed by Ishmael in his enormous clay chair and dragged by the island's wild sheep, and if you have ever wondered why horse-drawn carriages and dogsleds are far more common modes of travel than sheep-dragged sleighs, it is because sheep are not well-suited for employment in the transportation industry. The sheep meandered and detoured, lollygagged and moseyed, and occasionally stopped to nibble on wild grass or simply breathe in the morning air, and Ishmael tried to convince the sheep to go faster through his facilitation skills, rather than through standard shepherding procedures. "I don't want to force you," he kept saying, "but perhaps you sheep could go a bit faster," and the sheep would merely stare blankly at the old man and keep shuffling along.

But the Baudelaire orphans were on board the Little Engine That Couldn't not only because of the sheep's languor—a word which here means "inability to pull a large, wooden sleigh at a reasonable pace"—but because their own thoughts were not spurring them to action. Unlike the engine in the tedious story, no matter what Violet, Klaus, and Sunny told themselves, they could not imagine a successful solution to their difficulties. The children tried to tell themselves that they would do as Ishmael had suggested, and lead a safe life on the colony, but they could not imagine abandoning Kit Snicket on the coastal shelf, or letting her return to the world to see that justice would be served without accompanying her on this noble errand. The siblings tried to tell themselves that they would obey their parents' wishes, and stay sheltered from their unfortunate history, but they did not think that they could keep themselves away from the arboretum, or from reading what their parents had written in the enormous book. The Baudelaires tried to tell themselves that they would join Erewhon and Finn in the mutiny at breakfast, but they could not picture threatening the facilitator and his supporters with weapons, particularly because they had not brought any from the arboretum. They tried to tell themselves that at least they could be glad that Count Olaf was not a threat, but they could not quite approve of his being locked in a bird cage, and they shuddered to think of the fungus hidden in his gown and the scheme hidden in his head. And, throughout the entire journey over the brae and back toward the beach, the three children tried to tell themselves that everything was all right, but of course everything was *not* all right. Everything was all wrong, and Violet, Klaus, and Sunny did not quite know how a safe place, far from the treachery of the world, had become so dangerous and complicated as soon as they had arrived. The Baudelaire orphans sat in the sleigh, staring at Ishmael's clay-covered clay feet, and no matter how many times they thought they could, they thought they could, they thought they could think of an end to their troubles, they knew it simply was not the case.

Finally, however, the sheep dragged the sleigh across the beach's white sands and through the opening of the enormous tent. Once again, the joint was hopping, but the gathered islanders were in the midst of an argy-bargy, a word for "argument" that is far less cute than it sounds. Despite the presence of an opiate in seashells dangling from the waists of every colonist, the islanders were anything but drowsy and inactive. Alonso was grabbing the arm of Willa, who was shrieking in annoyance while stepping on Dr. Kurtz's foot. Sherman's face was even redder than usual as he threw sand in the face of Mr. Pitcairn, who appeared to be trying to bite Brewster's finger. Professor Fletcher was shouting at Ariel, and Ms. Marlow was stomping her feet at Calypso, and Madame Nordoff and Rabbi Bligh seemed ready to begin wrestling on the sand. Byam twirled his mustache at Ferdinand, while Robinson tugged his beard at Larsen and Weyden seemed to tear out her red hair for no reason at all. Jonah and Sadie Bellamy were standing face-to-face arguing, while Friday and Mrs. Caliban were standing back-to-back as if they would never speak to each other again, and all the while Omeros stood near Ishmael's chair with his hands held suspiciously behind his back. While Ishmael gaped at the islanders in amazement, the three children stepped off the sleigh and walked quickly toward Erewhon and Finn, who were looking at them expectantly.

"Where were you?" Finn said. "We waited as long as we could for you to return, but we had to leave your friend behind and begin the mutiny."

"You left Kit out there alone?" Violet said. "You promised you'd stay with her."

"And you promised us weapons," said Erewhon. "Where are they, Baudelaires?"

"We don't have any," Klaus admitted. "Ishmael was at the arboretum."

"Count Olaf was right," Erewhon said. "You failed us, Baudelaires."

"What do you mean, 'Count Olaf was right'?" Violet demanded.

"What do you mean, 'Ishmael was at the arboretum'?" Finn demanded.

"What do you mean, what do I mean?" Erewhon demanded.

"What you mean what you mean what I mean?" Sunny demanded.

"Please, everyone!" Ishmael cried from his clay chair. "I suggest we all take a few sips of cordial and discuss this cordially!"

"I'm tired of drinking cordial," Professor Fletcher said, "and I'm tired of your suggestions, Ishmael!"

"Call me Ish," the facilitator said.

"I'm calling you a bad facilitator!" retorted Calypso.

"Please, everyone!" Ishmael cried again, with a nervous tug at his beard. "What is all this argy-bargy about?"

"I'll tell you what it's about," Alonso said. "I washed up on these shores many years ago, after enduring a terrible storm and a dreadful political scandal."

"So what?" Rabbi Bligh asked. "Eventually, everyone washes up on these shores."

"I wanted to leave my unfortunate history

behind," Alonso said, "and live a peaceful life free from trouble. But now there are some colonists talking of mutiny. If we're not careful, this island will become as treacherous as the rest of the world!"

"Mutiny?" Ishmael said in horror. "Who dares talk of mutiny?"

"I dare," Erewhon said. "I'm tired of your facilitation, Ishmael. I washed ashore on this island after living on another island even farther away. I was tired of a peaceful life, and ready for adventure. But whenever anything exciting arrives on this island, you immediately have it thrown into the arboretum!"

"It depends on how you look at it," Ishmael protested. "I don't force anyone to throw anything away."

"Ishmael is right!" Ariel cried. "Some of us have had enough adventure for a lifetime! I washed up on these shores after finally escaping from prison, where I had disguised myself as a young man for years! I've stayed here for my own safety, not to participate in more dangerous schemes!"

"Then you should join our mutiny!" Sherman cried. "Ishmael is not to be trusted! We abandoned the Baudelaires on the coastal shelf, and now he's brought them back!"

"The Baudelaires never should have been abandoned in the first place!" Ms. Marlow cried. "All they wanted to do was help their friend!"

"Their friend is suspicious," claimed Mr. Pitcairn. "She arrived on a raft of books."

"So what?" said Weyden. "I arrived on a raft of books myself."

"But you abandoned them," Professor Fletcher pointed out.

"She did nothing of the sort!" cried Larsen. "You helped her hide them, so you could force those children to read!"

"We wanted to learn to read!" Friday insisted.

"You're reading?" Mrs. Caliban gasped in astonishment.

"You shouldn't be reading!" cried Madame Nordoff.

"Well, you shouldn't be yodeling!" cried Dr. Kurtz.

"You're yodeling?" Rabbi Bligh asked in astonishment. "Maybe we should have a mutiny after all!"

"Yodeling is better than carrying a flashlight!" Jonah cried, pointing at Finn accusingly.

"Carrying a flashlight is better than hiding a picnic basket!" Sadie cried, pointing at Erewhon.

"Hiding a picnic basket is better than pocketing a whisk!" Erewhon said, pointing at Sunny.

"These secrets will destroy us!" Ariel said. "Life here is supposed to be simple!"

"There's nothing wrong with a complicated life," said Byam. "I lived a simple life as a sailor for many years, and I was bored to tears until I was shipwrecked."

"Bored to tears?" Friday said in astonishment. "All I want is the simple life my mother and father had together, without arguing or keeping secrets."

"That's enough," Ishmael said quickly. "I suggest that we stop arguing."

"I suggest we continue to argue!" cried Erewhon.

"I suggest we abandon Ishmael and his supporters!" cried Professor Fletcher.

"I suggest we abandon the mutineers!" cried Calypso.

"I suggest better food!" cried another islander.

"I suggest more cordial!" cried another.

"I suggest a more attractive robe!"

"I suggest a proper house instead of a tent!"

"I suggest fresh water!"

"I suggest eating bitter apples!"

"I suggest chopping down the apple tree!"

"I suggest burning up the outrigger!"

"I suggest a talent show!"

"I suggest reading a book!"

"I suggest burning all books!"

"I suggest yodeling!"

"I suggest forbidding yodeling!"

"I suggest a safe place!"

"I suggest a complicated life!"

"I suggest it depends on how you look at it!"

"I suggest justice!"

"I suggest breakfast!"

"I suggest we stay and you leave!"

"I suggest you stay and we leave!"

"I suggest we return to Winnipeg!"

The Baudelaires looked at one another in despair as the mutinous schism worked its way through the colony. Seashells hung open at the waists of the islanders, but there was no cordiality evident as the islanders turned against one another in fury, even if they were friends, or members of the same family, or shared a history or a secret organization. The siblings had seen angry crowds before, of course, from the mob psychology of the citizens in the Village of Fowl Devotees to the blind justice of the trial at the Hotel Denouement, but they had never seen a community divide so suddenly and so completely. Violet, Klaus, and Sunny watched the schism unfold and could imagine what the other schisms must have been like, from the schism that split V.F.D., to the schism that drove their parents away from the very same island, to all the other schisms in the world's sad history, with every person suggesting something different, every story like a layer of an onion, and every unfortunate event like a chapter in an enormous book. The Baudelaires watched the terrible argy-bargy and wondered how they could have hoped the island would be a safe place, far from the treachery of the world, when eventually every treachery washed up on its shores, like a castaway tossed by a storm at sea, and divided the people who lived there. The arguing voices of the islanders grew louder and louder, with everyone suggesting something but nobody listening to anyone else's suggestions, until the schism was a deafening roar that was finally broken by the loudest voice of all.

"SILENCE!" bellowed a figure who entered the tent, and the islanders stopped talking at once, and stared in amazement at the person who stood glaring at them in a long dress that bulged at the belly.

"What are you doing here?" gasped someone from the back of the tent. "We abandoned you on the coastal shelf!"

The figure strode into the middle of the tent, and I'm sorry to tell you that it was not Kit Snicket, who was still in a long dress that bulged at the belly on top of her library raft, but Count Olaf, whose bulging belly, of course, was the diving helmet containing the Medusoid Mycelium, and whose orange and yellow dress the Baudelaires suddenly recognized as the dress Esmé Squalor wore on top of the Mortmain Mountains, a hideous thing fashioned to look like an enormous fire, which had somehow washed onto the island's shores like everything else. As Olaf paused to give the siblings a particularly wicked smile, the children tried to imagine the secret history of Esmé's dress, and how, like the ring Violet still held in her hand, it had returned to the Baudelaires' story after all this time.

"You can't abandon me," the villain snarled to the islander. "I'm the king of Olaf-Land."

"This isn't Olaf-Land," Ishmael said, with a stern tug on his beard, "and you're no king, Olaf."

Count Olaf threw back his head and laughed, his tattered dress quivering in mirth, a phrase which here means "making unpleasant rustling noises." With a sneer, he pointed at Ishmael, who still sat in the chair. "Oh, Ish," he said, his eyes shining bright, "I told you many years ago that I would triumph over you someday, and at last that day has arrived. My associate with the weekday for a name told me that you were still hiding out on this island, and—"

"Thursday," Mrs. Caliban said.

Olaf frowned, and blinked at the freckled woman. "No," he said. "Monday. She was trying to blackmail an old man who was involved in a political scandal."

"Gonzalo," Alonso said.

Olaf frowned again. "No," he said. "We'd gone bird-watching, this old man and I, when we decided to rob a sealing schooner owned by—"

"Humphrey," Weyden said.

"No," Olaf said with another frown. "There was some argument about his name, actually, as a baby adopted by his orphaned children also bore the same name."

"Bertrand," Omeros said.

"No," Olaf said, and frowned yet another time. "The adoption papers were hidden in the hat of a banker who had been promoted to Vice President in Charge of Orphan Affairs."

"Mr. Poe?" asked Sadie.

"*Yes,*" Olaf said with a scowl, "although at

the time he was better known under his stage name. But I'm not here to discuss the past. I'm here to discuss the future. Your mutineering islanders let me out of this cage, Ishmael, to force you off the island and crown me as king!"

"King?" Erewhon said. "That wasn't the plan, Olaf."

"If you want to live, old woman," Olaf said rudely, "I suggest that you do whatever I say."

"You're already giving us suggestions?" Brewster said incredulously. "You're just like Ishmael, although your outfit is prettier."

"Thank you," Count Olaf said, with a wicked smile, "but there's another important difference between me and this foolish facilitator."

"Your tattoo?" Friday guessed.

"No," Count Olaf said, with a frown. "If you were to wash the clay of Ishmael's feet, you'd see he has the same tattoo as I do."

"Eyeliner?" guessed Madame Nordoff.

"No," Count Olaf said sharply. "The difference is that Ishmael is unarmed. He abandoned his weapons long ago, during the V.F.D. schism, refusing to use violence of any sort. But today, you'll all see how foolish he is." He paused, and ran his filthy hands along his bulging belly before turning to the facilitator, who was taking something from Omeros's hands. "I have the only weapon that can threaten you and your supporters," he bragged. "I'm the king of Olaf-Land, and there's nothing you and your sheep can do about it."

"Don't be so sure about that," Ishmael said, and raised an object in the air so everyone could see it. It was the harpoon gun that had washed ashore with Olaf and the Baudelaires, after being used to fire at crows at the Hotel Denouement, and at a self-sustaining hot air mobile home in the Village of Fowl Devotees, and at a cotton-candy machine at a county fair when the Baudelaires' parents were very, very young. Now the weapon was adding another chapter to its secret history, and was pointing right at Count Olaf. "I had Omeros keep this weapon handy," Ishmael said, "instead of tossing it in the arboretum, because I thought you might escape from that cage, Count Olaf, just as I escaped from the cage you put me in when you set fire to my home."

"I didn't set that fire," Count Olaf said, his eyes shining bright.

"I've had enough of your lies," Ishmael said, and stood up from his chair. Realizing that the facilitator's feet were not injured after all, the islanders gasped, which requires a large intake of breath, a dangerous thing to do if spores of a deadly fungus are in the air. "I'm going to do what I should have done years ago, Olaf, and slaughter you. I'm going to fire this harpoon gun right into that bulging belly of yours!"

"*No!*" screamed the Baudelaires in unison, but even the combined voices of the three children were not as loud as Count Olaf's villainous laughter, and the facilitator never heard the children's cry as he pulled the bright red trigger of this terrible weapon. The children heard a *click!*

and then a *whoosh!* as the harpoon was fired, and then, as it struck Count Olaf right where Ishmael had promised, they heard the shattering of glass, and the Medusoid Mycelium, with its own secret history of treachery and violence, was free at last to circulate in the air, even in this safe place so far from the world. Everyone in the tent gasped—islanders and colonists, men and women, children and orphans, volunteers and villains and everyone in between. Everyone breathed in the spores of the deadly fungus as Count Olaf toppled backward onto the sand, still laughing even as he gasped himself, and in an instant the schism of the island was over, because everyone in this place—including, of course, the Baudelaire orphans—was suddenly part of the same unfortunate event.

C H A P T E R

Twelve

It is a curious thing, but as one travels the world getting older and older, it appears that happiness is easier to get used to than despair. The second time you have a root beer float, for instance, your happiness at sipping the delicious concoction may be not quite as enormous as when you first had a root beer float, and the

twelfth time your happiness may be still less enormous, until root beer floats begin to offer you very little happiness at all, because you have become used to the taste of vanilla ice cream and root beer mixed together. However, the second time you find a thumbtack in your root beer float, your despair is much greater than the first time, when you dismissed the thumbtack as a freak accident rather than part of the scheme of the soda jerk, a phrase which here means "ice cream shop employee who is trying to injure your tongue," and by the twelfth time you find a thumbtack your despair is even greater still, until you can hardly utter the phrase "root beer float" without bursting into tears. It is almost as if happiness is an acquired taste, like coconut cordial or ceviche, to which you can eventually become accustomed, but despair is something surprising each time you encounter it. As the glass shattered in the tent, the Baudelaire orphans stood and stared at the standing figure of Ishmael, but even as they felt the Medusoid Mycelium drift into their bodies, each tiny spore feeling like the footstep of an ant walking down their throats, they could not believe that their own story could contain such despair once more, or that such a terrible thing had happened.

"What happened?" Friday cried. "I heard glass breaking!"

"Never mind the breaking glass," Erewhon said. "I feel something in my throat, like a tiny seed!"

"Never mind your seedy throat," Finn said. "I see Ishmael standing up on his own two feet!"

Count Olaf cackled from the white sand where he lay. With one dramatic gesture he yanked the harpoon out of the mess of broken helmet and tattered dress at his stomach, and threw it at Ishmael's clay feet. "The sound you heard was the shattering of a diving helmet," he sneered. "The seeds you feel in your throats are the spores of the Medusoid Mycelium, and the man standing on his own two feet is the one who has slaughtered you all!"

"The Medusoid Mycelium?" Ishmael repeated in astonishment, as the islanders gasped again. "On these shores? It can't be! I've spent my life trying to keep the island forever safe from that terrible fungus!"

"Nothing's safe forever, thank goodness," Count Olaf said, "and you of all people should know that eventually everything washes up on these shores. The Baudelaire family has finally returned to this island after you threw them off years ago, and they brought the Medusoid Mycelium with them."

Ishmael's eyes widened, and he jumped off the edge of the sleigh to stand and confront the Baudelaire orphans. As his feet landed on the ground, the clay cracked and fell away, and the children could see that the facilitator had a tattoo of an eye on his left ankle, just as Count Olaf had said. "*You* brought the Medusoid Mycelium?" he asked. "You had a deadly fungus with you all this time, and you kept it a secret from us?"

"You're a fine one to talk about keeping secrets!" Alonso said. "Look at your healthy feet, Ishmael! Your dishonesty is the root of the trouble!"

"It's the mutineers who are the root of the trouble!" cried Ariel. "If they hadn't let Count Olaf out of the cage, this never would have happened!"

"It depends on how you look at it," Professor Fletcher said. "In my opinion, all of us are the root of the trouble. If we hadn't put Count Olaf in the cage, he never would have threatened us!"

"We're the root of the trouble because we failed to find the diving helmet," Ferdinand said. "If we'd retrieved it while storm scavenging, the sheep would have dragged it to the arboretum and we would have been safe!"

"Omeros is the root of the trouble," Dr. Kurtz said, pointing at the young boy. "He's the one who gave Ishmael the harpoon gun instead of dumping it in the arboretum!"

"It's Count Olaf who's the root of the trouble!" cried Larsen. "He's the one who brought the fungus into the tent!"

"I'm not the root of the trouble," Count Olaf snarled, and then paused to cough loudly before continuing. "I'm the king of the island!"

"It doesn't matter whether you're king or not," Violet said. "You've breathed in the fungus like everyone else."

"Violet's right," Klaus said. "We don't have time to stand here arguing." Even without his commonplace book, Klaus could recite a poem about the fungus that was first recited to him by Fiona shortly before she had broken his heart. "*A single spore has such grim power / That you may die within the hour,*" he said. "If we don't quit our fighting and work together, we'll all end up dead."

The tent was filled with ululation, a word which here means "the sound of panicking islanders." "Dead?" Madame Nordoff shrieked. "Nobody said the fungus was deadly! I thought we were merely being threatened with forbidden food!"

"I didn't stay on this island to die!" cried Ms. Marlow. "I could have died at home!"

"Nobody is going to die," Ishmael announced to the crowd.

"It depends on how you look at it," Rabbi Bligh said. "Eventually we're all going to die."

"Not if you follow my suggestions," Ishmael insisted. "Now first, I suggest that everyone take a nice, long drink from their seashells. The cordial will chase the fungus from your throats."

"No, it won't!" Violet cried. "Fermented coconut milk has no effect on the Medusoid Mycelium!"

"That may be so," Ishmael said, "but at least we'll all feel a bit calmer."

"You mean drowsy and inactive," Klaus corrected. "The cordial is an opiate."

"There's nothing wrong with cordiality," Ishmael said. "I suggest we all spend a few minutes discussing our situation in a cordial manner.

We can decide what the root of the problem is, and come up with a solution at our leisure."

"That does sound reasonable," Calypso admitted.

"Trahison des clercs!" Sunny cried, which meant "You're forgetting about the quick-acting poison in the fungus!"

"Sunny's right," Klaus said. "We need to find a solution now, not sit around talking about it over beverages!"

"The solution is in the arboretum," Violet said, "and in the secret space under the roots of the apple tree."

"Secret space?" Sherman said. "What secret space?"

"There's a library down there," Klaus said, as the crowd murmured in surprise, "cataloging all of the objects that have washed ashore and all the stories those objects tell."

"And kitchen," Sunny added. "Maybe horseradish."

"Horseradish is the one way to dilute the

poison," Violet explained, and recited the rest of the poem the children had heard aboard the *Queequeg*. "*Is dilution simple? But of course! / Just one small dose of root of horse.*" She looked around the tent at the frightened faces of the islanders. "The kitchen beneath the apple tree might have horseradish," she said. "We can save ourselves if we hurry."

"They're lying," Ishmael said. "There's nothing in the arboretum but junk, and there's nothing underneath the tree but dirt. The Baudelaires are trying to trick you."

"We're not trying to trick anyone," Klaus said. "We're trying to save everyone."

"The Baudelaires knew the Medusoid Mycelium was here," Ishmael pointed out, "and they never told us. You can't trust them, but you can trust me, and I suggest we all sit and sip our cordials."

"Razoo," Sunny said, which meant "You're the one not to be trusted," but rather than translate, her siblings stepped closer to Ishmael so they could speak to him in relative privacy.

"Why are you doing this?" Violet asked. "If you just sit here and drink cordial, you'll be doomed."

"We've all breathed in the poison," Klaus said. "We're all in the same boat."

Ishmael raised his eyebrows, and gave the children a grim smile. "We'll see about that," he said. "Now get out of my tent."

"Hightail it," Sunny said, which meant "We'd better hurry," and her siblings nodded in agreement. The Baudelaire orphans quickly left the tent, looking back to get one more glimpse of the worried islanders, the scowling facilitator, and Count Olaf, who still lay on the sand clutching his belly, as if the harpoon had not just destroyed the diving helmet, but wounded him, too.

Violet, Klaus, and Sunny did not travel back to the far side of the island by sheep-dragged sleigh, but even as they hurried over the brae they felt as if they were aboard the Little Engine That Couldn't, not only because of the desperate nature of their errand, but because of the poison they felt working its wicked way through the Baudelaire systems. Violet and Klaus learned what their sister had gone through deep beneath the ocean's surface, when Sunny had nearly perished from the fungus's deadly poison, and Sunny received a refresher course, a phrase which here means "another opportunity to feel the stalks and caps of the Medusoid Mycelium begin to sprout in her little throat." The children had to stop several times to cough, as the growing fungus was making it difficult to breathe, and by the time they stood underneath the branches of the apple tree, the Baudelaire orphans were wheezing heavily in the afternoon sun.

"We don't have much time," Violet said, between breaths.

"We'll go straight to the kitchen," Klaus said, walking through the gap in the tree's roots as the Incredibly Deadly Viper had shown them.

"Hope horseradish," Sunny said, following

her brother, but when the Baudelaires reached the kitchen they were in for a disappointment. Violet flicked the switch that lit up the kitchen, and the three children hurried to the spice rack, reading the labels on the jars and bottles one by one, but as they searched their hopes began to fade. The children found many of their favorite spices, including sage, oregano, and paprika, which was available in a number of varieties organized according to their level of smokiness. They found some of their least favorite spices, including dried parsley, which scarcely tastes like anything, and garlic salt, which forces the taste of everything else to flee. They found spices they associated with certain dishes, such as turmeric, which their father used to use while making curried peanut soup, and nutmeg, which their mother used to mix into gingerbread, and they found spices they did not associate with anything, such as marjoram, which everyone owns but scarcely anyone uses, and powdered lemon peel, which should only be used in emergencies, such as when fresh lemons have become extinct. They found spices used practically everywhere, such as salt and pepper, and spices used in certain regions, such as chipotle peppers and vindaloo rub, but none of the labels read HORSERADISH, and when they opened the jars and bottles, none of the powders, leaves, and seeds inside smelled like the horseradish factory that once stood on Lousy Lane.

"It doesn't have to be horseradish," Violet said quickly, putting down a jar of tarragon in frustration. "Wasabi was an adequate substitute when Sunny was infected."

"Or Eutrema," Sunny wheezed.

"There's no wasabi here, either," Klaus said, sniffing a jar of mace and frowning. "Maybe it's hidden somewhere."

"Who would hide horseradish?" Violet asked, after a long cough.

"Our parents," Sunny said.

"Sunny's right," Klaus said. "If they knew about Anwhistle Aquatics, they might have known of the dangers of the Medusoid Mycelium. Any horseradish that washed up on the island would have been very valuable indeed."

"We don't have time to search the entire arboretum to find horseradish," Violet said. She reached into her pocket, her fingers brushing against the ring Ishmael had given her, and found the ribbon the facilitator had been using as a bookmark, which she used to tie up her hair so she might think better. "That would be harder than trying to find the sugar bowl in the entire Hotel Denouement."

At the mention of the sugar bowl, Klaus gave his glasses a quick polish and began to page through his commonplace book, while Sunny picked up her whisk and bit it thoughtfully. "Maybe it's hidden in one of the other spice jars," the middle Baudelaire said.

"We smelled them all," Violet said, between wheezes. "None of them smelled like horseradish."

"Maybe the scent was disguised by another spice," Klaus said. "Something that was even more bitter than horseradish would cover the smell. Sunny, what are some of the bitterest spices?"

"Cloves," said Sunny, and wheezed. "Cardamom, arrowroot, wormwood."

"Wormwood," Klaus said thoughtfully, and flipped the pages of his commonplace book. "Kit mentioned wormwood once," he said, thinking of poor Kit alone on the coastal shelf. "She said tea should be as bitter as wormwood and as sharp as a two-edged sword. We were told the same thing when we were served tea right before our trial."

"No wormwood here," Sunny said.

"Ishmael also said something about bitter tea," Violet said. "Remember? That student of his was afraid of being poisoned."

"Just like we are," Klaus said, feeling the mushrooms growing inside him. "I wish we'd heard the end of that story."

"I wish we'd heard every story," Violet said, her voice sounding hoarse and rough from the poison. "I wish our parents had told us everything, instead of sheltering us from the treachery of the world."

"Maybe they did," Klaus said, his voice as rough as his sister's, and the middle Baudelaire walked to the reading chairs in the middle of the room and picked up *A Series of Unfortunate Events*. "They wrote all of their secrets here. If they hid the horseradish, we'll find it in this book."

"We don't have time to read that entire book," Violet said, "any more than we have time to search the entire arboretum."

"If we fail," Sunny said, her voice heavy with fungus, "at least we die reading together."

The Baudelaire orphans nodded grimly, and embraced one another. Like most people, the children had occasionally been in a curious and somewhat morbid mood, and had spent a few moments wondering about the circumstances of their own deaths, although since that unhappy day on Briny Beach when Mr. Poe had first informed them about the terrible fire, the children had spent so much time trying to avoid their own deaths that they preferred not to think about it in their time off. Most people do not choose their final circumstances, of course, and if the Baudelaires had been given the choice they would have liked to live to a very old age, which for all I know they may be doing. But if the three children had to perish while they were still three children, then perishing in one another's company while reading words written long ago by their mother and father was much better than many other things they could imagine, and so the three Baudelaires sat together in one of the reading chairs, preferring to be close to one another rather than having more room to sit, and together they opened the enormous book and turned back the pages until they reached the moment in history when their parents arrived on the island and began taking notes. The entries in the book alternated between the handwriting of the Baudelaire father and the handwriting of the Baudelaire mother, and the children could imagine their parents sitting in these same chairs, reading out loud what they had written and suggesting things to add to the register of crimes, follies, and misfortunes of mankind that comprised *A Series of Unfortunate Events*. The children, of course, would have liked to savor each word their parents had written—the word "savor," you probably know, here means "read slowly, as each sentence in their parents' handwriting was like a gift from beyond the grave"—but as the poison of the Medusoid Mycelium advanced further and further, the siblings had to skim, scanning each page for the words "horseradish" or "wasabi." As you know if you've ever skimmed a book, you end up getting a strange view of the story, with just glimpses here and there of what is going on, and some authors insert confusing sentences in the middle of a book just to confuse anyone who might be skimming. Three very short men were carrying a large, flat piece of wood, painted to look like a living room. As the Baudelaire orphans searched for the secret they hoped they would find, they caught glimpses of other secrets their parents had kept, and as Violet, Klaus, and Sunny spotted the names of people the Baudelaire parents had known, things they had whispered to these people, the codes hidden in the whispers, and many other intriguing details, the children hoped they would have the opportunity to reread *A Series of Unfortunate Events* on a less frantic occasion. On that afternoon, however, they read faster and faster, looking desperately for the one secret that might save them as the hour began to pass and the Medusoid Mycelium grew faster and faster inside them, as if the deadly fungus also did not have time to savor its treacherous path. As they read more and more, it grew harder and harder for the Baudelaires to breathe, and when Klaus finally spotted one of the words he had been looking for, he thought for a moment it was just a vision brought on by all the stalks and caps growing inside him.

"Horseradish!" he said, his voice rough and wheezy. "Look: 'Ishmael's fearmongering has stopped work on the passageway, even though we have a plethora of horseradish in case of any emergency.'"

Violet started to speak, but then choked on the fungus and coughed for a long while. "What does 'fearmongering' mean?" she said finally.

"'Plethora'?" Sunny's voice was little more than a mushroom-choked whisper.

"'Fearmongering' means 'making people afraid,'" said Klaus, whose vocabulary was unaffected by the poison, "and 'plethora' means 'more than enough.'" He gave a large, shuddering wheeze, and continued to read. "'We're attempting a botanical hybrid through the tuberous canopy, which should bring safety to fruition despite its dangers to our associates in utero. Of course, in case we are banished, Beatrice is hiding a small amount in a vess—'"

The middle Baudelaire interrupted himself with a cough that was so violent he dropped the book to the floor. His sisters held him tightly as his body shook against the poison and one pale hand pointed at the ceiling. "'Tuberous canopy,'" he wheezed finally. "Our father means the roots above our heads. A botanical hybrid is a plant made from the combination of two other plants." He shuddered, and his eyes, behind his glasses, filled with tears. "I don't know what he's talking about," he said finally.

Violet looked at the roots over their heads, where the periscope disappeared into the network of the tree. To her horror she found that her vision was becoming blurry, as if the fungus was growing over her eyes. "It sounds like they put the horseradish into the roots of the plant, in order to make everyone safe," she said. "That's what 'bringing safety to fruition' would be, the way a tree brings its crop to fruition."

"Apples!" cried Sunny in a strangled voice. "Bitter apples!"

"Of course!" Klaus said. "The tree is a hybrid, and its apples are bitter because they contain horseradish!"

"If we eat an apple," Violet said, "the fungus will be diluted."

"Gentreefive," Sunny agreed in a croak, and lowered herself off her siblings' laps, wheezing desperately as she tried to get to the gap in the roots. Klaus tried to follow her, but when he stood up the poison made him so dizzy that he had to sit back down and clasp his throbbing head. Violet coughed painfully, and gripped her brother's arm.

"Come on," she said, in a frantic wheeze.

Klaus shook his head. "I'm not sure we can make it," he said.

Sunny reached toward the gap in the roots and then curled to the floor in pain. "Kikbucit?" she asked, her voice weak and faint.

"We can't die here," Violet said, her voice so feeble her siblings could scarcely hear her. "Our parents saved our lives in this very room, many years ago, without even knowing it."

"Maybe not," Klaus said. "Maybe this is the end of our story."

"Tumurchap," Sunny said, but before anyone could ask what she meant, the children heard another sound, faint and strange, in the secret space beneath the apple tree their parents had hybridized with horseradish long ago. The sound was sibilant, a word which might appear to have something to do with siblings, but actually refers to a sort of whistle or hiss, such as a steam engine might make as it comes to a stop, or an audience might make after sitting through one of Al Funcoot's plays. The Baudelaires were so desperate and frightened that for a moment they thought it might be the sound of Medusoid Mycelium, celebrating its poisonous triumph over the three children, or perhaps just the sound of their hopes evaporating. But the sibilance was not the sound of evaporating hope or celebrating fungus, and thank goodness it was not the sound of a steam engine or a disgruntled theatrical audience, as the Baudelaires were not strong enough to confront such things. The hissing sound came from one of the few inhabitants of the island whose story contained not one but two shipwrecks, and perhaps because of its own sad history, this inhabitant was sympathetic to the sad history of the Baudelaires, although it is difficult to say how much sympathy can be felt by an animal, no matter how friendly. I do not have the courage to do much research on this matter, and my only herpetological comrade's story ended quite some time ago, so what this reptile was thinking as it slid toward the children is a detail of the Baudelaires' history that may never be revealed. But even with this missing detail, it is quite clear what happened. The snake slithered through the gap in the roots of the tree, and whatever the serpent was thinking, it was quite clear from the sibilant sound that came hissing through the reptile's clenched teeth that the Incredibly Deadly Viper was offering the Baudelaire orphans an apple.

CHAPTER Thirteen

It is a well-known but curious fact that the first bite of an apple always tastes the best, which is why the heroine of a book much more suitable to read than this one spends an entire afternoon eating the first bite of a bushel of apples. But even this anarchic little girl—the word "anarchic" here means "apple-loving"—never tasted a bite as wonderful as the Baudelaire orphans' first bite of the apple from the tree their parents had hybridized with horseradish. The apple was not as bitter as the Baudelaire orphans would have guessed, and the horseradish gave the juice of the apple a slight, sharp edge, like the air on a winter morning. But of course, the biggest appeal of the apple offered by the Incredibly Deadly Viper was its immediate effect on the deadly fungus growing inside them. From the moment the Baudelaire teeth bit down on the apple—first Violet's, and then Klaus's, and then Sunny's—the stalks and caps of the Medusoid Mycelium began to shrink, and within moments all traces of the dreaded mushroom had withered away, and the children could breathe clearly and easily. Hugging one another in relief, the Baudelaires found themselves laughing, which is a common reaction among people who have narrowly escaped death, and the snake seemed to be laughing, too, although perhaps it was just appreciating the youngest Baudelaire scratching behind its tiny, hooded ears.

"We should each have another apple," Violet said, standing up, "to make sure we've consumed enough horseradish."

"And we should collect enough apples for

all of the islanders," Klaus said. "They must be just as desperate as we were."

"Stockpot," Sunny said, and walked to the rack of pots on the ceiling, where the snake helped her take down an enormous metal pot that could hold a great number of apples and in fact had been used to make an enormous vat of applesauce a number of years previously.

"You two start picking apples," Violet said, walking to the periscope. "I want to check on Kit Snicket. The flooding of the coastal shelf must have begun by now, and she must be terrified."

"I hope she avoided the Medusoid Mycelium," Klaus said. "I hate to think of what that would do to her child."

"Phearst," Sunny said, which meant something like, "We should rescue her promptly."

"The islanders are in worse shape than Kit," Klaus said. "We should go to Ishmael's tent first, and then go rescue Kit."

Violet peered through the periscope and

frowned. "We shouldn't go to Ishmael's tent," she said. "We need to fill that stockpot with apples and get to the coastal shelf as quickly as we can."

"What do you mean?" Klaus said.

"They're leaving," Violet said, and I'm sorry to say it was true. Through the periscope, the eldest Baudelaire could see the shape of the outrigger and the figures of its poisoned passengers, who were pushing it along the coastal shelf toward the library raft where Kit Snicket still lay. The three children each peered through the periscope, and then looked at one another. They knew they should be hurrying, but for a moment none of the Baudelaires could move, as if they were unwilling to travel any farther in their sad history, or see one more part of their story come to an end.

If you have read this far in the chronicle of the Baudelaire orphans—and I certainly hope you have not—then you know we have reached the thirteenth chapter of the thirteenth volume in this sad history, and so you know the end is near, even though this chapter is so lengthy that you might never reach the end of it. But perhaps you do not yet know what the end really means. "The end" is a phrase which refers to the completion of a story, or the final moment of some accomplishment, such as a secret errand, or a great deal of research, and indeed this thirteenth volume marks the completion of my investigation into the Baudelaire case, which required much research, a great many secret errands, and the accomplishments of a number of my comrades, from a trolley driver to a botanical hybridization expert, with many, many typewriter repairpeople in between. But it cannot be said that *The End* contains the end of the Baudelaires' story, any more than *The Bad Beginning* contained its beginning. The children's story began long before that terrible day on Briny Beach, but there would have to be another volume to chronicle when the Baudelaires were born, and when their parents married, and who was playing the violin in the candlelit restaurant when the Baudelaire parents first laid eyes on one another, and what was hidden inside that violin, and the childhood of the man who orphaned the girl who put it there, and even then it could not be said that the Baudelaires' story had not begun, because you would still need to know about a certain tea party held in a penthouse suite, and the baker who made the scones served at the tea party, and the baker's assistant who smuggled the secret ingredient into the scone batter through a very narrow drainpipe, and how a crafty volunteer created the illusion of a fire in the kitchen simply by wearing a certain dress and jumping around, and even then the beginning of the story would be as far away as the shipwreck that left the Baudelaire parents as castaways on the coastal shelf is far away from the outrigger on which the islanders would depart. One could say, in fact, that no story really has a beginning, and that no story really has an end, as all of the world's stories are as jumbled as the items in the arboretum, with their details and secrets all heaped together so that the whole story, from beginning to end, depends on how you look at it. We might even say that the world is always in medias res—a Latin phrase which means "in the midst of things" or "in the middle of a narrative"—and that it is impossible to solve any mystery, or find the root of any trouble, and so *The End* is really the middle of the story, as many people in this history will live long past the close of Chapter Thirteen, or even the beginning of the story, as a new child arrives in the world at the chapter's close. But one cannot sit in the midst of things forever. Eventually one must face that the end is near, and the end of *The End* is quite near indeed, so if I were you I would not read the end of *The End*, as it contains the end of a notorious villain but also the end of a brave and noble sibling, and the end of the colonists' stay on the island, as they sail off the end of the coastal shelf. The end of *The End* contains all these ends, and that does not depend on how you look at it, so it might be best for you to stop looking at *The End* before the end of *The End* arrives, and to stop reading *The End* before you read the end, as the stories that end in *The End* that began in *The Bad Beginning* are beginning to end now.

The Baudelaires hurriedly filled their stockpot with apples and ran to the coastal shelf, hurrying over the brae as quickly as they could. It was past lunchtime, and the waters of the sea were already flooding the shelf, so the water was much deeper than it had been since the children's arrival. Violet and Klaus had to hold the stockpot high in the air, and Sunny and the Incredibly Deadly Viper climbed up on the elder Baudelaires' shoulders to ride along with the bitter apples. The children could see Kit Snicket on the horizon, still lying on the library raft as the waters rose to soak the first few layers of books, and alongside the strange cube was the outrigger. As they drew closer, they saw that the islanders had stopped pushing the boat and were climbing aboard, pausing from time to time to cough, while at the head of the outrigger was the figure of Ishmael, seated in his clay chair, gazing at his poisoned colonists and watching the children approach.

"Stop!" Violet cried, when they were close enough to be heard. "We've discovered a way to dilute the poison!"

"Baudelaires!" came the faint cry of Kit high atop the library raft. "Thank goodness you're here! I think I'm going into labor!"

As I'm sure you know, "labor" is the term for the process by which a woman gives birth, and it is a Herculean task, a phrase which here means "something you would rather not do on a library raft floating on a flooding coastal shelf." Sunny could see, from her stockpot perch, Kit holding her belly and giving the youngest Baudelaire a painful grimace.

"We'll help you," Violet promised, "but we need to get these apples to the islanders."

"They won't take them!" Kit said. "I tried to tell them how the poison could be diluted, but they insist on leaving!"

"No one's forcing them," said Ishmael calmly. "I merely suggested that the island was no longer a safe place, and that we should set sail for another one."

"You and the Baudelaires are the ones who got us into this mess," came the drowsy voice of Mr. Pitcairn, thick with fungus and coconut cordial, "but Ishmael is going to get us out."

"This island used to be a safe place," said Professor Fletcher, "far from the treachery of the world. But since you've arrived it's become dangerous and complicated."

"That's not our fault," Klaus said, walking closer and closer to the outrigger as the water continued to rise. "You can't live far from the treachery of the world, because eventually the treachery will wash up on your shores."

"Exactly," said Alonso, who yawned. "You washed up and spoiled the island forever."

"So we're leaving it to you," said Ariel, who coughed violently. "You can have this dangerous place. We're going to sail to safety."

"Safe here!" Sunny cried, holding up an apple.

"You've poisoned us enough," said Erewhon, and the islanders wheezed in agreement "We don't want to hear any more of your treacherous ideas."

"But you were ready to mutiny," Violet said. "You didn't want to take Ishmael's suggestions."

"That was before the Medusoid Mycelium arrived," Finn said hoarsely. "He's been here the longest, so he knows how to keep us safe. At his suggestion, we all drank quite a bit of cordial while he figured out the root of the trouble." She paused to catch her breath as the sinister fungus continued to grow. "And the root of the trouble, Baudelaires, is you."

By now the children had reached the outrigger, and they looked up at Ishmael, who raised his eyebrows and stared back at the frantic

Baudelaires. "Why are you doing this?" Klaus asked the facilitator. "You know we're not the root of the problem."

"In medias res!" Sunny cried.

"Sunny's right," Violet said. "The Medusoid Mycelium was around before we were born, and our parents prepared for its arrival by adding horseradish to the roots of the apple tree."

"If they don't eat these bitter apples," Klaus pleaded, "they'll come to a bitter end. Tell the islanders the whole story, Ishmael, so they can save themselves."

"The whole story?" Ishmael said, and leaned down from his chair so he could talk to the Baudelaires without the others hearing. "If I told the islanders the whole story, I wouldn't be keeping them safe from the world's terrible secrets. They almost learned the whole story this morning, and began to mutiny over breakfast. If they knew all these island's secrets there'd be a schism in no time at all."

"Better a schism than a death," Violet said.

Ishmael shook his head, and fingered the wild strands of his woolly beard. "No one is going to die," he said. "This outrigger can take us to a beach near Lousy Lane, where we can travel to a horseradish factory."

"You don't have time for such a long voyage," Klaus said.

"I think we do," Ishmael said. "Even without a compass, I think I can get us to a safe place."

"You need a *moral* compass," Violet said. "The spores of the Medusoid Mycelium can kill within the hour. The entire colony could be poisoned, and even if you make it to shore, the fungus could spread to anyone you meet. You're not keeping anyone safe. You're endangering the whole world, just to keep a few of your secrets. That's not parenting! That's horrid and wrong!"

"I guess it depends on how you look at it," Ishmael said. "Good-bye, Baudelaires." He sat up straight and called out to the wheezing islanders. "I suggest you start rowing," he said, and the colonists reached their arms into the water and began to paddle the outrigger away from the children. The Baudelaires hung on to the side of the boat, and called to the islander who had first found them on the coastal shelf.

"Friday!" Sunny cried. "Take apple!"

"Don't succumb to peer pressure," Violet begged.

Friday turned to face the children, and the siblings could see she was terribly frightened. Klaus quickly grabbed an apple from the stock-pot, and the young girl leaned out of the boat to touch his hand.

"I'm sorry to leave you behind, Baudelaires," she said, "but I must go with my family. I've already lost my father, and I couldn't stand to lose anyone else."

"But your father—" Klaus started to say, but Mrs. Caliban gave him a terrible look and pulled her daughter away from the edge of the outrigger.

"Don't rock the boat," she said. "Come here and drink your cordial."

"Your mother is right, Friday," Ishmael said

firmly. "You should respect your parent's wishes. It's more than the Baudelaires ever did."

"We are respecting our parents' wishes," Violet said, hoisting the apples as high as she could. "They didn't want to shelter us from the world's treacheries. They wanted us to survive them."

Ishmael put his hand on the stockpot of apples. "What do your parents know," he asked, "about surviving?" and with one firm, cruel gesture the old orphan pushed against the stockpot, and the outrigger moved out of the children's grasp. Violet and Klaus tried to take another step closer to the islanders, but the water had risen too far, and the Baudelaire feet slipped off the surface of the coastal shelf, and the siblings found themselves swimming. The stockpot tipped, and Sunny gave a small shriek and climbed down to Violet's shoulders as several apples from the pot dropped into the water with a splash. At the sound of the splash, the Baudelaires remembered the apple core that

Ishmael had dropped, and realized why the facilitator was so calm in the face of the deadly fungus, and why his voice was the only one of the islanders' that wasn't clogged with stalks and caps.

"We have to go after them," Violet said. "We may be their only chance!"

"We can't go after them," Klaus said, still holding the apple. "We have to help Kit."

"Split up," Sunny said, staring after the departing outrigger.

Klaus shook his head. "All of us need to stay if we're going to help Kit give birth." He gazed at the islanders and listened to the wheezing and coughing coming from the boat fashioned from wild grasses and the limbs of trees. "They made their decision," he said finally.

"Kontiki," Sunny said. She meant something along the lines of, "There's no way they'll survive the journey," but the youngest Baudelaire was wrong. There was a way. There was a way to bring the islanders a single apple that they could share, each taking a bite of the precious bitter fruit that might tide them over—the phrase "tide them over," as you probably know, means "help deal with a difficult situation"—until they reached someplace or someone who could help them, just as the three Baudelaires shared an apple in the secret space where their parents had enabled them to survive one of the most deadly unfortunate events ever to wash up on the island's shores. Whoever brought the apple to the islanders, of course, would need to swim very stealthily to the outrigger, and it would help if they were quite small and slender, so they might escape the watchful eye of the outrigger's facilitator. The Baudelaires would not notice the disappearance of the Incredibly Deadly Viper for quite some time, as they would be focused on helping Kit, and so they could never say for sure what happened to the snake, and my research into the reptile's story is incomplete, so I do not know what other chapters occurred in its history, as Ink, as some prefer to call the snake, slithered from one place to the next, sometimes taking shelter from the treachery of the world and sometimes committing treacherous acts of its own—a history not unlike that of the Baudelaire orphans, which some have called little more than the register of crimes, follies, and misfortunes of mankind. Unless you have investigated the islanders' case yourself, there is no way of knowing what happened to them as they sailed away from the colony that had been their home. But there was a way they could have survived their journey, a way that may seem fantastic, but is no less fantastic than three children helping a woman give birth. The Baudelaires hurried to the library raft, and lifted Sunny and the stockpot to the top of the raft where Kit lay, so the youngest Baudelaire could hold the wheezing woman's gloved hand and the bitter apples could dilute the poison inside her as Violet and Klaus pushed the raft back toward shore.

"Have an apple," Sunny offered, but Kit shook her head.

"I can't," she said.

"But you've been poisoned," Violet said. "You must have caught a spore or two from the islanders as they floated by."

"The apples will harm the baby," Kit said. "There's something in the hybrid that's bad for people who haven't been born yet. That's why your mother never tasted one of her own bitter apples. She was pregnant with you, Violet." One of Kit's gloved hands drifted down over the top of the raft and patted the hair of the eldest Baudelaire. "I hope I'm half as good a mother as yours was, Violet," she said.

"You will be," Klaus said.

"I don't know," Kit said. "I was supposed to help you children on that day when you finally reached Briny Beach. I wanted nothing more than to take you away in my taxi to someplace safe. Instead, I threw you into a world of treachery at the Hotel Denouement. And I wanted nothing more than to reunite you with your friends the Quagmires. Instead, I left them behind." She uttered a wheezy sigh, and fell silent.

Violet continued to guide the raft toward the island, and noticed for the first time that her hands were pushing against the spine of a book whose title she recognized from the library Aunt Josephine kept underneath her bed—*Ivan Lachrymose—Lake Explorer*—while her brother was pushing against *Mushroom Minutiae*, a book that had been part of Fiona's mycological library. "What happened?" she asked, trying to imagine what strange events would have brought these books to these shores.

"I failed you," Kit said sadly, and coughed. "Quigley managed to reach the self-sustaining hot air mobile home, just as I hoped he would, and helped his siblings and Hector catch the treacherous eagles in an enormous net, while I met Captain Widdershins and his stepchildren."

"Fernald and Fiona?" Klaus said, referring to the hook-handed man who had once worked for

Count Olaf, and the young woman who had broken his heart. "But they betrayed him—and us."

"The captain had forgiven the failures of those he had loved," Kit said, "as I hope you will forgive mine, Baudelaires. We made a desperate attempt to repair the *Queequeg* and reach the Quagmires as their aerial battle continued, and arrived just in time to see the balloons of the self-sustaining hot air mobile home pop under the cruel beaks of the escaping eagles. They tumbled down to the surface of the sea, and crashed into the *Queequeg*. In moments we were all castaways, treading water in the midst of all the items that survived the wreck." She was silent for a moment. "Fiona was so desperate to reach you, Klaus," she said. "She wanted you to forgive her as well."

"Did she—" Klaus could not bear to finish his question. "I mean, what happened next?"

"I don't know," Kit admitted. "From the

depths of the sea a mysterious figure approached—almost like a question mark, rising out of the water."

"We saw that on a radar screen," Violet remembered. "Captain Widdershins refused to tell us what it was."

"My brother used to call it 'The Great Unknown,'" Kit said, clasping her belly as the baby kicked violently. "I was terrified, Baudelaires. Quickly I fashioned a Vaporetto of Favorite Detritus, as I'd been trained to do."

"'Vaporetto'?" Sunny asked.

"It's an Italian term for 'boat,'" Kit said. "It was one of many Italian phrases Monty taught me. A Vaporetto of Favorite Detritus is a way of saving yourself and your favorite things at the same time. I gathered all the books in reach that I enjoyed, tossing the boring ones into the sea, but everyone else wanted to take their chances with the great unknown. I begged the others to climb aboard as the question mark approached, but only Ink managed to reach me. The others . . ." Her voice trailed off, and for a moment Kit did nothing but wheeze. "In an instant they were gone—either swallowed up or rescued by that mysterious thing."

"You don't know what happened to them?" Klaus asked.

Kit shook her head. "All I heard," she said, "was one of the Quagmires calling Violet's name."

Sunny looked into the face of the distraught woman. "Quigley," the youngest Baudelaire could not help asking "or Duncan?"

"I don't know," Kit said again. "I'm sorry, Baudelaires. I failed you. You succeeded in your noble errands at the Hotel Denouement, and saved Dewey and the others, but I don't know if we'll ever see the Quagmires and their companions again. I hope you will forgive my failures, and when I see Dewey again I hope he will forgive me, too."

The Baudelaire orphans looked at one

another sadly, realizing it was time at last to tell Kit Snicket the whole story, as she had told them. "We'll forgive your failures," Violet said, "if you'll forgive ours."

"We failed you, too," Klaus said. "We had to burn down the Hotel Denouement, and we don't know if anyone escaped to safety."

Sunny gripped Kit's hand in hers. "And Dewey is dead," she said, and everyone burst into tears. There is a kind of crying I hope you have not experienced, and it is not just crying about something terrible that has happened, but a crying for all of the terrible things that have happened, not just to you but to everyone you know and to everyone you don't know and even the people you don't want to know, a crying that cannot be diluted by a brave deed or a kind word, but only by someone holding you as your shoulders shake and your tears run down your face. Sunny held Kit, and Violet held Klaus, and for a minute the four castaways did nothing but weep, letting their tears run down their faces and into the sea, which some have said is nothing but a library of all the tears in history. Kit and the children let their sadness join the sadness of the world, and cried for all of the people who were lost to them. They cried for Dewey Denouement, and for the Quagmire triplets, and for all of their companions and guardians, friends and associates, and for all of the failures they could forgive and all of the treacheries they could endure. They cried for the world, and most of all, of course, the Baudelaire orphans cried for their parents, who they knew, finally, they would never see again. Even though Kit Snicket had not brought news of their parents, her story of the Great Unknown made them see at last that the people who had written all those chapters in *A Series of Unfortunate Events* were gone forever into the great unknown, and that Violet, Klaus, and Sunny would be orphans forever, too.

"Stop," Kit said finally, through her fading tears. "Stop pushing the raft. I cannot go on."

"We have to go on," Violet said.

"We're almost at the beach," Klaus said.

"The shelf is flooding," Sunny said.

"Let it flood," Kit said. "I can't do it, Baudelaires. I've lost too many people—my parents, my true love, and my brothers."

At the mention of Kit's brothers, Violet thought to reach into her pocket, and she retrieved the ornate ring, emblazoned with the initial R. "Sometimes the things you've lost can be found again in unexpected places," she said, and held the ring up for Kit to see. The distraught woman removed her gloves, and held the ring in her bare and trembling hand.

"This isn't mine," she said. "It belonged to your mother."

"Before it belonged to our mother," Klaus said, "it belonged to you."

"Its history began before we were born," Kit said, "and it should continue after we die. Give it to my child, Baudelaires. Let my child be part of my history, even if the baby is an orphan, and all alone in the world."

"The baby will not be alone," Violet said fiercely. "If you die, Kit, we will raise this child as our own."

"I could not ask for better," Kit said quietly. "Name the baby after one of your parents, Baudelaires. The custom of my family is to name a baby for someone who has died."

"Ours too," Sunny said, remembering something her father had told her when she had inquired about her own name.

"Our families have always been close," Kit said, "even if we had to stay apart from one another. Now, finally, we are all together, as if we are one family."

"Then let us help you," Sunny said, and with a weepy, wheezy nod, Kit Snicket let the Baudelaires push her Vaporetto of Favorite Detritus off the coastal shelf and onto the shores of the island, where eventually everything arrives, just as the outrigger disappeared on the horizon. The children gazed at the islanders for the last time—at least as far as I know—and then at the cube of books, and tried to imagine how the injured, pregnant, and distraught woman could get to a safe place to birth a child.

"Can you lower yourself down?" Violet asked.

Kit shook her head. "It hurts," she said, her voice thick with the poisonous fungus.

"We can carry her," Klaus said, but Kit shook her head again.

"I'm too heavy," she said weakly. "I could fall from your grasp and hurt the baby."

"We can invent a way to get you to the shore," Violet said.

"Yes," Klaus said. "We'll just run to the arboretum to find what we need."

"No time," Sunny said, and Kit nodded in agreement.

"The baby's coming quickly," she said. "Find someone to help you."

"We're alone," Violet said, but then she and her siblings gazed out at the beach where the raft had arrived, and the Baudelaires saw, crawling out of Ishmael's tent, the one person for whom they had not shed a tear. Sunny slid down to the sand, bringing the stockpot with her, and the three children hurried up the slope to the struggling figure of Count Olaf.

"Hello, orphans," he said, his voice even wheezier and rougher from the spreading poison of the Medusoid Mycelium. Esmé's dress had fallen away from his skinny body, and he was crawling on the sand in his regular clothes, with one hand holding a seashell of cordial and the other clutching at his chest. "Are you here to bow before the king of Olaf-Land?"

"We don't have time for your nonsense," Violet said. "We need your help."

Count Olaf's eyebrow raised, and he gave the children an astonished glare. "*You* need *my* help?" he asked. "What happened to all those island fools?"

"They abandoned us," Klaus said.

Olaf wheezed horridly, and it took the siblings a moment to realize he was laughing.

"How do you like them apples?" he sputtered, using an expression which means "I find this situation quite remarkable."

"We'll give you apples," Sunny said, gesturing to the stockpot, "if you help."

"I don't want fruit," Olaf snarled, and tried to sit up, his hand still clutching his chest. "I want the fortune your parents left behind."

"The fortune isn't here," Violet said. "None of us may ever see a penny of that money."

"Even if it were here," Klaus said, "you might not live to enjoy it."

"Mcguffin," Sunny said, which meant "Your scheming means nothing in this place."

Count Olaf raised the seashell to his lips, and the Baudelaires could see that he was trembling. "Then maybe I'll just stay here," he said hoarsely. "I've lost too much to go on—my parents, my true love, my henchfolk, an enormous amount of money I didn't earn, even the boat with my name on it."

The three children looked at one another, remembering their time on that boat and recalling that they had considered throwing him overboard. If Olaf had drowned in the sea, the Medusoid Mycelium might never have threatened the island, although the deadly fungus eventually would have washed up on its shores, and if the villain were dead then there would be no one on the beach who might help Kit Snicket and her child.

Violet knelt on the sand, and grabbed the villain's shoulders with both hands. "We have to go on," she said. "Do one good thing in your life, Olaf."

"I've done lots of good things in my life," he snarled. "I once took in three orphans, and I've been considered for several prestigious theatrical awards."

Klaus knelt down beside his sister, and stared into the villain's shiny eyes. "You're the one who made us orphans in the first place," he said, uttering out loud for the first time a secret all three Baudelaires had kept in their hearts for almost as long as they could remember. Olaf closed his eyes for a moment, grimacing in pain, and then stared slowly at each of the three children in turn.

"Is that what you think?" he said finally.

"We know it," Sunny said.

"You don't know anything," Count Olaf said. "You three children are the same as when I first laid eyes on you. You think you can triumph in this world with nothing more than a keen mind, a pile of books, and the occasional gourmet meal." He poured one last gulp of cordial into his poisoned mouth before throwing the seashell into the sand. "You're just like your parents," he said, and from the shore the children heard Kit Snicket moan.

"You have to help Kit," Violet said. "The baby is arriving."

"Kit?" Count Olaf asked, and in one swift gesture he grabbed an apple from the stockpot and took a savage bite. He chewed, wincing in pain, and the Baudelaires listened as his wheezing settled and the poisonous fungus was diluted by their parents' invention. He took another bite, and another, and then, with a horrible groan, the villain rose to his feet, and the children saw that his chest was soaked with blood.

"You're hurt," Klaus said.

"I've been hurt before," Count Olaf said, and he staggered down the slope and waded into the waters of the flooded coastal shelf. In one smooth gesture he lifted Kit from the raft and carried her onto the shores of the island. The distraught woman's eyes were closed, and as the Baudelaires hurried down to her they were not sure she was alive until Olaf laid her carefully down on the white sands of the beach, and the children saw her chest heaving with breath. The villain stared at Kit for one long moment, and then he leaned down and did a strange thing. As the Baudelaire orphans looked on, Count Olaf gave Kit Snicket a gentle kiss on her trembling mouth.

"Yuck," said Sunny, as Kit's eyes fluttered open.

"I told you," Count Olaf said weakly. "I told you I'd do that one last time."

"You're a wicked man," Kit said. "Do you think one kind act will make me forgive you for your failings?"

The villain stumbled a few steps away, and then sat down on the sand and uttered a deep sigh. "I haven't apologized," he said, looking first at the pregnant woman and then at the Baudelaires. Kit reached out and touched the man's ankle, right on the tattoo of an eye that had haunted the children since they had first seen it. Violet, Klaus, and Sunny looked at the tattoo, remembering all of the times it had been disguised and all the times it had been revealed, and they thought of all the other places they had seen it, for if you looked carefully, the drawing of an eye also spelled out the initials V.F.D., and as the children had investigated the Volunteer Fire Department, first trying to decode the organization's sinister mysteries and then trying to participate in its noble errands, it seemed that these eyes were watching them, though whether the eyes were noble or treacherous, good or evil, seemed even now to be a mystery. The whole story of these eyes, it seemed, might always be hidden from the children, kept in darkness along with all the other eyes watching all the other orphans every day and every night.

"'The night has a thousand eyes,'" Kit said hoarsely, and lifted her head to face the villain. The Baudelaires could tell by her voice that she was reciting the words of someone else. "'And the day but one; yet the light of the bright world dies with the dying sun. The mind has a thousand eyes, and the heart but one: yet the light of a whole life dies when love is done.'"

Count Olaf gave Kit a faint smile. "You're not the only one who can recite the words of our associates," he said, and then gazed out at the sea. The afternoon was nearly over, and soon the island would be covered in darkness. "'Man hands on misery to man,'" the villain said. "'It deepens like a coastal shelf. Get out as early as you can—'" Here he coughed, a ghastly sound, and his hands clutched his chest. "'And don't have any kids yourself,'" he finished, and uttered a short, sharp laugh. Then the villain's story came to an end. Olaf lay back on the sand, far from the treachery of the world, and the children stood on the beach and stared into his face. His eyes shone brightly, and his mouth opened as if he wanted to tell them something, but the Baudelaire orphans never heard Count Olaf say another word.

Kit gave a cry of pain, thick with poisonous fungus, and clutched her heaving belly, and the Baudelaires hurried to help her. They did not even notice when Count Olaf closed his eyes for the last time, and perhaps this is a good time for you to close your eyes, too, not just to avoid reading the end of the Baudelaires' story, but to imagine the beginning of another. It is likely your own eyes were closed when you were born, so that you left the safe place of your mother's womb—or, if you are a seahorse, your father's yolk sac—and joined the treachery of the world without seeing exactly where you were going. You did not yet know the people who were helping you make your way here, or the people who would shelter you as your life began, when you were even smaller and more delicate and demanding than you are now. It seems strange that you would do such a thing, and leave yourself in the care of strangers for so long, only gradually opening your eyes to see what all the fuss was about, and yet this is the way nearly everyone comes into the world. Perhaps if we saw what was ahead of us, and glimpsed the crimes, follies, and misfortunes that would befall us later on, we would all stay in our mother's wombs, and then there would be nobody in the world but a great number of very fat, very irritated women. In any case, this is how all our stories begin, in darkness with our eyes closed, and all our stories end the same way, too, with all of us uttering some last words—or perhaps someone else's—before slipping back into darkness as our series of unfortunate events comes to an end. And in this way, with the journey taken by Kit Snicket's baby, we reach the end of A Series of Unfortunate Events as well. For some time, Kit Snicket's labor was very difficult, and it seemed to the children that things were moving in an aberrant—the word "aberrant" here means "very, very wrong, and causing much grief"—direction. But finally, into the world came a baby girl, just as, I'm very, very sorry to say, her mother, and my sister, slipped away from the world after a long night of suffering—but also a night of joy, as the birth of a baby is always good news, no matter how much bad news the baby will hear later. The sun rose over the coastal shelf, which would not flood again for another year, and the Baudelaire orphans held the baby on the shore and watched as her eyes opened for the first time. Kit Snicket's daughter squinted at the sunrise, and tried to imagine where in the world she was, and of course as she wondered this she began to cry. The girl, named after the Baudelaires' mother, howled and howled, and as her series of unfortunate events began, this history of the Baudelaire orphans ended.

This is not to say, of course, that the Baudelaire orphans died that day. They were far too busy. Although they were still children, the Baudelaires were parents now, and there was quite a lot to do. Violet designed and built the equipment necessary for raising an infant, using the library of detritus stored in the shade of the apple tree. Klaus searched the enormous bookcase for information on child care, and kept careful track of the baby's progress. Sunny herded and milked the wild sheep, to provide nourishment for the baby, and used the whisk Friday had given her to make soft foods as the baby's teeth came in. And all three Baudelaires planted seeds from the bitter apples all over the island, to chase away any traces of the Medusoid Mycelium—even though they remembered it grew best in small, enclosed spaces—so the deadly fungus had no chance to harm the child and so the island would remain as safe as it was on the day they arrived. These chores took all day, and at night, while the baby was learning to sleep, the Baudelaires would sit together in the two large reading chairs and take turns reading out loud from the book their parents had left behind, and sometimes they would flip to the back of the book, and add a few lines to the history themselves. While reading and writing, the siblings found many answers for which they had been looking, although each answer, of course, only brought forth another mystery, as there were many details of the Baudelaires' lives that seemed like a strange, unreadable shape of some great unknown. But this did not concern them as much as you might think. One cannot spend forever sitting and solving the mysteries of one's history, and no matter how much one reads, the whole story can never be told. But it was enough. Reading their parents' words was, under the circumstances, the best for which the Baudelaire orphans could hope.

As the night grew later they would drop off to sleep, just as their parents did, in the chairs in the secret space beneath the roots of the bitter apple tree, in the arboretum on an island far, far from the treachery of the world. Several hours later, of course, the baby would wake up and fill the space with confused and hungry cries. The Baudelaires took turns, and while the other two children slept, one Baudelaire would carry the baby, in a sling Violet had designed, out of the arboretum and up to the top of the brae, where they would sit, infant and parent, and have breakfast while staring at the sea. Sometimes they would visit Kit Snicket's grave, where they would lay a few wildflowers, or the grave of Count Olaf, where they would merely stand silent for a few moments. In many ways, the lives of the Baudelaire orphans that year is not unlike my own, now that I have concluded my investigation. Like Violet, like Klaus, and like Sunny, I visit certain graves, and often spend my mornings standing on a brae, staring out at the same sea. It is not the whole story, of course, but it is enough. Under the circumstances, it is the best for which you can hope.

© Scott Irvine

BRETT HELQUIST was born in Ganado, Arizona, grew up in Orem, Utah, and now lives in Brooklyn, New York. He is hopeful that with the publication of the last book in A Series of Unfortunate Events, he'll be able to step outside more often in the daytime, and sleep better at night.

LEMONY SNICKET is the author of all 170 chapters of A Series of Unfortunate Events. He is almost finished.

To My Kind Editor:

The end of THE END can be found at the end of THE END.

With all due respect,

Lemony Snicket

Lemony Snicket

Book the Last

CHAPTER FOURTEEN

A SERIES OF UNFORTUNATE EVENTS

BOOK THE FIRST
THE BAD BEGINNING

BOOK THE SECOND
THE REPTILE ROOM

BOOK THE THIRD
THE WIDE WINDOW

BOOK THE FOURTH
THE MISERABLE MILL

BOOK THE FIFTH
THE AUSTERE ACADEMY

BOOK THE SIXTH
THE ERSATZ ELEVATOR

BOOK THE SEVENTH
THE VILE VILLAGE

BOOK THE EIGHTH
THE HOSTILE HOSPITAL

BOOK THE NINTH
THE CARNIVOROUS CARNIVAL

BOOK THE TENTH
THE SLIPPERY SLOPE

BOOK THE ELEVENTH
THE GRIM GROTTO

BOOK THE TWELFTH
THE PENULTIMATE PERIL

BOOK THE THIRTEENTH
THE END

A Series of Unfortunate Events

BOOK THE LAST

CHAPTER FOURTEEN

by

Lemony Snicket

Illustrated by
BRETT HELQUIST

EGMONT

Chapter Fourteen

Ô Mort, vieux capitaine, il est temps! levons l'ancre!
Ce pays nous ennuie, ô Mort! Appareillons!
Si le ciel et la mer sont noirs comme de l'encre,
Nos coeurs que tu connais sont remplis de rayons!

For Beatrice –

We are like boats passing in the night –

particularly you.

C H A P T E R

Fourteen

The last entry in the Baudelaire parents' handwriting in *A Series of Unfortunate Events* reads as follows:

> *As we suspected, we are to be castaways once more. The others believe that the island should stay far from the treachery of the world, and so this safe place is too dangerous for us. We will leave by a boat B has built and named after me. I am heartbroken, but I have been heartbroken before, and this might be the best for which I can hope. We cannot truly shelter our children, here or anywhere else, and so it might be best for us*

and for the baby to immerse ourselves in the world. By the way, if it is a girl we will name her Violet, and if it is a boy we will name him Lemony.

The Baudelaire orphans read this entry one evening after a supper of seaweed salad, crab cakes, and roast lamb, and when Violet finished reading all three children laughed. Even Kit's baby, sitting on Sunny's knee, uttered a happy shriek.

"Lemony?" Violet repeated. "They would have named me Lemony? Where did they get that idea?"

"From someone who died, presumably," Klaus said. "Remember the family custom?"

"Lemony Baudelaire," Sunny tried, and the baby laughed again. She was nearly a year old, and looked very much like her mother.

"They never told us about a Lemony," Violet said, and ran her hair through her hands. She had been repairing the water filtration system all day and was quite tired.

Klaus poured his sisters more coconut milk, which the children preferred to drink fresh. "They didn't tell us a lot of things," he said. "What do you think it means, 'I've been heart-broken before'?"

"You know what 'heartbroken' means," Sunny said, and then nodded as the baby murmured "Abelard." The youngest Baudelaire was best at deciphering the infant's somewhat unusual way of speaking.

"I think it means we should leave," Violet said.

"Leave the island?" Klaus said. "And go where?"

"Anywhere," Violet said. "We can't stay here forever. There's everything we might need, but it's not right to be so far from the world."

"And its treachery?" Sunny asked.

"You'd think we would have had enough treachery for a lifetime," Klaus said, "but there's more to life than safety."

"Our parents left," Violet said. "Maybe we should honor their wishes."

"Chekrio?" the baby said, and the Baudelaires considered her for a moment. Kit's daughter was growing up very quickly, and she eagerly explored the island at every opportunity. All three siblings had to keep a close eye on her, particularly in the arboretum, which was still heaping with detritus even after a year of cataloging. Many of the items in the enormous library were dangerous for babies, of course, but the infant had never had a serious injury. The baby had heard about danger, too, mostly from the register of crimes, follies, and misfortunes of mankind from which the Baudelaires read out loud each evening, although they had not told the infant the whole story. She did not know all of the Baudelaires' secrets, and indeed there were some she would never know.

"We can't shelter her forever," Klaus said.

"In any case, treachery will wash up on these shores."

"I'm surprised it hasn't already," Violet said. "Plenty of things have been shipwrecked here, but we haven't seen a single castaway."

"If we leave," Sunny asked, "what will we find?"

The Baudelaires fell silent. Because no castaways had arrived in the year, they had little news of the world, aside from a few scraps of newspaper that had survived a terrible storm. Judging from the articles, there were still villains loose in the world, although a few volunteers also appeared to have survived all of the troubles that had brought the children to the island. The articles, however, were from *The Daily Punctilio*, and so the children could not be sure they were accurate. For all they knew, the islanders had spread the Medusoid Mycelium, and the entire world might be poisoned. This, however, seemed unlikely, as the world, no matter how monstrously it may be threatened, has never been known to succumb entirely. The Baudelaires also thought of all the people they hoped to see again, although, sadly, this also seemed unlikely, though not impossible.

"We won't know until we get there," Violet said.

"Well, if we're leaving, we'd better hurry," Klaus said. He stood up and walked to the bench, where the middle Baudelaire had fashioned a calendar he believed to be fairly accurate. "The coastal shelf will flood soon."

"We won't need much," Sunny said. "We have quite a bit of nonperishable food."

"I've cataloged quite a bit of naval equipment," Violet said.

"I have some good maps," Klaus said, "but we should also make room for some of our favorite detritus. I have some novels by P. G. Wodehouse I've been meaning to get to."

"Blueprints," Violet said thoughtfully.

"My whisk," Sunny said, looking at the item that Friday had smuggled her long ago, which had turned out to be a very handy utensil even after the baby had outgrown whisked foods.

"Cake!" shrieked the baby, and her guardians laughed.

"Do we take this?" Violet asked, holding up the book from which she had read out loud.

"I don't think so," Klaus said. "Perhaps another castaway will arrive, and continue the history."

"In any case," Sunny said, "they'll have something to read."

"So we're really leaving," Violet said, and they really were. After a good night's sleep, the Baudelaires began to prepare for their voyage, and it was true they didn't need much. Sunny was able to pack a great deal of food that would be perfect for the journey, and even managed to sneak in a few luxuries, such as some roe she had harvested from local fishes, and a somewhat bitter but still tasty apple pie. Klaus rolled several maps into a neat cylinder, and added a number of useful and entertaining items from the vast library. Violet added some blueprints and equipment to the pile, and then selected a boat from all the shipwrecks that lay in the arboretum. The eldest Baudelaire had been surprised to find that the boat that looked best for the task was the one on which they had arrived, although by the time she was done repairing and readying it for the voyage she was not surprised after all. She repaired the hull of the boat, and fastened new sails to the masts, and finally she looked at the nameplate reading COUNT OLAF, and with a small frown, she tore through the tape and removed it. As the children had noticed on their voyage to the island, there was another nameplate underneath, and when Violet read what it said, and called her siblings and adopted daughter over to see, yet another question about their lives was answered, and yet another mystery had begun.

Finally, the day for departure arrived, and as the coastal shelf began to flood the Baudelaires carried the boat—or, as Uncle Monty might have put it, "vaporetto"—down to the beach and began to load all of their supplies. Violet, Klaus, and Sunny gazed at the white sands of the beach, where new apple trees were beginning to grow. The children spent nearly all of their time in the arboretum, and so the side of the island where the colony had been now felt like the far side of the island, rather than where their parents had lived. "Are we ready to immerse ourselves in the world?" Violet asked.

"I just hope we don't immerse ourselves in the sea," Klaus said, with a small smile.

"Me too," Sunny said, and smiled back at her brother.

"Where's the baby?" Violet said. "I want to

make sure these life jackets I've designed will fit properly."

"She wanted to say good-bye to her mother," Sunny said. "She'll be along soon."

Sure enough, the tiny figure of Kit's daughter could be seen crawling over the brae, toward the children and their boat. The Baudelaires watched her approach, wondering what the next chapter in this infant's life would be, and indeed that is difficult to say. There are some who say that the Baudelaires rejoined V.F.D. and are engaged in brave errands to this day, perhaps under different names to avoid being captured. There are others who say that they perished at sea, although rumors of one's death crop up so often, and are so often revealed to be untrue. But in any case, as my investigation is over, we have indeed reached the last chapter of the Baudelaires' story, even if the Baudelaires had not. The three children climbed into the boat, and waited for the baby to crawl to the water's edge, where she could pull herself into a standing position by clinging to the back of the boat. Soon the coastal shelf would flood, and the Baudelaire orphans would be on their way, immersing themselves in the world and leaving this story forever. Even the baby clutching the boat, whose story had just begun, would soon vanish from this chronicle, after uttering just a few words.

"Vi!" she cried, which was her way of greeting Violet. "Kla! Sun!"

"We wouldn't leave without you," Violet said, smiling down at the baby.

"Come aboard," Klaus said, talking to her as if she were an adult.

"You little thing," Sunny said, using a term of endearment she had made up herself.

The baby paused, and looked at the back of the boat, where the nameplate had been affixed. She had no way of knowing this, of course, but the nameplate had been nailed to the back of the boat by a person standing on the very spot she was standing—at least, as far as my research has shown. The infant was standing on a spot in someone else's story, during a moment of her own, but she was thinking neither of the story far in the past nor of her own, which stretched into the future like the open sea. She was gazing at the nameplate, and her forehead was wrinkled in concentration. Finally, she uttered a word. The Baudelaire orphans gasped when they heard it, but they could not say for sure whether she was reading the word out loud or merely stating her own name, and indeed they never learned this. Perhaps this last word was the baby's first secret, joining the secrets the Baudelaires were keeping from the baby, and all the other secrets immersed in the world. Perhaps it is better not to know precisely what was meant by this word, as some things are better left in the great unknown. There are some words, of course, that are better left unsaid—

but not, I believe, the word uttered by my niece, a word which here means that the story is over.

Beatrice.